Dyi

"Finally, a protagonist w[...]
—*Riverfront Times* (St. Louis, MO)

"Laugh-out-loud humor adds to the brisk action."
—*South Florida Sun-Sentinel*

Praise for the
Dead-End Job Mystery Series

"One way for a fugitive to hide in plain sight is to work at low-wage jobs, which is what Helen Hawthorne has been doing in Elaine Viets's quick-witted mysteries."
—Marilyn Stasio, *The New York Times Book Review*

"Wickedly funny."
—*The Miami Herald*

"A stubborn and intelligent heroine, a wonderful South Florida setting, and a cast of more or less lethal bimbos.... I loved this book."
—#1 *New York Times* bestselling author Charlaine Harris

"Hair-raising.... Viets keeps the action popping until the cliff-hanger ending."
—*Publishers Weekly*

"Hilarious."
—*Kirkus Reviews*

"A fast-paced story and nonstop wisecracks.... Elaine Viets knows how to turn minimum wage into maximum hilarity."
—Nancy Martin, author of *Little Black Book of Murder*

"Elaine Viets reaches the right equilibrium with well-placed humor and lively plotting."
—*South Florida Sun-Sentinel*

"A quick summer read for fans of humorous mysteries with clever premises."
—*Library Journal*

Also by Elaine Viets

A DOG GONE MURDER

JOSIE MARCUS, MYSTERY SHOPPER

Elaine Viets

AN OBSIDIAN MYSTERY

OBSIDIAN
Published by the Penguin Group
Penguin Group (USA) LLC, 375 Hudson Street,
New York, New York 10014

USA | Canada | UK | Ireland | Australia | New Zealand | India | South Africa | China
penguin.com
A Penguin Random House Company

First published by Obsidian, an imprint of New American Library,
a division of Penguin Group (USA) LLC

First Printing, November 2014

ISBN 978-0-451-46598-6

Printed in the United States of America
10 9 8 7 6 5 4 3 2 1

For Alan and Molly Portman and the Princesses.
I wouldn't have this book without you.

Acknowledgments

Writing a novel is a team effort, and this time I needed a slew of friends. Thank you, Alan Portman and Molly Portman, for your tween-parenting tips and information, and to the Princesses for their help.

I couldn't have written this book without the IT expertise of William Simon and Alan Portman. They worked hours to save this novel after a computer disaster. Mystery writers and Sisters in Crime Marcia Talley and Hank Phillippi Ryan also bailed me out.

Thank you to Sandra Harding, my NAL editor, who reads my novels with the best kind of critical eye; the editing and production staff at NAL; and copy editor Eileen G. Chetti.

Special thanks to my friend Jinny Gender, who gave me her canine expertise when we visited dog day-care centers. Two more award-winning mystery writers, Twist Phelan and Julie Compton, gave me legal advice. Dr. Wil Ostmann of Union, Missouri, answered the veterinary questions.

Thank you, MarySue Carl and your clever first- and second-period biology classes at Arroyo High School in El Monte, California, for help with Amelia's tween talk. Go Blue Pride!

Jaspurr is a big rescue cat who belongs to Mike and Maria Kight. He's on a diet now.

The real Oscar belongs to mystery writer Kathryn O'Sullivan and her husband, Paul. Kathryn's mother, Judith, made a generous donation to charity to see her family in this novel.

Doc Cross and his wife, Grace, really do believe in

peace and love and drive a magic bus. They are owned by Sasha and Daisy. Doc grows his own vegetables. Unfortunately, I live too far away to enjoy his tomatoes.

Flaco's Cocina is an off-beat Mexican restaurant near St. Louis. Maplewood, Missouri, is a real place. If you visit Schlafly Bottleworks, Airedale Antics, Kakao Chocolate, Foundation Grounds, and the Book House, you've just started exploring its downtown.

Thank you, Rachelle L'Ecuyer, community development director for the city of Maplewood. The Tiffany Diner is a real place in downtown Maplewood, with good, cheap food, and its own "honor library." Its sign reads BORROW, RETURN, STEAL, DONATE.

Laura Hyzy, the new veterinarian at Dr. Ted Scottsmeyer's clinic, is named in honor of the late Laura Hyzy. Her friends Liz Mellett, Lenore Boehm, and Jack and Judy Cater made a generous donation to charity to have her name in this novel. Franklin is her fictional father.

Thank you, Liz Aton, Valerie Cannata, Kay Gordy, Jack Klobnak, Bob Levine, Janet Smith, Anne Watts, and my St. Louis rock, Karen Grace.

Special thanks to Detective R. C. White, Fort Lauderdale Police Department (retired), and to the law enforcement men and women who answered my questions on police procedure. Some police and medical sources had to remain nameless.

Thanks to poison expert Luci Zahray, who knows interesting ways to kill people.

David Hendin is still the world's best agent. Thank you, Don Crinklaw, my ace-reporter husband and first reader.

Many booksellers have kept this series going. Thank you. And thanks to the librarians for your help and advice. The Internet will never replace smart people.

I blog for the Femmes Fatales and rely on your encouragement and advice. Read our blog at www.femmes fatales.typepad.com.

Thanks also to the authors at the Kill Zone. TKZ aims to inspire, anger, amuse, and entertain readers at www .killzoneauthors.blogspot.com.

Questions or comments? Please e-mail me at eviets@ aol.com.

Chapter 1

"A dog can't talk," Amelia Marcus said. Her tween scorn should have melted the TV set.

"Sure he can," Josie Marcus said. "As soon as Uncle Bob shuts up, you'll hear him."

Josie, Amelia's mother, was snuggled next to her new husband, Dr. Ted Scottsmeyer, on the comfortably squishy black leather couch in their basement family room. Amelia was sprawled in the recliner, but she wasn't alone. Two tabby cats, brown-striped Harry and orange Marmalade, were curled in her lap. Festus, the black Lab, snored next to her chair.

The family was watching a TV commercial for Uncle Bob's Doggy Day Camp. Uncle Bob, a pudgy, round-faced man, wore clownish blue overalls, a red flannel shirt, and a white bone for a bow tie. Bob had his arm around a curly-haired black Labradoodle, as awkward as a blind date.

"He looks like a big baby with a bad haircut," Amelia said.

Josie frowned at the spite in her daughter's voice, but Ted cheerfully ignored it.

"Can't argue with you there," Ted said.

"The dog looks smarter than he does," Amelia said, still looking for a fight.

"Right again," Ted said.

The black dog had more dignity than Uncle Bob,

Josie thought. The odd couple sat on the steps of a rustic log cabin, Uncle Bob's day-camp headquarters.

Uncle Bob shot out words like a machine pistol. *"Don't take my word for it,"* he said. *"Ask Ralph the Talking Dog. Ralph, how is life for the poor pups who don't go to Uncle Bob's?"*

"Ruff!" Ralph the Labradoodle said.

"That's right," Uncle Bob said. *"They're all alone at home while the lucky dogs at Uncle Bob's run, jump, and play with their friends and our certified Doggy Camp Counselors. So don't let your dog live a life that's . . ."* He paused dramatically.

"Ruff!" Ralph said on cue, and wagged his tail.

"That's just stupid," Amelia said.

"So stupid it's funny," Josie said, and giggled. She couldn't help it. Her twelve-year-old was being such a sourpuss tonight.

"All his commercials are lame," Amelia said. "Last time he ate a peanut butter dog treat. That's gross."

"It did sort of turn my stomach," Josie said. "Watching him play fetch on his hands and knees with a bunch of dogs was pretty desperate."

What happened to my little girl's sense of humor? she wondered. Josie studied her daughter's blossoming figure, shoulder-length glossy brown hair, and the sprinkling of chocolate freckles across her nose, and reminded herself once again that Amelia was no little girl. Lately her daughter's moods changed from silly to snarly to boy crazy in seconds.

This evening, she was stuck in surly mode. Worse, she tried to pick a fight with her stepfather, Ted. I'm darn lucky to find a man like Ted, especially at age thirty-four. How long will he tolerate my daughter's rude behavior?

"Ads like Uncle Bob's give St. Louis TV color," Josie said. "Otherwise, all we'd watch would be bland ads for big-box stores and franchises."

"The ads may be awful, but that's why you remember them," Ted said. "Bad ads help small businesses fight the giants. Remember Becky the Queen of Carpet advertising Becky's Carpet and Tile Superstore?"

Amelia groaned. "She was even stupider than Uncle Bob."

"But you remembered her," Ted said. "Especially when Becky rode that corny flying carpet over the Arch."

"Whatever happened to her friend Wanda the Princess of Tile?" Josie asked. "She used to fly with her, too."

"Maybe she got rolled up in a carpet and dumped in the river," Ted said.

"Hmpf!" Amelia said, and lapsed into sullen silence.

"Is Uncle Bob's Doggy Day Camp any good?" Josie asked.

"I don't know," Ted said. "Most of our clinic clients take their dogs to Westminster Dog Day Care. It's closer to our clinic."

Ted, a vet with a small practice, was the co-owner of the St. Louis Mobo-Pet Clinic in the nearby Village of Rock Road. Their Fresno Court house was a short drive away in Maplewood, a colorful old suburb of St. Louis.

Josie was proud of their new—well, new to them— house, a pocket-sized precursor of the McMansion. Built in the thirties, the Tudor Revival cottage was a soft yellow-gold brick, a pleasant contrast to the city's sooty red brick. The house was beautifully crafted, with art-glass windows, an arched wooden front door with wrought-iron hinges, and satiny, caramel-colored woodwork.

The basement family room was paneled in warm honey-colored knotty pine, and a braided rug made it cozy.

Josie and Ted had spent that fine September afternoon raking leaves in the yard, and now she was pleasantly tired.

"It's eight thirty, Amelia," Josie said. "You have school tomorrow. Time for bed."

The expected protest didn't materialize. Amelia shrugged and headed upstairs, striped Harry riding her shoulder and orange Marmalade draped over her arm. Festus stayed by Ted, but the big black Lab would join Amelia later.

Josie rested her head on Ted's strong shoulder, enjoying her man. His long legs were stretched out. Ted was six feet tall, with thick brown hair. He smelled like coffee and cinnamon with a faint tang of wood smoke. He liked to cook and was kind to animals. He put up with her daughter's bad moods. No, Ted even seemed to enjoy Amelia most of the time.

They'd be married a year in November, and Josie had never expected to be this happy. She'd been a single mom struggling to raise her daughter on a mystery shopper's salary. She wouldn't have made it if Jane, Josie's mother, hadn't let her daughter and granddaughter live in the downstairs apartment in Jane's two-family flat at a greatly reduced rent. Josie had dated a few men, then given up on love. She didn't have time to date. If Amelia's cat, Harry, hadn't needed to see a vet, she wouldn't have met Ted.

"Thank you for putting up with Amelia," she said, and kissed his ear.

Ted shrugged. "It's not easy being twelve," he said. "She's doing a pretty good job. And Uncle Bob's commercial was stupid."

"And funny," Josie said.

"Give her time to sort out her opinions," Ted said. "She still has a lot to think about."

Josie didn't want to think about anything. She just wanted a quiet evening with her new husband.

After the ten o'clock news, Ted stretched and said, "I'm tired. Let's go upstairs."

"Amelia should be asleep by now," Josie said hopefully.

"We'll be very, very quiet," Ted said.

They tiptoed upstairs and walked through the newly renovated midcentury modern kitchen, a chic turquoise with a checkerboard floor. Ted opened the back door to let Festus outside. The Lab trotted across the deck and out into the yard. Josie checked the kitchen phone for messages. Nothing.

"You look worried," Ted said.

"I am," she said. "I haven't heard from Mom since Friday afternoon and we usually talk at least once a day. I left her another message at dinnertime, and she still hasn't called back. I haven't heard from her in two and a half days."

"Your mom's not alone," he said. "If anything was wrong, we'd hear from her downstairs renter, Franklin Hyzy. She was probably out with Frank this beautiful weekend."

"Probably," Josie said. But a nagging voice said something was wrong. If she didn't hear from her mother by tomorrow afternoon, she'd drive over to Jane's house.

Ted opened the front door and the couple stepped out onto the small front porch to study their peaceful street, softly silvered with moonlight. The other three houses on Fresno Court were dark.

"Did you see the change on the empty house next door?" Josie asked. "The real estate agent's sign with the 'sold' banner is finally gone. I wonder if new neighbors will be moving in soon."

She locked the door and Ted whistled for Festus to come out of the backyard. The Lab raced by them and bounded upstairs to Amelia's room.

Ted and Josie climbed the stairs together, hand in hand. The narrow hallway was softly lit by graceful wall sconces with amber shades, the original nineteen thirties Virden lights. Amelia's cozy purple bedroom with its dramatically slanted ceiling was the first room.

Josie put her fingers to her lips and checked on her daughter. Amelia seemed to be asleep. Harry slept by her head, Marmalade was curled near her hip, and Festus snored on her feet.

Josie kissed her daughter on the forehead.

"There's hardly room for her in that bed with all the animals," she whispered to Ted and smiled. Amelia's window overlooked the backyard of the sold house. Josie closed Amelia's curtains and made a mental note to check them at bedtime if they had neighbors again.

Back out in the hall, she whispered, "Sure hope the new neighbors will be better than the last woman with the yappy dog."

"Wouldn't take much to be better than she was," Ted said.

"I'd like a family about our age," Josie said.

"With a quiet dog or a cat they'll take to the clinic," Ted said.

Amelia's voice floated out of her purple bedroom. "I hope it's a family with a boy my age," she said.

Just what we don't need, Josie thought, and tried not to sigh.

Chapter 2

"Amelia Marcus, you are not going to school dressed like a prostitot," Josie said. I am so not ready for this fight at seven thirty on a Monday morning, she thought.

Amelia's red skating skirt was shockingly short, showing her long, coltish legs and nearly exposing her panties. There was more material in the girl's white top than in her skirt.

Josie knew something was off when she saw Amelia waiting by the front door, backpack at her feet, a suspiciously innocent look on her face. Most Mondays, Josie had to remind Amelia at least three times that they had to leave for school.

"Mom," Amelia protested, making the three-letter word four syllables.

The skimpy skirt was easily fixed. Josie used to pull that same stunt on her mother. "That skirt's too short for school," Josie said. "Unroll it."

Amelia angrily yanked on her skirt and the waistband unrolled. Now the red skirt was an acceptable length.

That's when Josie's alert ears picked up an odd rattle, and she noticed her daughter wasn't wearing a bra. "Let me see that top," she said.

"Mom, it's not low cut," Amelia said. "It's not sleeveless and it doesn't show my stomach."

"So why does it rattle?" Josie said. "White cotton

doesn't make that noise. Turn around so I can see your back."

Amelia reluctantly swung to the right and Josie saw her daughter's slender, pale back and more—way more. The top was backless and held together with chains. The fabric had been cut away from neck to hip, and the edges hemmed crookedly. The tarnished brass chains were too heavy for the light fabric. They sagged and dragged it down.

"Where did you get that top?" Josie asked, fighting not to sound accusing. That top must have cost more than a hundred bucks before the amateur alterations, and Josie hadn't bought it. She braced herself for the answer. Please, please don't let my girl be a shoplifter, she prayed.

"I made it," Amelia said.

"I can see you've recycled the top," Josie said. "But where did you get it?"

"At the garage sale next to Emma's house last Saturday," Amelia said. "We went to it."

Josie felt weak with relief. Emma, Amelia's best friend, was funny and studious, with strict parents. No way the girls would go on a shoplifting spree.

"Why did you cut it up?" Josie asked.

Amelia's words poured out in a rush. "I got this top for seventy-five cents because it had a big stain on the back. I bought it with my own money. Emma found these chains in her mom's sewing box and I cut out the back and sewed the chains myself."

"I see that," Josie said. "You made this in your room?"

"No, at Emma's," Amelia said. "We didn't make a mess."

"I'm glad you didn't, but you're still not wearing it to school."

"But, Mom, there's one just like it at Charlotte Russe," Amelia said. "It's twenty-three dollars."

"Charlotte Russe, prostitot headquarters," Josie said.

"Prostitot's not even a word," Amelia said. "Charlotte Russe has awesome clothes. Everybody at school wears them, and you won't let me."

"Oh, Amelia," Josie said. "If everyone at school—" She skidded to a stop. Josie caught herself before she said *jumped off a bridge, would you follow them?*

Whew. That was close, Josie thought. Amelia is self-shortening her skirts the way I did at her age, and I'm channeling my mother.

Josie quickly switched her sentence to "—dresses like that, you're still not wearing that top to school."

"But it only shows my back," Amelia said.

"And a lot of side boob when you move," Josie said. "That's too much skin for school. Go change. Put on a bra and another shirt."

"But, Mom, I'm gonna be late."

"Then you'd better rush. You should have thought of that before you sprung that outfit on me right before we're supposed to leave for school, Amelia. You know you can't wear that top, or you wouldn't have sneaked it into the house."

"I didn't sneak it," Amelia said. "I *put* it in my purse because it was easier to carry. When I got home Saturday, I fed the animals, then we ate dinner, and I forgot."

"Fine," Josie said. "But we're wasting time talking. Hurry."

Amelia ran upstairs and was back down two minutes later, in a crisp white button-down shirt, a pink scarf draped around her neck.

"Very chic," Josie said.

Amelia's smile was a pleasant surprise. "The white top was kinda lame."

"Not really your style," Josie agreed.

"YOLO," Amelia said and shrugged.

"YOLO," short for "you only live once," had replaced the all-purpose teen "whatever." Josie didn't like the new phrase or its philosophy but hoped if she kept quiet, Amelia would find another favorite word.

"Let's go," Josie said, and they ran out into the sun-drenched fall day and to Josie's beat-up gray Honda.

She navigated the back streets in tense silence, relieved that rush-hour traffic was light for a Monday. Soon she was on Lindbergh Boulevard, driving through a rich ghetto in west St. Louis County. Barring an accident, they'd be at the Barrington School for Boys and Girls in fifteen minutes.

This fall, Amelia was in ninth grade, the last year of middle school at Barrington. A late July birthday meant Amelia was nearly eight months younger than some of her classmates, but she was still bright enough to win a scholarship. By Barrington standards, Maplewood was "inner city." Josie thought that meant it had older brick homes, real sidewalks, and an undeserved reputation for crime. Many Barrington mothers bragged they hadn't been in "the city" for decades and saw St. Louis as hopelessly crime-ridden.

Oh well, she thought. Thanks to Barrington's sheltered suburban view, my daughter qualifies for the school's diversity program. It's still a struggle to pay the stiff fees and the four-figure stipend, but my Amelia does well there.

Josie's battered gray Honda Accord breezed past artfully landscaped multimillion-dollar homes. Many of the Barrington students lived in these mansions. Amelia pointed to a private drive leading off Lindbergh. The street's sign, a black shield, said OAKLEIGH HEIGHTS ROAD — PRIVATE in gold script.

"Kate Rivington, the new girl in my class, lives on that street," Amelia said. "I'm invited to a party at her house on Friday night. Can I go, Mom? Palmer's mom will drive us."

"Isn't Emma going?" Josie said.

"She can't make it," Amelia said. "But everyone else is going. And you like Palmer and her mom."

"I do, but I don't know anything about this new family," Josie said. She thought some of the Barrington trust-fund babies were poor little rich kids raised by nannies and housekeepers. Some middle schoolers were already experimenting with alcohol and sex and forming vicious cliques.

Palmer Lindell's parents, Priscilla and Gifford, were involved and protective. Maybe a little too protective, but Josie didn't consider that a fault at Amelia's age.

"The Rivingtons are from Philadelphia, Mom. Kate's dad works with Palmer's father. He's a C-something. CFO, COO, CEO, some kinda big deal. Kate's older brother has a scholarship to City University. Please, Mom? I have to tell her if I'm going."

"The Rivingtons sound good, but let me talk with Priscilla first," Josie said. "If Mrs. Lindell says they're okay, you can go."

"Yes!" Amelia gave a fist pump. "Can I have a new outfit? Please?"

"I think you're due for one," Josie said. "We might even find something at Charlotte Russe. Not all their clothes are bad. We can look at styles online."

She turned right off Lindbergh and was soon at Barrington School. The austere redbrick and white trim Georgian campus looked especially fine against the china blue sky, surrounded by the blazing red oaks and orange sweet gums. Josie carefully negotiated the turn into the curved driveway and parked behind a black Beemer.

"Bye, Mom," Amelia said. She grabbed her backpack and hurried off to join her friend Emma. Josie missed the days when her little girl used to kiss her good-bye.

Back at home, Josie poured herself a cup of coffee, checked her phone messages, and saw her mother hadn't called yet. Something was wrong. Josie knew it.

If Mom doesn't call me by noon, I'm going to her flat, Josie thought. She called Jane again and got her voice mail. She could be out walking her dog, Josie decided.

Rather than worry about her mother, Josie called Priscilla Lindell. Palmer's mother was as prim as her name, trophy-wife thin, and perfectly manicured, with her blond hair sprayed into submission. She was a stay-at-home mom. Many of the Barrington mothers looked down their patrician noses at Josie and her pink-collar job.

But Josie had seen Priscilla stand up to Barrington's formidable head of school, Miss Apple, and defend her daughter. Priscilla had spirit. The two women respected each other.

Priscilla knew all about the party. "I'll come by for Amelia about seven. I think it will be good for both our girls," she said. "Simon and Eve Rivington are solid people. She's already on three boards and he's CFO of my husband's corporate real estate agency. Eve assured me that they will both be home."

"Good," Josie said. "Some of these class parties can get out of hand. I'd like Amelia home by nine. Will that work for you? I can pick up the girls."

"Would you? Gifford and I would like to go to dinner, but we'll be home before nine."

"My pleasure," Josie said.

"Twelve is such a worrisome age for girls, isn't it?" Priscilla said. "And I fear it's only going to get worse. You heard that Jace Parkington got sent home from school last Friday?"

"What for?" Josie asked. Jace and her clique were troublemakers.

"Inappropriate dress," Priscilla said. "She wore a pair of low-cut skinny jeans with holes in them—deliberate holes. I think they're called 'destroyed.' Her teacher caught her showing off her tattoo."

"She has a tattoo at twelve?" Josie asked.

"A rose. It was below her hipbone. Her jeans were cut so low, everyone could see the tattoo. Her teacher caught her showing it off to the high school boys and sent her home. The housekeeper had to pick her up. At least the tattoo was temporary.

"I'm so glad our girls don't dress like that, aren't you, Josie?"

"Amelia would never get out of this house in that outfit," Josie said truthfully.

Chapter 3

"Hey, Josie, you like dogs?" *Crunch! Crunch!*

Harry the Horrible, head of the St. Louis branch of Suttin Services, called Josie the moment she hung up from talking to Palmer's mom.

I hope he has a mystery-shopping assignment, Josie thought. I could use the money for Amelia's party dress.

Crack! Crunch! Harry sounded like Festus with a bone.

"Sure, I like dogs," Josie said.

"Figured you'd have to, being married to a vet and all," he said. "That's why I called you first. I need a mystery shopper with a buncha dogs. You must have dogs coming out your ears."

"Why do I need dogs for this assignment?" Josie asked warily.

"The Certified Pet Care Centers want a mystery shopper"—*crack!*—"to check out three dog day-care places."

Chomp.

What is he eating? Josie wondered. The man is a junk-food junkie.

"CPCC is a big deal." *Slurp!* "Their seal on a day-care or boarding facility is a guarantee that it has high-class pet care. It's worth thousands in extra business each year."

Crunch! Crunch!

Was he chewing gravel?

"People are nuts about their dogs," Harry said. "They'll pay anything to make them happy. Treat them like children. Better than children. Nobody gets little Fenster a berry facial, but they'll buy one for the dog. They feed mutts filet mignon. Board their dog in suites that are nicer than my bedroom."

That last one wouldn't surprise Josie. She'd seen Harry's office, a dark, sunless cave carpeted in fast-food wrappers and crumpled take-out bags. She'd never been to Harry's home, but he was short, hunched, and, like his name, hairy, from his ears to his toes. She knew about his hairy toes from the awful August when she saw him in shorts and sandals. The sight was seared into her brain. Only his dome was follicle-free. Harry was the only person who didn't think that was funny.

Crack! Crunch!

"So what do I have to do, Harry?" she asked.

"Mystery-shop three different dog day-care centers. Treat three dogs to the best each place has to offer."

"And the client pays for everything?"

"Yep, treats, grooming, supervised play, the whole shebang. But you have to bring a different dog to each place. They asked for different personalities and sizes. They want a big dog, sixty pounds or more, for one assignment."

Festus, Josie thought. The black Lab was the clinic blood-donor dog. He deserved some pampering.

"And a medium dog, about fifteen, sixteen pounds."

Stuart Little, my mother's shih tzu, Josie thought. It will give me an excuse to call her again and go to her house.

"And a little dog that weighs ten pounds or less," Harry said. "A small breed like a yappy or something."

"You mean a Yorkie?" Josie asked.

"Yeah, the ones that wear the bows in their hair. They yap a lot."

"Would a Chihuahua do?" Josie asked. My best friend, Alyce, has one named Bruiser, she thought. She loves mystery-shopping with me.

"Sure," he said. "But no puppies." *Crunch!* "They have to be adult dogs. At least one has to have hair long enough to be groomed."

"That would be the shih tzu," Josie said.

"Good," he grunted. "You gotta tour the facility, talk to the owner or manager, and answer the questions on the checklist I'll fax you. You can either leave the dog that same day or make an appointment and come back. The dog can stay a full day or a half day.

"With your husband being a vet, you should be able to get your hands on a pack of dogs."

"I don't think we can use Ted's patients for this assignment," Josie said. "But I can get you three dogs I know well. One's mine, one is my mother's, and the third belongs to a friend."

"Fine with me," he said. *Crack!*

"What about cats?" Josie asked. Harry didn't like being away from his home or his pal Amelia, but laid-back Marmalade, the clinic's feline blood donor, would love the attention. The orange tabby was a real ham.

"Nope," he said. "Dogs only. The three day-care places are Westminster Dog Day Care in Maplewood, Bow-Wow Heaven in North County, and Uncle Bob's Doggy Day Camp in South County."

"I've seen Uncle Bob's ads on TV," Josie said. "I don't know the other places."

"Uncle Bob and Bow-Wow have a bunch of locations, but the CPCC wants you to mystery-shop only the ones on the list. I've seen the Web sites for these dog places. They're like resorts, with massages, fitness training, even lap pools. Your job is to make sure they're as good as they look."

Crunch!

"Do you have a dog?" Josie asked. "Maybe I could take your pet to a day-care place."

"Nope," he said. "Animals are too much work. I don't get why people are so nuts about them. Do you know people actually let dogs sleep on their beds?"

"What's wrong with that?" Josie asked, uneasy.

Her mother-in-law, Lenore Scottsmeyer Hall, had criticized Josie for letting the family pets sleep on Amelia's bed. She'd said it looked "Third World." But Lenore was a rich doctor's wife in a Boca Raton mansion—and Josie was happy Ted's mother stayed in Florida most of the time. Harry looked like he slept under a bridge.

Crack! "Animals are dirty," he said. "Dogs are covered with ticks and fleas."

"Not our dog," Josie said. "And our cats take baths all the time."

"So they're covered in cat spit. And they scratch around in litter boxes," Harry said. "That's like playing in a toilet."

It is?

Crack! Crack! Crack! Harry sounded like he was breaking the bones of a small forest animal

"What are you eating?" Josie asked, eager to change the subject.

"Dessert," he said.

"At ten in the morning?"

"You know what they say: Life is short. Eat dessert first."

Harry's arteries had to be a lard logjam. Josie couldn't understand why he hadn't keeled over from a heart attack.

"I'm eating a Twinkie log," he said.

"What's that?"

"A frozen Twinkie dipped in white chocolate and rolled in crushed cashews."

"For real?" Josie asked.

Crack!

It sounded like he was chomping a chunk of firewood.

"Hey, don't knock it if you haven't tried it," Harry said. "You should have one. I get them at the Carnival Diner."

"I'm afraid to eat a Twinkie log, Harry. I want to see my daughter grow up. Are you having another course after you eat the log?"

"White Castle pâté," he said proudly. "The classiest way to serve my favorite burger."

"Pâté" was one four-letter word Josie never thought she'd hear Harry use.

"Your husband would love it," he said.

"I'm not much of a cook," Josie said.

"Don't have to be. The recipe is a snap." *Crack!* "Here, I'll give it to you. You grind up fifteen sliders in a blender with water."

"Do I leave the buns on?" Josie asked.

"The whole enchilada, except it's a hamburger," Harry said. "Buns, pickles, onions."

"How much water?"

"Enough to make the burgers liquid," Harry said. "There's a trick to it: You gotta mash up the burgers three at a time or you'll burn out your blender. Keep scraping the sides and adding water. Then pour the glop in a greased loaf pan."

Josie tried to block the mental picture of pulverized sliders pouring into a greased baking pan.

"You really need that extra grease with White Castles?" she asked.

"Just a touch. I like to put some raw bacon in the pan first. Then bake it at three twenty-five for forty-five minutes, take it out of the pan—that's when you'll be glad you greased it—and let it cool.

"Then comes the piece dee resistance," he said in fractured French. "You ice it with half yogurt and half sour cream and sprinkle it with fresh parsley."

"Will it still taste the same if I leave off the parsley?" Josie asked.

"You can laugh, but real men like real food," Harry said. "You've been married for almost a year, and you're no spring chicken. Kinda cute for a MILF, but—"

"Harry! This conversation is not appropriate," Josie said.

"Sorry. Don't say anything, okay? Or corporate will make me go to another one of those sensitivity classes."

"My lips are sealed," Josie said.

"I didn't mean to get personal, but men like man food—meat—and variety. White Castle pâté will fulfill those needs. Don't forget the candles to set the mood. I've got one burning now on my desk."

"What kind of candle?" Josie asked. The mood in the office was always glum.

"A slider-scented candle, shaped like a White Castle box." Harry took a deep breath. "I'm inhaling one now. Ambrosia."

Josie swore she could smell onions reeking through the holes in her phone.

"Now, that's romance," he said. "Serve that pâté to Ted by candlelight tonight and I guarantee you'll thank me tomorrow."

Josie felt herself blushing. The idea of Harry even hinting at ways to improve her love life was too terrible to contemplate.

Chapter 4

Ew, Josie thought, as she hung up the phone. After talking to Harry, I want another shower.

I could complain to Suttin headquarters about my boss's improper conversation, but mystery-shopping assignments are scarce these days. I suspect the St. Louis office is barely hanging on: Harry is the only full-time employee. If Suttin fires my boss, it might close the local office. I can't risk that. Ted makes good money, but he's still paying off his share of the loan for the clinic expansion, and we have our new house. We need my small income.

Besides, I don't actually work in the office. It's not like I see Harry every day or he chases me around his desk.

Josie rationalized her way out of her dilemma, then tackled her next worry. She called her mother and got Jane's voice mail. Again.

"Hi, Mom, it's me," Josie began her message. "Can I borrow Stuart Little? My new mystery-shopping assignment is dog day care, and we're supposed to use real dogs. I can take Festus to one place, but they'd also like a dog who needs grooming. The client will pay for all Stuart's beauty treatments, plus treats and supervised playtime. He'll have fun. I'd like to scout the place this afternoon. Want to go with me? Please call. I haven't heard from you since Friday, and I'm worried."

She hung up. I sounded too plaintive, she decided. I'm

thirty-four and whining for my mommy. Maybe Ted was right. Mom's an adult and has an active life. If anything was wrong, Mrs. Mueller, the busybody next door, would call me to gloat—or make me feel guilty.

Josie still felt uneasy. She checked the kitchen clock. Ten thirty. At noon, I'm driving over there. Mom's silence has gone on too long.

If Josie couldn't wash that icky conversation with Harry out of her mind, she could clean something while she waited. She poured herself a fresh mug of coffee and headed down to the basement laundry room. Amelia's striped cat padded after her.

"Shouldn't you be sleeping on Amelia's bed, dude?" she asked, scratching Harry's warm brown ears. "That's okay. I can use the company, Harry. It's not your fault you have the same name as my boss the troll."

The laundry room was plain and practical, with a washer-dryer, a white Formica sorting table, and sturdy white-painted shelves for supplies.

She sorted clothes from the basket under the laundry chute. Harry curled up on Amelia's crumpled pastel shirts and socks, while Josie threw in a load of whites. Soon she was soothed by the wash-day sounds and smells: the rhythmic churning of the washer, the sharp sting of bleach, the clean scent of the detergent. Fifteen minutes later, the dryer was rumbling in concert.

By eleven forty-five, Josie had folded one load and shooed away Harry when he settled on the pile of towels warm from the dryer. She reloaded the washer and the dryer, then climbed the stairs to put away the clean laundry.

Josie checked her voice mail and was relieved to hear that Jane had called fifteen minutes ago and left this message:

"Josie, of course I'll go with you this afternoon, but I don't want to take Stuart today. I want to see this facility

first before I leave him. Come by at twelve thirty, and we'll have lunch. I made your favorite chicken salad with the grapes."

Yes! Josie thought. Mom's okay, and I get lunch, too. At first, the message made her smile. Mom hadn't originally wanted Stuart Little. Ted had talked her into taking the shih tzu when his owner refused to pay the dog's vet bills and abandoned him. Now Jane was so protective, she wouldn't let her dog stay anyplace until she inspected it first.

But Jane's message nagged at Josie, and she replayed it. Mom doesn't quite sound like herself, she decided. Well, I'll know soon enough. She changed into a fresh blouse and clean jeans and hurried to her Honda for the short drive.

Jane's house was a two-story redbrick flat with a white-painted porch. When Josie was nine, her father had divorced her mother and moved to Chicago, where he started another family. Jane and Josie lost their comfortable life. This flat and its small income were the only things Jane had rescued from her wrecked marriage. Her lawyer ex-husband never paid the promised child support and Jane didn't have the money to take him to court. She took a safe, dull job at a bank to support her daughter.

Josie never saw her father again. She and her mom lived in the upstairs flat until Josie went to college. During her junior year, Josie had ended her engagement to a sweet, safe accountant. She had been dazzled by Nate. She wanted to believe the lean, brown-haired Canadian was rich, and that was why he owned his own plane and flew her to New York for dinner and the Cayman Islands for scuba diving on the weekends. Their romance was all-consuming. For Josie it was almost a form of madness.

Jane had disapproved of Nate and his effect on Josie. Then Josie discovered she was pregnant with Amelia.

She was sure they'd marry. But before she could tell Nate the happy news, her lover was arrested for smuggling drugs into the US.

Josie blamed herself for ignoring the telltale signs that Nate was dealing. She refused to bring her baby into his shadowy, dangerous world. She dropped out of college to become a mystery shopper.

Jane was deeply disappointed in Josie and refused to forgive her until she finally saw her baby granddaughter. Jane fell in love with Amelia. The downstairs flat was empty at the time, and Jane insisted Josie and Amelia move in. They stayed for the next eleven years.

For nine of those years, Josie didn't date. Then she met such disastrous men, she resolved to live without love. Nate, Amelia's father, had triggered Josie's current happiness. He'd been locked away in prison until Amelia was ten. Then Nate was released from prison and showed up on Josie's doorstep. Her handsome lover was now a hopeless alcoholic.

Josie was horrified, and tried to shelter Amelia from Nate's drinking. She knew only her father's good side before his sudden death. She had a photo of Nate as a brash boy with a striped tabby and wanted a cat like her father's.

Josie and Amelia found Harry at the Humane Society. Josie knew nothing about cat care. She fed Harry only dry food, and the cat became so lethargic Amelia feared her cat was dying. Josie called the St. Louis Mobo-Pet Clinic. Ted was on duty that day and parked the clinic's big blue van in front of her mother's flat.

Josie was impressed by Ted's gentleness with the skittish, frightened cat. Ted calmed Harry and examined him. Harry's problem turned out to be minor and easily treated. A combination of canned and dried food would keep Harry healthy.

Funny how our love story started right here with a

constipated cat, Josie thought as she parked her car in front of her mother's house. The red brick was warmed by the fall sunshine and framed by fiery red and orange trees. Jane's yellow mums made bright golden mounds in their pots on the porch.

Mom's flowers look better than Mrs. Mueller's, Josie thought. The neighbor's bronze mums look straggly this year. I like the bushes Mrs. M put in to separate her front yard from Mom's. But what's wrong with Mom's grass?

Josie got out of her Honda and saw deep tire tracks. From a car? she wondered. They were gouged into Jane's velvety grass from the curb to the sidewalk, and then a good twenty feet from the sidewalk through the yard, stopping right before the vehicle plowed into the bushes.

It looked like the car had backed up and tried to follow the first set of tracks, then branched off and created a second set. A good third of the lawn was chewed up.

The tire tracks had been covered with new sod, but the scars were still raw and ugly.

I was right, Josie thought, hurrying up the sidewalk. I knew something was wrong. A car jumped the curb and drove across Mom's yard. But who was it and why didn't she tell me?

On her mother's porch, Josie checked out the downstairs flat, where she'd lived with Amelia for more than eleven years. She saw no sign of Franklin Hyzy, the new tenant. She knocked on her mother's front door and Jane called down, "Come on up, Josie."

Woof! Stuart Little said, waving his furry flag of a tail.

Josie stopped at the top of the steep stairs to scratch the dog's silky ears, then followed the plastic runner across her mother's pale green wall-to-wall carpet to Jane's kitchen, the homiest room in the flat.

Josie smelled cinnamon-apple cake and fresh coffee and saw chicken salad heaped on two rose-flowered china plates. A cut-glass vase of fall leaves was the centerpiece. Jane made even a casual lunch with her daughter an occasion.

Josie's mother wore a comfortable blue pantsuit and a helmet of perfectly coiffed gray hair. She hugged her daughter, and Josie breathed in her scent of Estée Lauder and noticed the small spot of thinning hair on her crown was expertly hidden by Jane's stylist. Her mother was gracefully fighting the advances of age.

"Sit down and eat your salad," Jane said. "Have a warm roll. Coffee?"

"Please," Josie said.

"Now, tell me about this mystery-shopping assignment," Jane said quickly, before Josie could ask about the lawn.

Josie did, skipping Harry's sly advice about her love life.

"I thought we could take Stuart Little to Uncle Bob's Doggy Day Camp," Josie said. "This is a spectacular salad, Mom. I like it even better with red grapes instead of green ones."

"I can see," Jane said. "Your plate's empty already. More?"

"No, thanks," Josie said.

"I'm not sure about taking Stuart to day care," Jane said as she cut Josie a generous slice of apple cake and refilled her cup.

"What's wrong?" Josie asked. "You don't want to leave Stuart there because of the stupid TV ads?"

"No, the ads don't bother me," Jane said. "The problem is Frank Hyzy works there now."

"But that's good," Josie said. "You like Frank. You still get along with him even though he lives downstairs, don't you?"

Jane's silence filled the warm kitchen.

"Don't you?" Josie prompted. The cake was gone. Josie mashed the last crumbs with her fork and ate them.

"I'm not sure," Jane said. "I don't know what to think anymore, Josie. He's an attractive man." She took a long drink of coffee.

"He sure is," Josie said. "He's a senior hunk with that thick, curly white hair and those brown eyes. He has good manners and a sense of humor. He's a widower. His grown daughter, Laura, is a vet at Ted's clinic and she fits in well. Frank is perfect, Mom."

"Not quite," Jane said. "You saw that mess on my lawn?"

"Looks like a car slammed into your yard," Josie said.

Jane put down her coffee cup with trembling hands. "It was a car," she said. "It happened late Friday night.

"Frank was driving, Josie, and he was drunk."

Chapter 5

"Frank drove his car onto your lawn Friday night?" Josie said. This sounded surreal. "Was he hurt?"

"No, thank goodness," Jane said. "It happened about three in the morning, so I guess it was really Saturday. Frank drove into my yard and then passed out. I didn't hear him. Stuart's barking woke me up. I looked out the window, recognized Frank's car, threw on some clothes, and ran down there. He was snoring with his head on the steering wheel."

Josie tried to reconcile steady, sensible Frank with an unconscious drunk on a bender. She saw his calm brown eyes, his tall body with the slightly narrow shoulders, his neat, precise style of dressing, but she couldn't picture him passed out at the wheel of his dark blue Lincoln.

"I didn't know he drank, Mom," she said. "I didn't notice any obvious signs. He has no broken veins in his face, his hands don't shake, and I've never noticed alcohol on his breath."

"I didn't either," Jane said. "But I did wonder if something was wrong recently. We went out twice in the last three weeks and he drank more than usual: He had almost a full bottle of wine at dinner one night, and I had to drive us home. He had four beers when we went bowling Tuesday. He said he was okay to drive, and he went very, very slow, but the police stopped him."

"Driving too slowly is probably why he was stopped, Mom," Josie said. "That can be one of the signs of a drunk driver."

"The nice woman police officer didn't test him for alcohol," Jane said. "She told him to give me the keys, and I drove the rest of the way. Frank said he was relieved. After his wife died, he had a DUI and wrecked their car. He was afraid he'd lose his license if he got caught driving drunk again."

"I'd never guess Frank has an alcohol problem," Josie said.

"He doesn't," Jane said. "He drinks a little too much because he's lonely. I noticed his garbage clanked when he took it out last Monday, but that could be ketchup bottles or mayonnaise jars."

"Ketchup and mayonnaise come in plastic now, Mom," Josie reminded her. "So does most everything else." Except liquor and beer bottles, she thought. I'm not the only Marcus woman who's deluded herself about a man.

"Did you call the police when you found him?" she asked.

"No need," Jane said. "There was no damage except to my grass. Then I shook him awake and helped him into his flat."

Josie tried to picture her mother, barely five feet five, helping six-foot-tall Frank into his home.

"I checked him for signs of a stroke or heart attack, but he smelled like a brewery, Josie. There was no mistaking it. Frank was drunk. A quiet, well-behaved drunk, but he'd definitely been shellacking the goldfish bowl."

Josie hid a smile at that old-fashioned term for drinking.

"I didn't want a scandal," Jane said. "After I settled him on his couch, I hurried outside and examined his car for signs that he'd hit something, but there were no dents.

Then I backed his car out of my yard. I tried to follow the tracks he'd made, but the lawn was too muddy. I parked the car safely on the street."

"What about Mrs. Mueller, our own personal Neighborhood Watch program?" Josie asked. "He nearly ran over her bushes. She should have been out there raising Cain."

"She was, uh, indisposed," Jane said.

"Indisposed?" Josie asked.

Jane looked trapped, and it took Josie a few seconds to figure out what was wrong. Jane hated discussing bodily functions. Mrs. M had never shown any signs of ordinary humanity. She did have a daughter Josie's age, but Cheryl must have been ordered from a catalogue. No one ever mentioned Mr. Mueller, but their nosy neighbor must have been married once upon a time. Mrs. Mueller certainly had a first name, but no one used it.

"You mean Mrs. Mueller was on the commode when Frank trashed your lawn?" Josie asked. She snickered.

"She had that stomach flu," Jane said. "Everyone's had it around here. I'm lucky I've escaped so far."

"This is priceless," Josie said, and giggled. "The best gossip of the whole year happens right next door and Mrs. M is marooned on the toilet."

"I was lucky," Jane said. "When I ran outside to see to Frank, I saw her bathroom light was on. I woke up Frank and helped him in as fast as I could. When I ran back out again, her bathroom light was still on . . ."

"Hee-hee," Josie said. "The nosy old bat was incommoded."

"No reason to be crude, Josie," Jane said. "I'd just parked Frank's car when she came out in that ugly chenille robe."

"Her head crowned with sponge rollers?" Josie asked. "If Frank saw her in that getup he'd be instantly sober."

"Please, Josie, it's not funny," Jane said.

"Sorry, Mom." Josie tamped down her glee and listened. To distract herself, she got up and poured them both more coffee and cut another piece of cake. Jane waved away her offer of a slice, so Josie took it.

"I didn't say a word about Frank," Jane said, "but Mrs. Mueller figured out what happened. 'Your renter was driving drunk, wasn't he?' she said, all high and mighty.

"'He did no such thing,' I told her.

"'It's a sin to lie, Jane Marcus. I can see the tracks in your yard and the mud on his tires. His Lincoln wrecked your lawn, and he was drunk. It's illegal to drive in that condition. I'm calling the police.'

"'Go ahead,' I told her. 'You didn't see anything. It's my yard, and I'll tell the police I want it like this and leave those tire tracks there permanently, and you'll have to live next to them.'

"'He nearly hit my azaleas,' Mrs. Mueller said.

"'But he didn't, did he?' I said. 'So it's none of your business.'"

Jane looked indignant and waved her arms as she told her tale and—Josie suspected—embellished her dialogue.

"Azaleas," Josie said. "So that's what those bushes are. They have those frothy pink flowers in the spring."

"That's right," Jane said. "Mrs. Mueller's azaleas are pink. I was thinking of getting white ones along my property line, but now I don't want anything she has."

"I'd grow cactus," Josie said. "With long, sharp spines. What happened next?"

"Mrs. Mueller threatened to have the police Breathalyze Frank, but I said he was asleep in his home and the police had no right to wake up a private citizen at this hour and force him to take a test."

"How did Mrs. M take that?" Josie asked.

"She was furious," Jane said. "She told me, 'You're condoning his alcoholism.' She griped and carried on, but I let it go in one ear and out the other until she said, 'You could have had a good neighbor. Rowena Crum wanted to rent your flat. She's a good, quiet church lady. But no, you had to let a drunk move into our neighborhood.'

"Church lady!" Jane said. "Rowena's her little spy, and I wouldn't let her rent my flat if she paid double. But I took the high road, and that made Mrs. Mueller even madder.

"She started to say something else, and then she got this funny look, pulled her robe tighter, and ran back inside. I saw her bathroom light go on. She didn't bother me the rest of the night."

Jane's hands were shaking again. She took a long drink of her coffee. When she seemed calmer, Josie said, "What did you do next, Mom?"

"I went back to check on Frank. He was dead to the world, snoring up a storm on the couch. I pulled off his shoes and covered him with a blanket, then turned off the lights, locked his door, and went upstairs.

"It took a while for me to calm down, Josie. I've been dating Frank, but it's not serious."

Josie thought it was. Jane had worked hard after her divorce to support her difficult daughter. She deserved a man who'd appreciate her. But if her mother needed that polite fiction to preserve her dignity, Josie wouldn't argue with her.

"After your father left, I learned to live alone, Josie. I like my freedom. I don't want a relationship with a man who has a drinking problem. Not at my time of life."

"Of course, Mom," Josie said. The two women sipped their coffee, and Josie thought of the silver locket Jane had given her engraved with ALWAYS MY DAUGHTER, NOW TOO MY FRIEND.

For many years they weren't friends. Jane had criticized her daughter and nagged her to date "nice" men. Jane's definition of "nice" was suitors of staggering dullness.

Since Josie had married Ted, Jane had mellowed. The two women were friends and sometimes coconspirators.

"You must have been worried sick," Josie said.

"It was four thirty when I finally fell asleep," Jane said. "When I woke up the next morning, Franklin's car was gone. He didn't come back until four that afternoon. He had a trunkload of sod. He knocked on my door with a big bouquet of pink roses and sea salt chocolate caramels from Kakao."

"My favorite," Josie said.

"Mine, too," Jane said. "He was freshly shaved and all spiffed up, though his eyes were still bloodshot. I never saw a man look so apologetic. I let him in. Mrs. Mueller was standing out on my sidewalk, arms folded across her chest, glaring at us. I glared right back at her and she went into her yard.

"I poured Frank some coffee, put his roses in water, and we had a long talk. Frank apologized for the damage he did and said he'd fix it that day. You can see he's covered the tire tracks with new sod. It will be a few weeks before it takes root.

"I told him I couldn't rent to a man with a drinking problem. Frank said he knew that. He admitted he's been lonesome since his wife died.

"'I need a job to keep busy,' Frank said, 'and I need it fast. We used to board our dogs at Uncle Bob's, and he knew me. I went straight there at eight this morning. Uncle Bob has a high turnover—he's as crazy in person as he is on TV—and he's always looking for help. He hired me as a camp counselor to play with the dogs and walk them. I started this morning. I spent the day walking the dogs that are boarded. I just got off and stopped by the nursery to get your sod. I'll have it down before dark.'

"He had all the sod down and watered by six o'clock, and he cleaned the muddy sidewalk."

"Is he going to join Alcoholics Anonymous, Mom?"

"Frank says he doesn't need to go to meetings," Jane said. "He needs to work."

"Do you believe that?" Josie asked.

"I don't know," Jane said. "I really—" She stopped. "I really like Frank. But when I had my problem a couple of years ago, I needed professional help."

Jane had had a serious shopping addiction, but after many months of counseling, she had it under control.

"I told him I'd see," Jane said. "He's on probation."

"Smart. Where are the roses? Did you throw them out?"

"I couldn't. They're too expensive," Jane said, and her face turned pink. "They're in my bedroom."

In your bedroom, Josie thought. And on probation. Right.

Chapter 6

Bark! Ruff! Yip! Yap! Ow-oooooh!

Josie and Jane heard Uncle Bob's Doggy Day Camp before they saw it that afternoon. The dogs seemed to be competing to see which one barked the loudest.

Josie rounded the corner and saw Uncle Bob's trademark log cabin sprawled on several acres in suburban South County.

"Looks like Camp Run-a-Muck, where you sent me the summer I was ten," she said.

"That was Camp Agnus Dei," Jane said, her voice crisp. "It was run by the St. Louis Archdiocese. I wanted you to meet good Catholic girls."

"With bad kidneys," Josie said. "I had the bunk under a bed wetter. And I got poison ivy."

She saw Jane's face tighten and felt bad. That miserable week was more than two decades ago, she reminded herself. Your mother worked through her own vacation to send you to camp. Grow up.

She pulled into the parking lot and Jane scanned the cars. "I don't see Frank's blue Lincoln," she said.

"Maybe he's parked in an employee lot," Josie said.

"Maybe he's lying about working here," Jane said.

"That's easy to check," Josie said. "I'll ask when we're inside."

She checked her mystery-shopping questions: *Is the*

facility clean and free of pet waste, inside and out? Were you greeted at the door? Is the equipment in the indoor and outdoor play areas well maintained? Are big dogs separated from small dogs by size? By temperament? Can you see into the grooming area? Were you greeted at the reception desk? Does the facility require dogs to have shots?

The client's list asked more than twenty questions. Josie had trained herself to remember details. She couldn't take the list in with her.

"Look at that outdoor dog gym, Mom," she said. "It's better than the kids' playground near our home."

The plastic slides, ramps, tunnels, and teeter-totter in kindergarten colors looked new. A small, spidery Chihuahua was carefully picking his way down a low ramp while a twentysomething woman with a glossy brown ponytail said, "Come on, Chico, come on. Good dog!" She wore a blue polo shirt with CAMP COUNSELOR on the back in bold yellow letters.

Nearby, another counselor, a clean-cut young man with pink skin and short blond hair, said wearily, "Come on, Lucky. One more race through the tube, then up the ramp, and your exercise is done for the day."

Mr. Pink patted the entrance to a tomato red tube the size of a sewer main next to a blue inverted V-shaped ramp. The fat yellow Lab grinned at him and wagged his tail but refused to move, much less race.

"Treat?" Mr. Pink said, holding up a dog biscuit.

Woof! Lucky said, and wagged his tail.

"Not till you finish your exercise."

Lucky whined, stretched out flat, and covered his face with his paws.

"Okay, you can have your treat, but don't tell anyone," Mr. Pink said.

Better to be Lucky than good, Josie thought. And Lucky is very good at working his trainer.

Woof! Ruff! Grrrr!

In a nearby fenced grassy area, a collie, a sheepdog, and a golden retriever were tugging on a rope toy and growling playfully at one another.

Josie and Jane walked along a wide sidewalk that wound through thick green zoysia with suspicious brown patches. Zoysia often browned out in the fall, but Josie didn't think that was the case here. She didn't detect an unpleasant odor. She'd still give the place high marks for outdoor cleanliness.

The reception area was decorated in bold red, bright blue, and sunny yellow. The woman behind the red reception desk looked like a pug in a blue shirt. She had a small flat face, slightly bulging brown eyes, a sturdy body, and short brown hair. She was Beverly, according to her name tag.

Josie felt an odd urge to pat Beverly's head and give her a treat from the basket on her desk.

Beverly smiled and welcomed them immediately, and Josie mentally ticked off another good mark. "Of course you can tour our day camp," Beverly said. "Uncle Bob himself will take you."

"Good," Josie said. "We heard good things about your place from Franklin Hyzy. Does he work here?"

"Frank? He's our new hire. He's a real sweetie. He's out running an errand now."

Jane flashed Josie a relieved smile.

"Let me call Uncle Bob for your tour," Beverly said. She pressed a button and the yellow door behind her opened. Uncle Bob paused in the doorway like an aging actress making an entrance.

He was bigger and rounder than he appeared on TV, Josie thought. He looks like an oversized infant in his trademark outfit: blue overalls, red flannel shirt, and white-plastic-bone bow tie. Josie checked his feet to see if he was wearing giant clown shoes, but he had on subdued black sneakers. Bob was fiftysomething but as energetic as a teenager.

"Well, hot diggity," he said, clapping his hands and smiling. "Do we have new customers here? Yes, we do."

He turned to Josie. "What's your baby's name, sweetheart?"

"Amelia," Josie said.

"Amelia!" He savored the name. "A little girl! What breed is she?"

Breed? Josie thought. "Oh, Amelia's my daughter," she said. "She's in ninth grade. You want to talk to my mother. She's thinking about day care for her dog."

"And who is your baby?" he asked Jane.

"Stuart Little," she said. "He's a shih tzu."

"We love shih tzus," Uncle Bob said. "Let me show you all the fun things we have for Stuart." He bounced down a hall like a beach ball to a glassed-in yellow room divided into four bays.

Josie heard the roar of a supersized dryer in the first section and saw a woman in a white lab coat drying a black Scottie. The dog's leash was clipped to a pole and he stood quietly, proud chest out, enjoying the warm air.

"That's Karen," Uncle Bob said. "She loves grooming small dogs."

In the second bay a white standard poodle was standing in a big sink, getting his face rubbed with blue gunk. The dog's eyes were closed and he looked blissfully happy. His pink tongue snaked out and slurped the blue goo.

"That's Charlie," Uncle Bob said. "He's getting a blueberry facial. You can see he likes it."

"Why does a dog need a facial?" Josie asked.

"Makes their fur soft," Uncle Bob said. "Gets rid of tear stains. And for wrinkled dogs like pugs, bulldogs, and shar-peis, it cleans those hard-to-reach facial folds." Charlie slurped more blueberry facial.

"We have full grooming services, facials, full-body massages, nail clipping, and nail polish," Bob said. "We offer skin and hair treatments, including emulsifying, exfoliating, moisturizing, and coat conditioning, as well as your usual trimming and ear plucking. We also have an acupuncturist."

"Goodness!" Jane said. Josie doubted her hardworking mother had ever been pampered as well as these dogs.

They followed Uncle Bob out into the hall and past a door with a paw-print sign on the handle: SH! SESSION IN PROGRESS.

"If your dog has emotional problems, we have a pet psychiatrist and a pet psychic," he said, whispering.

"Stuart is healthy in mind and body," Jane whispered back.

Bob turned down a hall and opened another glass door. "Our doggy hotel for long-term boarding," he said. "You should live so well. Each room has a different theme. This is our Hawaiian Island doggy vacation."

Josie looked through glass at a room painted with turquoise waves. A low cot rested under a real potted palm. An embarrassed-looking boxer lounged under a miniature tiki hut. A dog-sized opening led to a fenced gravel yard outside.

"And here's my favorite," Bob said. "The luxury cruise. It's not occupied now, but I'll show you how big and comfortable it is."

The room was painted to look like the deck of an ocean liner, with a blue-and-white-striped canvas overhead. The same canvas covered a low cot. The walls were lined with life preservers, and ocean blue peeked through mahogany railings. Live goldfish swam behind brass portholes at dog level.

Bob opened the ocean liner's glass door, got down on his hands and knees, and barked at the goldfish, then crawled to the corner and pretended to lap water from the bowl. Next he crawled to the gravel run and barked.

"If he goes out on that gravel, I'm leaving," Josie said.

Uncle Bob waggled his hindquarters, barked again, then stood up and dusted his knees.

Back in the hall, he said, "Our clients like the idea of their dogs going on a cruise when they do." He pointed out more theme rooms, including a ski lodge.

Josie and Jane followed him down another hall. "Here are the indoor playrooms for little dogs and big dogs," Bob said. "It's a sunny day, so all the doggies are playing outside now and both rooms are empty."

The rooms were long, narrow, and windowless, with white tile floors.

"How big are they?" Josie asked.

"Twelve by five," he said. "Plenty of room for six or eight dogs."

Not by my client's standards, Josie thought.

"Do you separate dogs by temperament as well as size?" she asked.

"I'm not sure what you mean," Uncle Bob said.

"I mean some small dogs, like Jack Russells, are bundles of energy and don't play well with miniature poodles or shih tzus."

"I've never seen that," Uncle Bob said. "Next you'll have me separating them by color." His laugh was forced.

Wrong answer, Bob, Josie thought, and smiled at him. They toured the outdoor play yards for big and small dogs and the gym. "This is all new equipment," Uncle Bob said. "None of that sun-faded crap you see in kids' playgrounds. We treat our dogs better than most children."

Sadly, Josie thought he was right.

"Now, back inside," Uncle Bob said. "I've saved the best till last."

He opened the door to a small, square room with

bone-print wallpaper and a glittering disco ball on the ceiling. "This is our party room, for birthdays, doggy weddings, bark mitzvahs, and disco dancing. You should see the dogs boogie to 'Stayin' Alive.' They all get *Saturday Night Fever*."

He deftly steered Josie and Jane next door to a gift shop lined with racks of clothes, packaged treats, toys, and bins of biscuits.

"We sell the disco clothes right here," he said, and pulled a tiny, pink-sequin-spangled dress off a rack. "Our girls love to have their hair and nails done at the salon and dress up. For the boys, we have this disco-fever suit like John Travolta wore in the movie."

He produced a white jacket, vest, and pants, with a black shirt. "Bet this would look good on your little man, huh, Jane?"

Jane was speechless. Josie examined the suit and said, "Very authentic. Genuine polyester."

Bob beamed.

"And if you're of the Jewish persuasion, we have everything for a bark mitzvah," he said, and showed them blue and white yarmulkes and prayer shawls with the Star of David.

Jane looked shocked. Josie thought religious garb for dogs was vaguely sacrilegious.

"Uh, no thanks," she said quickly.

"We'll cater your doggy party," Bob said. "All our treats are organic: ice cream, peanut butter cakes, chicken-flavored treats. No chocolate—that's bad for doggies—but we ice the party cakes in cream cheese."

"Very nice," Josie said.

Jane seemed stunned.

"It's time for my lunch," Bob said. "Not only do my doggies eat organic, so do I. Let me show you where we make our treats and cakes."

He led them to a pristine kitchen scented with grilling

meat. A pale, red-haired staffer was mixing something in a big bowl. "Heidi's making a peanut butter birthday cake for the collie outside," Bob said. "It's a surprise. She's also working on my lunch."

"Hope she doesn't get them mixed up," Josie said.

"No chance of that," Bob said, and gave her a toothy grin. "Heidi, how's my fillet?"

"Should be ready, sir," she said. Heidi set down the bowl, slipped on blue oven mitts, and took out a juicy fillet.

"That's an organic Niman Ranch grilled steak," he said. Josie's stomach growled.

"And here's my salad."

A big plastic bowl on the counter held what looked like the leaves that Josie had raked Sunday.

"Are those oak leaves?" she asked.

"Close," he said, and laughed loudly. "It's lettuce. Baby green oak lettuce and red oak lettuce, baby romaine, red romaine, and tango lettuce. The dandelion leaves are grown right here."

"On this lawn?" Josie asked, remembering the brown patches.

"I know what you're thinking," he said, wagging his finger. "We have a doggy-free garden patch back by the employee parking lot and a patio for our staff.

"Heidi mixes up this buttermilk ranch dressing fresh daily," he said. It was in a gravy bowl. Uncle Bob sure wasn't counting calories if he used that, Josie thought.

"Well, ladies, are you convinced this is the right place for your doggy?" he asked.

"I'd like to try a day of day care," Jane said. "Maybe tomorrow. I want Stuart groomed, too."

"Good, good," he said, guiding them through the door. "Right down the hall there is Beverly. She'll help you book an appointment. Little Stuart Little can really put on the dog."

Chapter 7

Frank was a restless shadow in the fall twilight, pacing back and forth on Jane's front porch, when Josie brought her mother home at seven thirty that night.

"Look, Josie," Jane said. "What's Frank doing outside? It's chilly."

Josie swiftly parked behind his big dark car and he loped down the sidewalk toward them. Josie was surprised her mother's well-groomed renter hadn't changed out of his stained and rumpled camp counselor shirt. Frank's white hair stuck up in unruly curls and his face was grim.

But he still remembered his old-school manners and opened Jane's car door.

"Are you okay, Frank?" she asked, her voice heavy with worry.

"No. I mean yes," he said, and threw up his arms in frustration. "Hell, I don't know what I mean, Jane. I have to tell you something. You, too, Josie. This concerns both of you. Can you stay for a minute?"

Me? Josie thought. Now what? "Sure, Frank," she said.

"Upstairs immediately," Jane said. "I don't want any eavesdroppers on our conversation." She glared at Mrs. Mueller's house and marched purposefully up the sidewalk, Josie and Frank trailing behind her.

Josie averted her eyes from the struggling new sod, as if avoiding an ugly scar on a pretty face. But not before she noticed it had been freshly watered.

Stuart met them at the top of Jane's stairs with a short, reproving *woof*, dancing back and forth.

"Poor dog. He needs to go outside," Jane said. "He's had to wait too long and he's been so good. Have a seat and we'll be back."

She opened the back door in the kitchen and Stuart pattered down the steep stairs as fast as his short legs could carry him. Josie hated the delay and didn't want to hear any bad news.

She'd had a pleasant day with her mother. After the visit to Uncle Bob's Doggy Day Camp, Jane had insisted on riding with Josie to pick up Amelia at school. Amelia had discussed her party plans with her grandmother. This was Amelia's first grown-up party with boys. "Kate's having a DJ and we're wearing dresses and everything, Grandma. She's invited the boys, too, but her parents will be there, so it's okay."

"Chaperones are important," Jane had said. "I don't care how modern you are."

Josie had enjoyed listening to Amelia rattle on about the party. She was grateful and just a little resentful. My daughter's surliness vanishes around Jane, but she won't talk to me like that, she thought.

She reminded herself that she and Jane had been at odds, too, and that had changed. She felt the silver pendant at her neck. *Always my daughter, now too my friend.*

At Ted and Josie's home, Amelia had talked Jane into staying to cook dinner with her. Amelia, who loved to cook, was proud of the family's newly renovated midcentury modern kitchen. She and Jane had decided to fix pot roast—a treat for Josie, who was an indifferent cook.

The pot roast was smothered in three kinds of mushrooms. By the time they'd put together a salad with walnut dressing and cranberries, and the oven fries were hot and crispy, Ted was home from the clinic. They'd enjoyed a leisurely meal. It was after seven when Josie finally drove her mother to the flat on Phelan Street.

Now Josie was upstairs in Jane's apartment, making stilted conversation with Frank in the kitchen. He pretended she didn't know about the car on the lawn as she quietly checked him for signs of alcohol. He smelled like breath mints but there was no hint that the breath freshener covered up booze. His eyes were clear. Worried, but clear.

Poor Frank, Josie thought. For the rest of his life, anyone who knows about the car incident will be checking him for alcohol. She also saw three light blond hairs on his creased shirt and hoped they were dog hairs.

"Would you like coffee, Frank?" she asked.

"No, thanks," he said. "I'm coffeed-out and jittery as a burglar at a cop convention."

Now what? she wondered. I can't ask if he wants a beer.

"But I would like some water," he said.

"How about some of Mom's apple cake, too?"

"That I'd never refuse," he said.

Josie gratefully hurried to the kitchen counter to fix Frank's cake and fill a glass with ice and water. By the time she carried his snack to the table, Jane and Stuart Little had returned.

Jane sat down at the table, and Stuart curled up at her feet. "Now," she said. "What's going on, Frank?"

"I've had a terrible day," he said. "Working at Uncle Bob's today was a nightmare. He hurt a little dog."

"On purpose?" Jane asked.

"Looked that way to me," Frank said. "Angel is a regular, a fluffy little caramel-colored Pomeranian. Looks like a feather duster. She's fifteen and feeble. Nearly blind, and white around the muzzle."

"A dog that old goes to day camp?" Josie asked.

"Sharon works all day and Angel needs care," Frank said. "She has to have a pill at noon, and if she gets startled she may be incontinent. Sharon doesn't want to leave her alone. She pays through the nose for Angel's care.

"Angel likes to hang out with her two friends, a toy poodle and a Yorkie. All three dogs are very small, arthritic, and old. They stay in an area we call the senior center. It's a special room with soft cushions, lots of food and treats. They're sheltered from the younger, more playful or aggressive dogs. Mostly, the senior dogs sleep. They may do a little gentle exercise, but they enjoy each other's company, and they like to eat together."

"Like old friends in a nursing home," Jane said.

"Exactly," Frank said. "They couldn't hurt a flea, and I mean that literally. I don't even think they have all their teeth. They're our special pets and we check on them a lot. If the dogs have an accident, we clean up after them.

"Anyway, the day camp was extra-busy this morning. Bob was in a sour mood. Bob doesn't like dogs."

"Not even Ralph the Talking Dog?" Josie asked.

"Especially Ralph," Frank said. "Bob loves being a local celebrity and taking people on tours of the day camp. He's happy to be the public face of the business. But the only time he's around dogs is for those TV commercials. The dogs don't like him, either. Ralph growls at him, so it takes forever to shoot the commercials."

Josie giggled.

"I don't understand," Jane said. "How did Bob get into the day-care business if he doesn't like dogs?"

"He took over his father's little boarding kennel. His wife, Candice, may be the brains of the operation. She's publicity shy but loves dogs and has a real head for business. She's the dog lover and takes care of Ralph, while Bob is the showman."

"He put on quite a show when we toured the place

today," Josie said. "The receptionist said you were running an errand."

"I was. A terrible one," he said.

Josie expected Frank to ask why they were at the day camp, but he skated right past her comment. He seemed anxious to unload his bad news.

"Bob took Angel back to the senior center. I suspect he handled her too roughly. Anyway, the poor little dog piddled on Bob's shoe.

"Bob was furious. He kicked her. Karen the groomer said so."

Jane gasped. "That's so cruel!"

"Damn right it is," Frank said. "Her bones are so fragile they're like dry twigs. He just left her there. Karen was going to fetch a dog for grooming when she saw Angel in the senior center, whimpering and dragging her front leg. She picked her up.

"Karen suspected the leg was broken and put her in a caddy so she couldn't move around and hurt herself. Then she found Bob in the staff kitchen and gave him holy hell."

"And he didn't fire her?" Josie asked.

"Wouldn't dare," Frank said. "She's his best groomer. Specializes in small dogs. If she left, she'd take a lot of business with her. She told Bob that dog was going to the vet immediately, or she'd quit on the spot.

"I was back there cleaning the kitchen floor and heard it all. Bob didn't want to take Angel to the regular vet we use. I think he was afraid the vet would know he'd kicked a dog. I suggested Dr. Ted's clinic. I said my daughter, Laura, worked there. Bob ordered me to take Angel to Laura's clinic.

"Since it was an emergency, I got your husband, Josie. I don't think my Laura had the experience to handle this case."

"I just saw Ted at dinner," Jane said. "He never mentioned it."

"He can't, Mom," Josie said. "Patient information is confidential."

"Bob told me to say that the dog had fallen off a grooming table," Frank said. "But I wasn't going to lie. I didn't tell Ted how Angel broke her leg, but he knew. Ted said that little dog had been kicked and her bones were like matchsticks. Smart man, your Ted."

"He sure is," Josie said, proudly.

"I was too upset to understand exactly what he did, but Ted said Angel was lucky she had a closed fracture. Lucky! Hah! With the pain she was in?"

"What's a closed fracture?" Jane asked.

"That means the bone was fractured," Frank said, "but the skin wasn't broken. He said in a young pup, a break like that would heal in a few weeks, but a senior dog like Angel would need maybe three or four months. He had to pin the bone."

"That poor dog!" Josie said.

Jane stayed silent, her mouth tight with anger.

"I was so mad, I asked Dr. Ted what I should do. He said this was a clear case of cruelty to animals. He would report it to the police and the Humane Society. Since I worked there and Karen witnessed the incident, he said we should report it to the Humane Society, too. I've already talked with Karen and she promised she would.

"Dr. Ted had to give Angel a shot to set her leg and pin it, but she was whimpering by the time I brought her back to the day camp. She slept for the rest of the day until her owner showed up.

"Sharon was furious. Bob made up some story about Angel jumping up on a table and falling off. 'You're a liar!' Sharon screamed. 'My Angel can't even jump up on a coffee table, she's so arthritic. I'm calling my lawyer.'

"I wanted to tell her what really happened, but Bob kept me too busy cleaning cages in the back. Then he made me clean the grooming rooms. It was hard, dirty work. By the time I could take a break, Sharon and Angel were gone. I was mad at myself. If I was any kind of a man, I would have told Sharon, then quit on the spot. But I didn't. I thought I needed this job to stay ..."

He stopped before he said "sober."

"Stay occupied," Frank finished. "But that was my last day at that place. I'm quitting first thing tomorrow. I know I promised you I'd find something to do, Jane, but I can't work for an animal abuser."

"I wouldn't expect you to," Jane said. She patted his hand.

"Listen to me, rattling on like that," Frank said. "I didn't even bother to ask: Why were you at Uncle Bob's?"

"I'm supposed to mystery-shop it," Josie said. "We were going to take Stuart Little for a day-care stay and grooming tomorrow."

"But I'm not putting my dog in jeopardy," Jane said. "Not after what you told me."

Chapter 8

"Is this mystery-shopping thing a big deal?" Frank said.

Jane's kitchen was now pleasantly warm on this chilly fall night, and Josie detected the odor of wet dog on Frank's rumpled clothes, a familiar smell to a vet's wife.

"Very," she said. "This information has to be kept confidential." She stopped and waited.

"Of course," he said. "I won't say anything, Josie, you know that." He took a sip of his water. His fingers were long, slender, and slightly freckled with liver spots.

Once she had Frank's assurance, Josie said, "Uncle Bob's is one of three St. Louis dog day-care centers up for accreditation as a Certified Pet Care Center."

"I've heard of them," Frank said. "So far as I know, only two local day-care centers have the CPCC seal of approval. Makes Uncle Bob crazy jealous. He's always scheming for ways to get a CPCC seal. We figured he was such a buffoon the organization wouldn't want him."

"No, they're interested," Josie said. "They're sniffing around, at least." She stopped in midthought and laughed. "I'm really getting into this dog assignment."

"That seal means thousands of extra dollars a year for a business," Frank said. "People believe the place is safe for their pets. Uncle Bob doesn't deserve it. Can't you tell the organization that Bob deliberately hurt a dog?"

Frank finally noticed the blondish hairs on his shirt

front and picked them off, then looked around for a place to throw them away.

Jane took the hairs and tossed them in the trash under the sink, then offered Frank more water and another slice of cake. "No, thanks," Frank said, patting his stomach. "Gotta watch my girlish figure."

Josie, hiding her impatience at the interruption, said, "Unfortunately, I can't report Bob's cruelty unless I witness it while I'm mystery-shopping."

"But Ted's reporting it," Frank said, "and I'm planning to. I'll go online tonight. Like I said, I talked to Karen, the groomer who saw him kick that little dog, and she's filing a complaint, too."

"The complaints still have to be investigated," Josie said. "That takes time."

"Meanwhile, Uncle Bob's Doggy Day Camp gets accreditation and more dogs stay there," Frank said. "More helpless animals could get hurt."

"Unless Uncle Bob's doesn't pass the mystery-shopping test," Josie said. "I guess I could take our dog, Festus, there Wednesday. He's a big, sturdy Lab."

"He's big, but Festus could get injured, too," Jane said. "That sweet dog would never hurt anyone, even to defend himself."

"At the clinic, the staff has to watch Festus to make sure the clients' kids don't hurt him," Josie said. "The little ones crawl on that poor dog, ride him like a horse, even pull his ears. He won't even snap at them. When he's had enough, he simply hides under Ted's desk in his office.

"Besides, I'm supposed to bring a dog who needs grooming. Ted clips his dog's nails and bathes him, but Festus doesn't need a haircut. Neither does Alyce's Chihuahua, Bruiser."

"Any chance Uncle Bob will fail the mystery-shopping?" Frank said.

"Too early to tell," Josie said. "He has a good staff and

a clean facility. Mom and I toured the place, and he failed to meet the client's standards in a few ways, but I don't know if those are enough to disqualify him. I'll have to mystery-shop the place to know for sure."

"If you don't do the job, some other mystery shopper will," Frank said, "someone who doesn't know that Uncle Bob hurt a dog."

"Right," Josie said. "I'm not going to deliberately wreck his chances, but I'll keep a sharp eye out. And when the cruelty investigation becomes public, I'll let the client know."

It wasn't enough, though. She knew it. So did Frank and Jane. They sat in thoughtful silence while Stuart Little moved from one to the other, begging for pats and scratches.

Josie absently scratched the shih tzu's ears and looked into his trusting brown eyes. This dog was already abandoned by his first owner, she thought. Jane can't send him undercover into a potentially dangerous situation. What am I going to do?

Frank slammed down his nearly empty water glass, and Josie jumped. "I can't let that bastard get that seal," he said. "But I can hold off quitting until tomorrow afternoon. Then I can be Stuart's bodyguard. What time are you planning to come?"

"His appointment is at nine o'clock," Josie said. "It's a morning of day care and an afternoon of grooming. We haven't canceled it yet."

"And you're picking him up at four o'clock?" Frank asked.

"Yes," Josie said.

"Then that's how we'll work it," Frank said. "I'll be at the front desk when you come to Uncle Bob's. Beverly, the receptionist, will question you about your dog's personality. You should say Stuart Little is afraid of other dogs and you don't want him in a playgroup. You want private playtime. I'll pipe up and say that Stuart knows me and I'll give him individual playtime, treats, and lunch and take him for a walk. I'll stay with him every minute until one o'clock."

"Can you do that?" Josie asked.

"Sure. The staff understands," he said. "Nobody likes that fat fraud."

"Frank, you're really not going to say anything to your coworkers about my assignment, are you?" Josie asked. "I could get fired if this information got out."

"Not a chance," Frank said. "I gave you my word, Josie.

"But I'll come in early, at seven o'clock," he said, "and do some of the nastier chores, like cage cleaning, to help out. That will give the others more time to work with the dogs. Once you hand over Stuart to me, he won't leave my sight until I personally escort him to Karen. Our top groomer would never, ever hurt an animal. She gets upset if a dog yelps when she's combing out a tangle.

"But you have to get Stuart enough spa treatments so he stays with her all afternoon," Frank said. "Maybe a half-hour massage, a facial, and aromatherapy. By the time Stuart's finished his spa afternoon, his time will be over. You can trust Karen to keep him safe. Remember, she's filing a cruelty complaint against Bob, too."

"Won't she be fired?" Josie asked.

"She's leaving," Frank said. "With her clientele, she can go anywhere. Karen says Westminster Dog Day Care here in Maplewood has been after her for months. They offered her more money. She told me she won't stay at Uncle Bob's, not after what he did to Angel. She'll probably quit. That's going to be a real whack in the wallet."

Frank smiled at the prospect of his enemy in financial pain, then turned to Jane.

"If you take Stuart to Uncle Bob's tomorrow, Jane, he'll be in good hands all day. Say yes."

"Well," Jane began.

Frank took her hands and looked into her eyes. "He'll be safe," he said. "I'll treat him as if he were my own child. Please trust me, Jane."

Frank's intensity made Josie feel like an intruder. He seemed to be begging Jane to forgive him for the lawn incident and promising that he had reformed. Stuart sat at Frank's feet, wagging his tail.

Jane blushed a pretty shade of pink and said, "Of course I trust you, Frank. Stuart can go, but only if you stay with him and Karen grooms him."

Josie felt weak with relief. "Thank you," she said. "Thank you both."

"I'm glad we have a deal," Frank said. "Order as many spa services as you want, Jane, and I'll pay for them."

"You're very kind, but that's not necessary," Josie said. "The client pays for everything and I'll make sure Stuart gets the royal treatment."

Frank picked up the dog and set him in his lap. "No dog's life for you, huh, buddy?" he said, as he rubbed Stuart's back. Stuart slurped Frank's face with his wet pink tongue.

"I have to head home," Josie said. "I'll see you both in the morning. And thank you, Frank, for your help."

It was close to nine o'clock when Josie pulled into the drive at Fresno Court. Warm golden lights glowed in the windows. The dark wood on the round-topped door looked old and satiny. The trees stretched their bright fall branches protectively around her home.

Josie had to make a quick switch from mystery shopper to Mom as soon as she walked through the door.

Amelia ambushed her, iPad in hand. "Mom, Mom, can I go shopping for dresses with Palmer after school this Wednesday? We want to go to Plaza Venetia. The party's this Friday. Her mom will pick us up at school, so you won't have to. I've already picked out some styles. They're on my iPad."

She waved her pink-cased tablet as she dragged Josie by the arm to the dining room table to look at dresses.

Ted came up the basement stairs. Josie was alarmed by how tired he looked. His shoulders were bowed and he had dark circles under his eyes. Had he looked that bad at dinner? She didn't think so, but she'd been busy with Jane, Amelia, and three hungry animals—Festus and the two cats. She hadn't really studied her husband.

Now she saw he was wearing her favorite khaki shirt with the zipper front. The color brought out the natural red highlights in his brown hair. She kissed his freshly washed hair and said, "Rough day?"

He nodded.

"Frank told me about the dog from Uncle Bob's," she said. She kissed him again and inhaled his scent of wood smoke and coffee.

"I called the Village of Rock Road Police Department from the clinic, and they said they'd notify the Summerdale cops. I just filed the complaint with the Humane Society on my computer, Josie," he said. "They may get to it faster than the cops. But Uncle Bob is a beloved local celebrity. He can make our lives difficult."

"He's a celebrity," Josie said, "but he's also a joke, Ted. Frank says his staff can't stand him. That little dog's leg was broken with a kick. You have the facts on your side."

"I can prove that. I couldn't ignore the damage done to that helpless old dog. It's going to take months for Angel to heal."

"Then Bob doesn't deserve to be in business," Josie said. "Your clients will stick by you. And I'm proud of you."

She kissed him again and lightly tugged on his shirt zipper. "Let me help Amelia and then I'll come downstairs. Do you want hot coffee or a cold beer?"

"Beer," he said. "Do I get a back rub with that?" He

winked at her. The basement family room's soundproofing gave the newlyweds privacy.

"Hurry," he whispered.

"Mom?" Amelia asked. She was sitting at the mission-style dining room table, a screenful of party dresses on her iPad. Even before Josie sat down, her daughter pushed the iPad in front of her and said, "What do you think of this?"

Amelia pointed to a skintight black sheath with a waterfall of chains down the back. The dress was cut to the top of the model's derriere.

"It's too low cut," Josie said.

"But it's just her back," Amelia said.

"And her back end," Josie said. "That dress will have to be dry-cleaned. You'll have to pay for that yourself, and it will add to the cost."

Amelia showed her a short pink strapless next. "Too bare," Josie said. "And two hundred dollars. Your budget is fifty and under."

"This dress has long sleeves," Amelia said.

"Long *sleeve*," Josie said. "Singular. One long sleeve and one bare arm and a naked shoulder."

"Doesn't that count as half sleeves?" Amelia said.

Josie hid a smile. "No averaging," she said. "The dress is too tight and too short. But I like this one." She pointed to the coral lace A-line with a ribbon sash. "And that blue bubble dress and this pink-and-black color-block A-line. Three good ones."

"They're between thirty-eight and fifty dollars," Amelia said.

"Even better," Josie said. "Good choices. You can go shopping with Palmer. I'll confirm the details with her mother tonight."

Josie knew this solo shopping trip was a rite of passage, and she had mixed feelings about it. "This is the first time you've shopped on your own, Amelia, so make sure the dress fits at the waist and the bust and that it isn't too short or too tight. Check the tags for the cleaning instructions. No plunging necklines or hems slit to the thigh."

"YOLO," Amelia said.

That word, Josie thought. When is it going out of style?

"I trust you and Palmer," she said. "I know you'll pick a good dress." And if I say any more about what a good, sensible girl Palmer is, I'll ruin that budding friendship, she thought.

Josie climbed off her soapbox and said, "It's after nine. Time for you to get ready for bed. Wednesday you can pick out a new party dress."

"Cool," Amelia said.

"I thought nobody says that," Josie said.

"It's back in," Amelia said.

We've come full circle, and I'm cool again, Josie thought.

Chapter 9

Jane hated taking her dog to Uncle Bob's Doggy Day Camp Tuesday. She never said so, but Josie could tell.

Sure, she was ready when Josie arrived at her home at eight in the morning. But then Jane started dithering: She couldn't find her purse. She'd misplaced her keys. She went back twice to check that the kitchen door was locked.

"We're going to be late, Mom," Josie said, and herded Jane and Stuart into her car.

Josie felt guilty. She was borderline rude and Jane was right to be worried. But Stuart would be protected by Frank. He'd promised. Josie tried to ignore the sod-covered tracks in Jane's lawn — proof that he wasn't always reliable.

Josie tried to distract her mother by talking about Amelia, but Jane answered in monosyllables.

Uncle Bob's Doggy Day Camp was in the South County town of Summerdale. It used to be a sleepy Sunday drive from downtown St. Louis before it grew into a prosperous suburb.

At Uncle Bob's, they were once again greeted by barks and yips. Josie parked in back by the side door, afraid a day-camp dog might frighten Stuart. They passed a yellow door with a TOP DOG — UNCLE BOB sign.

Josie watched the little shih tzu run toward the reception desk. "Look how happy Stuart is," she said. "And I see Frank waiting for us." Why was he frowning? she wondered.

Then she realized they'd arrived at a bad time. A woman was pounding on the lobby reception desk and shouting at the pug-faced Beverly. "I didn't want to bring my Angel back here!" the woman screamed. *Whap!* She slammed the red desktop with her bony hand.

The receptionist's slightly popped eyes bulged more.

Angel, Josie thought. Uncle Bob broke the dog's leg. That's Sharon, her owner.

"Angel didn't accidentally fall off a table!" Sharon was a series of triangles from her tented eyebrows to her ski-jump nose and sharp chin. Even her brown hair was a wedge. The reception area's cheery schoolroom colors— blue, red, and yellow—mocked her anger.

Sharon cradled a pink plastic carrier where a caramel Pomeranian shivered inside. Josie winced when she saw the miniature metal scaffolding on the frail dog's leg.

Jane twisted her hands while Stuart Little circled nervously at her feet. Mom's going to bolt, Josie thought.

"I'm here for one reason," Sharon said. "I took Angel to a new day-care center this morning, and she howled until they called me to pick her up. Angel misses her friends. That's why I brought her back."

"Right, Sharon," Beverly said, her voice shaky.

"I'm Ms. Pancera!" Sharon shrieked.

Beverly flinched. Angel whimpered.

"I want my Angel in the senior center," Sharon said. "Her day care is free. And that fat fool doesn't go near my baby. Heidi is the only person allowed to touch her. Got that?" She glared at Beverly.

"Y-yes," the receptionist said, stumbling over the word.

"Where is that son of bitch? Is he here this morning?"

"N-no," Beverly stuttered. "He's at the dentist."

"Good. Keep him out of my sight."

"I'll get Heidi," Frank volunteered, interrupting the

tirade. He was back in moments with the Pom's favorite staffer. Heidi's dark red hair was tied back in a ponytail and her face seemed dusted with flour.

"There's my little Angel," Heidi said, with a false, frightened smile. "Let's take you back to see Pepper and Baby. Your friends miss you."

She flinched slightly when she saw the little Pom's metal leg support.

"These are her pills and the instructions are on the bottles," Sharon told Heidi. "Call me if there are any problems. Otherwise, I'll be back at four."

The irate dog owner headed down the hall toward the back lot, and Josie quickly stepped up to the reception desk.

"Mom and I are here for day care and spa time for Stuart Little," Josie said.

"Well, aren't you a cutie?" Beverly said, smiling at the shih tzu. "Would you like a treat?"

Stuart sat up and begged.

"Nice manners," Beverly said. "You want Stuart here for a full day, correct?"

"Yes," Josie said. "Day care in the morning, grooming and spa services in the afternoon."

"You lucky dog," the short, sturdy receptionist said.

Everyone says that, Josie thought. I hope it's true.

"Here are his papers," Jane said. "Stuart's shots are up-to-date and he's been neutered. I brought his food." She pulled out a ziplock bag of kibble from her big pink purse.

"Good," Beverly said. "We recommend that. Some dogs don't tolerate different food."

Stuart seems very tolerant, Josie thought. He's on his third treat.

"I can see he's a sweetie," Beverly said. "But if he's going into a play group we have to know how he behaves with other dogs."

Frank, standing behind Beverly, shook his head no, and Jane waded in.

"No," she said. "I don't want Stuart playing with other dogs. He's too shy. But he needs exercise."

"I know this handsome fella," Frank said, and took Stuart's red leash. "I've finished my morning chores, so I'll give him personal playtime."

"That's six dollars for fifteen minutes," Beverly said.

"We'll take half an hour," Josie said, and Jane nodded.

Josie saw the long list of services and took charge. "What else do you suggest?" she asked.

"Treat time," Beverly said. "Gourmet cookies are three dollars each."

"He'll take two," Josie said. An hour gone, she thought.

"Our pool is chlorine- and chemical-free. Thirty dollars for thirty minutes," Beverly said.

"Done," Josie said.

"A light workout in the gym is thirty dollars," Beverly said.

Jane interrupted. "What if Stuart's too tired?"

"Then he'll sit with me in the small dog park," Frank said. "After he naps, he'll have lunch."

"His grooming starts at one o'clock," Beverly said.

"We want a full grooming," Jane said. "His coat washed and cut, ears cleaned and plucked, nails trimmed, and, er, glands cleaned."

Josie knew her prim mother couldn't say "anal glands." Especially in front of Frank.

"That's sixty dollars," Beverly said.

"Your groomer will take special care with the hair around his eyes?" Jane said. A tiny worry wrinkle showed between her eyes.

"Karen is the best," Beverly said.

"He'll be fine, Mom," Josie said.

"Stuart is a bug-eyed dog," Jane said. "If you don't

groom the hair right, it can grow into their eyes. Some poor dogs go blind."

"That's terrible," Josie said, eyeing the brown fringe hanging in Beverly's cute pug face.

"It's vital that bug-eyed dogs have groomers who know what they're doing," Jane said. "Otherwise, their eyes can pop out."

Josie's stomach flip-flopped. "That's more than I want to know, Mom." She focused on the calming blue wall. Mom's dithering again, she thought.

"What else do you have at the spa, Beverly?" she asked.

"A blueberry facial," Beverly said.

"Won't that stain Stuart's fur blue?" Jane asked.

"No, dogs love our facials."

"Sign him up," Josie said.

"What color polish do you want for his nails?" Beverly asked.

"Polish!" Jane said. "Stuart is a boy."

"Some of our dudes get their nails painted to match their neck scarves or collars," Beverly said. "It's dashing."

"No, thank you!" Jane said.

"What about a massage?" Beverly asked. "Karen can give Stuart a fifteen-minute or a half-hour massage."

"Half an hour," Josie said.

"Many dogs enjoy aromatherapy with their favorite fragrances."

"Like steak, hamburger, and chicken?" Josie asked.

Beverly smiled patiently. "A dog has a highly sensitive sense of smell, so we use small amounts of therapeutic-grade oil, usually lavender or spearmint."

"Go for it," Josie said.

"We can also streak his hair your favorite color—maybe blue to match your pretty pantsuit."

"Certainly not," Jane said.

"I guess you won't want the extreme makeover, then," Beverly said.

"Stuart is perfect," Jane said, bristling on behalf of her dog.

Frank took charge. "Let's go, buddy," he said. Josie silently thanked him. Her last sight of them was Stuart Little, tail wagging, eagerly following Frank through the yellow door.

I've just spent more on a dog than on my entire annual clothing budget, Josie thought. "We'll be back at four," she said, guiding her mother down the back hall, past Uncle Bob's TOP DOG lair.

The two women weren't out of the parking lot before Jane was fretting. "I'm so worried, Josie. After I saw poor little Angel—"

"Frank and Karen will protect Stuart," Josie said. "I know you're worried. Would you like to stay with me until we pick up Stuart?"

"No, take me to the church hall. I'm helping sort donations for the rummage sale."

"Good," Josie said. She dropped Jane off at the basement entrance of St. Philomena's hall. Jane joined a group of women laughing and carrying bags of clothes and books.

Hard work and some laughs with her friends will keep Mom busy until I pick her up again, Josie thought. She hit the supermarket, then cleaned house until three o'clock, when she swung by the church for Jane. She was relieved that her mother was smiling and pleasantly tired.

"I'm glad that's over," Jane said as she climbed into the car.

"I can't wait to see Stuart," Josie said. "I'll pay the bill; then I have to ask Uncle Bob a few questions for my mystery-shopping report."

"Stuart and I will be outside," Jane said. "I don't want to be in that place any longer than I have to be."

They made the rest of the trip in silence, while Josie prayed that Jane's dog was safe. Mom will never forgive me if he's hurt, she thought. I had no right to put that dog at risk. But I did, and now all I can do is hope.

Back at Uncle Bob's, Jane ran up the sidewalk so fast, Josie had trouble keeping up with her.

Beverly greeted them with a smile. "Wait till you see your boy," she said and pressed a button. Stuart Little came trotting out with Karen the groomer, his fur shiny, eyes bright, and wearing a jaunty red neckerchief.

"That's my handsome guy," Jane said, and kneeled down to hug and scratch Stuart. Josie paid the bill and asked, "May I talk to Uncle Bob for a moment, Beverly?"

"Sure," she said. "He's in his office, but I haven't seen him since lunch. His phone's off the hook. He does that when he wants to be left alone, and that's fine with me."

Did she really say that about her boss? Josie wondered.

"He had a dental appointment this morning and he wasn't feeling well," Bev said. Maybe she regretted her indiscreet remark, Josie thought.

"Who's a good doggy," Jane said, over and over, rumpling Stuart's fur and scratching his ears. "Let's go outside, boy."

Josie glanced at her watch. "I really need to get going," she said. "Maybe Frank can find Uncle Bob."

Beverly brushed her hair out of her eyes and looked uneasy. "Uh, Frank's no longer with us," she said. "He quit."

"When?" Josie said.

"Right after he took Stuart to the groomer, he went in to see Bob. Bob was just settling down to lunch and didn't want to talk, but Frank insisted. They . . . they had a fight."

"About what?" Josie asked.

"I couldn't hear," Beverly said quickly.

Too quickly, Josie thought. She knows darn well what they fought about.

"All I know is Frank shouted, 'I quit!' We all heard that.

"'Then get out of here,' Bob said, 'so I can eat my lunch.'

"'I hope you choke on it,' Frank said, and slammed the office door. He took his things and left. We're all sorry to see Frank go. He's a good man who knows how to handle dogs. That was about one fifteen. Bob's been in his office ever since. He likes to take afternoon naps."

"Then it's time to wake him up," Josie said.

"I don't want to get fired, too," Beverly said.

"You won't be," Josie said. "You can say you couldn't stop me."

Josie turned and marched down the hall to the yellow TOP DOG door and knocked hard. "Hello! Uncle Bob?"

No answer.

Josie knocked again, then opened the door. The room was painted in the same bright colors as the reception area. The yellow walls were crowded with framed photos of Uncle Bob gripping and grinning at celebrities from the governor to the mayor. His red desk, the size of a minivan, was heaped with papers, catalogues, treats, and toys.

Josie saw the partly eaten remains of his organic lunch in the center. A rare fillet congealed in a bloody puddle on a plate, and a few leaves of salad and some mushrooms were left in a plastic snap-top bowl.

"Bob?" she asked.

Now Josie was uneasy. Why would a big guy like Bob leave that much rare beef untouched?

"Bob?" The room's silence seemed thick and heavy.

Josie walked around the edge of the desk and stepped on a rubbery hand. Uncle Bob lay on his side like a deflated hot-air balloon.

"Bob!" she screamed. "Somebody call 911!"

Chapter 10

Three paramedics with a stretcher slammed through the door of Uncle Bob's Doggy Day Camp. The muscle-bound rescuers looked like they bench-pressed pianos.

"Where's the emergency?" said the tall paramedic with the buzz cut.

"Follow me," Beverly said. The receptionist raced down the hall to Bob's office. A Summerdale uniform followed, and Josie trailed behind the group.

The odor hit them before they reached the office door. Josie saw Bob curled up on the floor as if he had cramps, one arm flung out. She hoped she hadn't hurt his hand when she'd accidentally stepped on it, but Bob looked beyond ordinary pain. His pale, damp face was green-gray, like a fashionable wall.

"Jeez, it stinks," Beverly said, as the color fled her face. She backed into the hall and leaned against the wall. The cop, somewhere in his twenties, with a girlish pink complexion, stood stoically beside Bob's doorway.

The paramedics barged into Bob's office without any reaction. Josie stayed out of the way in the hall. She heard quick, clipped phrases but wasn't sure which man-mountain was talking. From the metallic rattle and muttered commands, she guessed they'd hoisted Bob onto the stretcher.

"Check the vitals." Was that the tall paramedic with

the buzz cut? Buzz's voice was strong and steady. "Is he breathing? No? Clear the airway."

A gravelly voice said, "There's a weird leaf in there. It's out."

Yuck, Josie thought. No wonder the paramedics wore protective gloves.

"We'll intubate." A baritone.

Were they using an endotracheal tube? Josie wondered. She watched the medical dramas. On TV, inserting the tube was always tricky. The TV doctor usually lost his nerve and a steady-handed newbie had to guide the tube into the windpipe.

It took several tense seconds to get the tube into Bob. "Okay, it's in," Baritone said.

"Start bagging him." That was Buzz.

This really is like TV, Josie thought. If she remembered right, squeezing the bag forced air into the patient's lungs. This was the part where the whole medical team cried, "He's gonna make it!" and triumphant music celebrated another TV victory over death.

But that didn't happen for Uncle Bob. Instead, Josie heard Buzz say, "He seems stable at the moment. There's a pulse and he has a blood pressure. Let's hook him up to the portable monitor and get an IV in."

That sounds hopeful, she thought.

"This dude has to be pushing fifty-five or sixty and he's at least a hundred pounds overweight," Gravel Voice said.

"One fifty, more like it," Baritone said. "It could be a heart attack or a stroke. Okay, he's hooked up to the EKG."

"Something's off here." Josie recognized Buzz's voice. "Those mushrooms in his salad look a little odd. Are the cops here yet?"

The Summerdale uniform appeared in the doorway. Josie thought the clean-cut blond cop could have stepped out of a recruiting poster.

"That you, Perkins? Better bag his lunch," Buzz said.

"Cops don't take orders from medics," Officer Perkins said.

"I'm not giving you an order," Buzz said. "I'm telling you these mushrooms look weird. Had a poisoning last summer. Some back-to-nature dude picked his own mushrooms in the woods and nearly died. You may want to have the detectives take a look. But, hey, no skin off my nose if you want to keep driving a patrol car."

Perkins gingerly stepped across the squalid floor to the desk, dumped the remains of the bloody steak into the plastic salad container, and said, "I'll tell the detectives."

Josie couldn't tell if his lip was curled in disgust at the smelly room, Uncle Bob, or the lunch.

Officer Perkins pointed at Beverly. "What do you know about these mushrooms, miss?"

"Nothing," Beverly said, her voice high and excited. "Candice, Bob's wife, brought them this morning, then left."

"She eat any?" the cop asked.

"No, she's been out all day."

"Where do they live?" he asked.

"They don't—" Beverly stopped and pulled on her fringe of bangs.

"They don't what?" the cop said.

"I can't tell you," Beverly said.

"You'd better, miss. This man is seriously ill. If he was poisoned, accidentally or on purpose, we need to know what it was to save his life."

"Bob and Candice are separated," Beverly said. "They don't live together, but they keep that a secret. A divorce would be bad for business."

"Where is she now?"

"I don't know. I'll get you her address and phone number."

Officer Perkins went to the far end of the hall to make a call, while Beverly went back to her desk for the information. Josie tuned back in to the paramedics' conversation.

"Why didn't this dude call for help?" Gravel Voice said.

"Looks like he tried," Baritone said. "His phone's off the hook.

"No sign of a brain bleed or stroke," he added. "No injection sites for a drug OD."

"No diabetes bracelet." That was Buzz.

"Okay, he's stable enough. Let's pack him up and get him to the rig. He needs to be at the hospital."

With a rush and a rattle of the stretcher, they were out the door. Josie saw no sign that Bob's massive chest was moving, and he was still unconscious. The red ambulance raced off, lights flashing and sirens screaming. The sirens set the day-camp dogs howling.

While one Summerdale uniform was trying to track down Uncle Bob's wife, another struggled to sort out the staff and customers already in the building. His name tag identified him as MAKEPEACE, which Josie thought was apt. On the porch, angry, worried owners were storming the day-camp door, demanding their dogs.

"I want my Angel and I want her now!" Josie heard a woman shriek as she pounded on the door.

Angel, she thought. That was the Pom with the broken leg. Sharon's dog.

The dogs inside the day camp picked up the fear and rage. They yapped, yipped, and yowled. A gray-muzzled basset's mournful *ah-ooohs* made the hair stand up on Josie's neck.

Josie spotted her mother in the frantic crowd. She must have come back when the ambulance arrived. Stuart Little had circled Jane's legs until she was tangled in his leash. Josie elbowed her way to her mother, sorted out the dog's leash, then picked him up and pushed through to an empty chair. Stuart shivered in her arms, his jaunty neckerchief wilted. The shih tzu didn't calm down until Jane sat down and held him.

"Sh, boy," Jane said, petting her dog. "It's okay."

"Good thing Ted picked up Amelia at school," Josie said.

"Is she at home alone?" Jane asked.

"She's at the clinic," Josie said. "She still wants to be a vet, and she likes helping out at the clinic. I'd better let Ted know what's going on."

Josie speed-dialed Ted and was relieved when he answered his cell phone.

"I only have a minute," she said. "Mom and I picked up Stuart at Uncle Bob's. I found Bob passed out in his office. He's on his way to the hospital."

"Good Lord," Ted said. "What happened?"

"I don't know," Josie said. "He may have eaten poisoned mushrooms."

"Is he going to make it?"

"I can't tell," Josie said, "but he was barely breathing when the paramedics wheeled him out."

"Did someone try to kill him?"

"Nobody knows yet," Josie said. "The police just got here and the paramedics think his illness is suspicious. I expect Mom and I will be questioned. I don't know how long it will take before we're released. Since I found Bob, they'll probably keep me longer than Mom. I'll give her my keys and she can drive my car home as soon as they cut her loose."

"Jane can call me," Ted said. "I'll pick her up."

"How's Amelia?" Josie asked.

"Ecstatic. She's holding a genuine Oscar," Ted said. "We'll give you the details later."

His voice turned soft and serious. "Take care of yourself, Josie. Stay safe. And call me if I can help. I love you, and I'm lucky to have you."

Josie saw her mother's cheeks turn pink and knew she'd heard the conversation.

"Such a thoughtful boy," Jane said, and covered a yawn. "I am feeling a little tired, Josie. I think I'll take Ted up on his offer for a ride home if I'm done before you."

Josie realized Jane's skin was papery gray. This day had taken its toll on her.

"I'm so sorry, Mom," Josie said. "I should have never gotten you into this."

"There's no way you could have predicted this," Jane said. "It's crazy."

And getting crazier. The reception desk was a tornado of demanding dog owners. The staff looked confused and frightened.

Little Beverly hopped up on the reception desk and shouted, "Quiet! People! It's me, Bev. Now that Bob's in the hospital, I'm in charge. Staff, return to your assigned duties. Customers, line up at the desk, and I'll settle your bills and deliver your dogs, as soon as the police say you can go."

"Where's Candice?" red-haired Heidi asked.

"We're trying to reach her," Bev said. "Bob's in good hands at the hospital. The best way we can help him is to stay here, keep the dogs calm, and get them to their owners."

With that, the front door opened, and the crowd parted. Josie saw a man in a retro suit and skinny-brimmed hat, holding up a gold badge. He was about her age—midthirties—with short brown hair and blue eyes.

"Detective Radley Dobbs, Summerdale Crimes Against Persons," he said. "Who called 911?"

"I did," Beverly said. "But she found Uncle Bob."

She pointed straight at Josie.

Chapter 11

"Who called 911?" Detective Radley Dobbs had demanded.

When Beverly pointed at Josie, all eyes swung toward her. Angry eyes, all of them. These people wanted to pick up their pets and go home. The staff wanted to leave. Thanks to Josie, they were at the mercy of a detective with a late-fifties wardrobe fetish.

Josie shrank back from their glares. "I—," she said, and her voice died.

"Is there a room where we can talk?" Detective Dobbs asked Beverly.

"The visitors' office on your left," the receptionist said.

"Everybody, stay here," Dobbs said. "Officer Makepeace will take your names, contact information, and reason for being here. The customers can go. The staff will stay until I talk to them."

More glares. Even Officer Makepeace is mad at me, Josie thought. And poor Mom looks frantic with worry. At least I know she'll be going home soon.

"Down the hall," Detective Dobbs said to Josie, and made sure she walked in front of him. She felt the hostile stares as she made her way to the small visitors' office, painted in Uncle Bob's kindergarten color scheme. Dobbs stood by the red desk and Josie sat in the blue customer chair. The banana yellow walls looked bilious.

"Wait here," he said, and shut the door on her. Josie guessed he was going to examine Uncle Bob's office. She paced the cramped room like a caged canine, studying more than a dozen framed photos of Uncle Bob, including one with his arm around Ralph the Talking Dog. Josie thought Ralph didn't look too happy, but she could have read that into the photo—she definitely wasn't happy.

The big schoolhouse clock ticked off twenty-six minutes before Dobbs returned. He sat behind the red desk, took off his skinny-brimmed hat, pulled at his French cuffs, then asked Josie's name and why she was at the day camp.

"My mother and I dropped off Stuart Little, her shih tzu, for day care and spa time this morning," Josie said.

"What time?" he asked. Josie noticed his suit was gray with an understated windowpane grid. Was it new or vintage? she wondered.

"What time, Ms. Marcus?" Detective Dobbs asked again.

Josie forced herself to focus. "Sorry. About nine o'clock," she said. "We asked for a full day of supervised play, treats, and grooming."

Josie was relieved he didn't ask her to list everything she'd ordered for Stuart. The dog's indulgences embarrassed her. She didn't mention that she was mystery-shopping the day camp, either. She didn't need another complication.

"We came back about four o'clock to pick up Mom's dog. I wanted to speak with Uncle Bob. Bev, the receptionist, said he was in his office, but he'd taken his phone off the hook. She thought he was asleep. I didn't want to wait any longer. Mom was tired. I opened the door and found him. I screamed for Bev to call 911."

"What did you see when you entered his office?" he asked. Was that a pocket square in his suit coat? she wondered. Why am I obsessing about his suit? Concentrate.

"I noticed his partly eaten lunch on his desk," Josie said. "It was a salad and most of a fillet. There was no sign of Bob, but I didn't think he'd leave that steak untouched. I walked around the desk and stepped on his hand. That's when I found him."

"What did you hear when you walked in?" His tiepin was a tiny pair of handcuffs. Josie tore her eyes away from it to answer.

"Nothing," she said. "Bob wasn't groaning or anything. I heard dogs barking, but they always bark here."

"What did you smell?"

"The office smelled bad," Josie said. "Like he'd been sick—thrown up and had . . . you know . . ." Now I'm sounding like Mom, she thought. Grow up. "He'd had diarrhea. But I didn't notice the smell until after I found him."

"How could you miss it?"

"I don't know," Josie said. "Something felt off about his office, even when I was outside in the hall and the door was shut. I may have thought the bad smell had to do with the dogs. I was annoyed he didn't answer my knock. I thought he was avoiding me. Mom and I had spent a lot of money at this place and he'd been really friendly when he was after our money. Now he was ignoring me. I barged into his office and didn't see him at first. Then I found Bob passed out on the floor and called Bev."

"What was the mood in the office when you arrived this afternoon to pick up your dog?"

"Busy," Josie said. "Professional. The day camp was shorthanded because a staff member had quit."

Frank, she thought. Frank quit and I led this detective right to him. Well, he'll find out anyway.

But Josie was frightened now. She didn't want to make trouble for Frank, who had a good reason to hate Uncle Bob. Would Frank kill him because he broke the little dog's leg? He might punch Bob, but Josie didn't think he'd try something sneaky like poison mushrooms. But she didn't think Frank drank, either.

"Hello, Ms. Marcus," the detective said. "May I have your attention?"

"Yes, I'm sorry," Josie said. "I found his body. I mean, I found Bob. It was very upsetting and I still feel strange. What was your question again?"

"Did you know the staff member who quit?" he asked.

"Franklin Hyzy," Josie said. "My mother lives in a two-family flat in Maplewood and Frank rents the downstairs apartment."

"Do you know why Mr. Hyzy quit?" he asked.

"I wasn't here when it happened," Josie said, dodging the question.

"What was the reaction of the staff after they learned that the owner was near death?"

"I stayed in the hall by Bob's office," Josie said. "Bev, the receptionist, was with me. She looked sick. The rest of the staff stayed back by the reception desk. They looked worried, but I didn't hear them say anything."

"Did you notice anything unusual about the color of the victim's face?"

"His skin seemed clammy," Josie said. "It was an odd gray-green."

"Was he vomiting?" he asked.

"No, not when I saw him. But he'd definitely been sick before."

"Did he say anything to you?"

"No, he was unconscious."

"Did you touch anything?"

"The door when I came in," Josie said. "And I stepped on his hand, but not on purpose. He was on the floor and I didn't see him. That's when I backed out of the room and shouted for Bev to call 911."

"Were you present when the paramedics treated the victim?"

"I was out in the hall with Bev. I didn't go in, but I could hear them. One of the EMS guys said something was off about Bob's lunch."

"Off how?"

"He said the mushrooms looked strange and called in Officer Perkins. The officer said he didn't take orders from medics, but he must have decided to scrape the rest of Bob's lunch into the plastic salad bowl and have it analyzed. I think that's when Officer Perkins called you."

"Did the paramedics suspect suicide, murder, or accidental poisoning?"

"I don't know," Josie said. "One mentioned he'd been called out on an accidental poisoning case when a back-to-nature guy picked his own mushrooms, but they were mostly interested in Bob. They were in a hurry to get him to the hospital."

"Do you know Bob personally?"

"No," Josie said. "I saw his ads on TV, but that's all. I'd never met him before yesterday, when he gave Mom and me a tour of the day camp."

"So you don't know if he had any health issues?" Detective Dobbs asked.

"No."

"What about the mushrooms? What do you know about them?"

"Nothing," Josie said. "I never saw any mushrooms. Bob talked about how the day-camp dogs ate only organic treats and he had an organic lunch of salad and Niman Ranch beef. He showed me his salad when we toured the place. It looked like it had been raked off a lawn."

"Do you know if he hunted wild mushrooms?" the detective asked.

"He never mentioned that," Josie said. "I didn't see any mushrooms, but it didn't look like a regular salad."

"What did it look like?" he said.

"The spring mix you get at the supermarket," Josie said. "Some of the leaves were round, some were curly, some were green, and others were purple or red. It definitely wasn't iceberg or romaine lettuce."

"Officer Perkins thought this might be a potential crime," he said. "I can see that the victim collapsed on the floor alone in his office, apparently with no signs of a struggle or anything out of the ordinary. It looks like a medical issue, except for those mushrooms. So what's going on here, Ms. Marcus?"

"I don't know," Josie said. "The paramedics thought the mushrooms looked strange, and Bev told them Bob's wife Candice brought them. She said the couple doesn't live together, but they pretend their marriage is okay for the sake of the business. I think Officer Perkins was trying to track down Candice. That's all I know. Can I go home, please?"

"After you sign a statement," he said.

"What about Mom?" Josie asked. "She's sixty-seven and I'm worried about her. She doesn't look good."

"She's probably been released by now, Ms. Marcus. You can check on her as soon as you sign your statement."

After another half hour, Josie was free to leave. By that time, the day-camp lobby was empty. Beverly was at her reception desk and no staffers were in sight. Officer Makepeace was guarding the front door when it was flung open.

A short, brittle woman with long dyed-black hair stood in the doorway. She was skinny, with a skunk stripe of gray-white roots down her center part and an angry face. She carried a wide-brimmed hat.

"Where is that bastard?" she asked. "He's supposed to meet me at the house at five, and it's six thirty."

"Candice," Bev said.

"Mrs. Manning," Candice corrected her.

"There's a problem," Bev said, her voice shaking. "We've tried to reach you, but your phone was off. It's Bob. He was taken to the hospital."

The remaining color drained from Candice's sallow face. "What? What happened? What hospital?"

"Summerdale General," Bev said. "We're not sure what's wrong, but it's serious."

"Then I'm on my way there," Candice said.

"Not till you talk to Detective Dobbs," Officer Makepeace said.

Candice barely came to his shoulder, but she looked him right in the eye. "Am I under arrest?" she asked.

"No, but—"

"If he wants to talk to me, he can find me at the hospital."

The tiny dark woman clapped the big hat on her head, turned on her heel, and marched out, leaving Makepeace openmouthed.

Chapter 12

Josie called Ted from her car in the day-care parking lot.

"Josie," he said, "how are you?"

"Exhausted and itchy," she said. "I hope I didn't get fleas at Uncle Bob's. How's Mom?"

"I took her home," Ted said. "She was too tired to have dinner with us. I fixed her an omelet while Amelia walked Stuart Little; then she went to bed."

"Was Frank home?" Josie asked.

"His lights were on, but we didn't see him. Why are we talking on the phone? Come home. Amelia and I made beef stew and a salad for dinner."

"I'm on my way," Josie said. "I love you." She never got tired of saying that to her new husband.

Josie felt better as soon as she saw the warm lights of their home glowing in the fall dusk. The streetlights turned the trees into fiery torches and the air smelled of wood smoke and spicy fallen leaves.

Amelia held the front door open and hugged her. "Mom," she said, "you're home."

Josie was grateful for the temporary truce in the mother-daughter wars. She was enveloped in more hugs and kisses, fragrant cooking smells, and furry animals. Festus the Lab insisted on an ear scratch, Harry the cat gave her a head-bump greeting, and Ted kissed her, all at the same time. Marmalade interrupted with a demand for dinner.

Josie showered and decided the itching was dog hair. She brushed her brown hair, added a slash of lipstick, and was soon smiling and seated at the table. Ted put a salad bowl brimming with red tomato cubes, cucumber chunks, and fresh basil on the table.

"After Jane told us about Uncle Bob's lunch, we thought you'd like a country salad," he said. "No mushrooms. I made Jane's old-fashioned beef stew with potatoes, carrots, and onions."

"It's 'shroom-free, too," Amelia said.

"Perfect," Josie said, and dug into her salad.

"Your mom told us what happened," Ted said, "but why did that police detective question you?"

"You aren't a suspect, are you, Mom?" Amelia said. "If you go to jail, can I still go to the party?"

"I'm not a suspect and I'm not going to jail," Josie said. "Would you want to go to the party if your mother was a jailbird?"

"It might be kind of cool," Amelia said. "You could do the perp walk, like on TV."

Josie looked up and saw her daughter was teasing her. I am tired, she thought. Too tired to recognize a joke.

"It's too warm to wear a jacket over my head," she said, and smiled. "The detective just wanted information about Uncle Bob. From what I can figure out, the paramedics think he may have been poisoned by the mushrooms, but nobody knows if it was accidental or on purpose. Frank, Mom's renter, quit today, and I told Detective Dobbs, but I didn't say why he left."

Ted heard the doubt in her voice. "You did the right thing. He'd find out anyway," he said. "He'll know that Frank also filed a cruelty complaint against Bob. But so did two other people, me and Karen the groomer. We didn't all kill him."

"You don't think Frank would kill Uncle Bob, do you?" Josie asked.

"Of course not," Ted said. "He might punch the creep. I wanted to when I saw Angel. But poison strikes me as a woman's weapon."

"Me, too, and I've got a good candidate," Josie said. "Bob and his wife split, and Candice is one scary-looking lady."

"Are you going to turn in your mystery-shopping report, Mom?" Amelia asked.

"I'll have to, but it's not complete. Bob couldn't answer some of my questions. I'll leave those blank and explain what happened."

Josie had eaten most of her stew. "I don't want to talk about Bob anymore," she said. "Tell me something good. Amelia, I want to know about that Oscar. What's it feel like to hold one?"

Josie savored a mouthful of tender beef while Amelia talked. Josie enjoyed her daughter's enthusiasm. Her dark hair was shoulder-length now. Josie liked the cinnamon sprinkling of freckles on Amelia's nose but didn't say anything. They had a silent ongoing battle over Amelia's attempts to hide them with makeup.

"This Oscar wasn't very heavy," Amelia said. "He weighs eight pounds, two ounces." She giggled. "I weighed him myself. He's real cuddly."

"Oscars don't look cuddly," Josie said. "They're metal, right?"

Amelia's giggles turned into laughter, and Ted joined her.

"What am I missing?" Josie asked.

"Oscar is a cat, Mom," Amelia said. "A tabby like Harry. He's owned by Kathryn O'Sullivan. Her husband, Paul, is a film director, and he likes to hold up Oscar and say, 'I'd like to thank the academy . . .'

"When Kathryn brought her cat in for his checkup, she

asked if I wanted to hold a real Oscar. He likes me, too, and he doesn't like most people. He's a shelter cat, and she says he sleeps in the shower during storms because he's afraid of rain."

"Poor Oscar," Josie said.

"He's fine," Ted said. "Happy and healthy. More stew?"

"No, thanks," Josie said. "Don't tell Mom, but it's better than hers."

"There's apple pie for dessert," Amelia said.

Josie finished her pie first and loaded the dishwasher while Ted lingered over dessert and Amelia rattled on about the Friday night party.

"Kate's going to have a DJ and everything," she said.

"What kind of music do you like, Amelia?" Ted asked.

"Taylor Swift, the Smiths, and One D."

Amelia saw Ted's puzzled look and said, "That's One Direction. I also like Rick Ross, Hoodie Allen, and Justin Bieber. We hate the Bieb but listen anyway. Kanye West, sometimes, and Austin Mahone."

"I've heard of some of those," Ted said.

"It's about time for bed," Josie said.

"Can I text Emma and Palmer first?"

"Make it quick," Josie said.

Amelia hoisted Harry up onto her shoulder, and Festus and Marmalade padded behind her upstairs to her purple bedroom.

After the table was cleared and the dishwasher was turned on, Ted said, "Let's watch the news and see if there's more about Bob. I'm having a bedtime beer. What about you?"

"White wine," Josie said. "I'll check on Amelia and meet you downstairs."

Amelia had fallen asleep without any fuss, possibly hoping to make tomorrow's shopping expedition come sooner, Josie thought. Her daughter had one arm around

Harry. Festus and Marmalade slept at the foot of the bed. There was hardly room for Amelia with that menagerie, but she wouldn't have it any other way.

Josie kissed her daughter's forehead and headed downstairs to the cozy basement family room. She snuggled up to Ted on the big, soft couch, and he put his arm around her.

"I must be getting old," Ted said. "I only knew about half the musicians Amelia named."

"I only know them because she listens to them on YouTube," Josie said. "The last person I recognized on the cover of *Rolling Stone* was the pope."

"Paul McCartney made the cover, too," he said. "I think he was in another band before Wings." He grinned at her. "Why did you make a face when Amelia mentioned Taylor Swift?"

"Taylor's music is okay, but she reminds me of a sickly-sweet high school suck-up. Twelve-year-olds listening to hours of her breakup songs is weird. I finally played Carly Simon's 'You're So Vain' and Amelia admitted that there were breakup songs before Ms. Swift.

"I'd never tell her, but I like One Direction. Their videos remind me of the young Beatles."

"The band before Wings?" he said, and winked.

"That one. But parental approval would be the kiss of death. Wait—the local news is on. Turn up the sound."

On Channel Seven, Uncle Bob smiled from the screen, but Honey Butcher, the hair-sprayed blond anchor, looked dead serious.

"Our city lost a beloved local celebrity today," she said, "when Robert Jarvis Manning—known to St. Louisans as Uncle Bob—died this evening at Summerdale General Hospital."

A photo of the sprawling redbrick hospital flashed on the screen.

"What!" Josie said. "He's dead?"

Honey continued. "Uncle Bob was found unconscious at his dog day-care center about four o'clock this afternoon and rushed to Summerdale, where he died three hours later."

"I can't believe he's dead," Josie said. "I hated what he did to Angel, but I still feel like somebody punched me in the gut."

"Of course you do," Ted said. "You found him."

Honey faked sincere sadness, like an undertaker in a designer dress. "Police are investigating his death as a possible homicide," she said. "No arrests have been made at this time."

"He was murdered," Josie said. "I guess the mushrooms did kill him. I wonder if his wife is a suspect."

Honey lowered her voice as if confiding to the TV audience and said, "Uncle Bob's wife of twenty-two years, Candice Ellen Manning, was with him at the hospital when he passed away. She gave Channel Seven this exclusive interview at the couple's Summerdale home this evening."

"But they don't live together," Josie said. Now she was sitting straight up, talking to the TV. On-screen, the newly minted widow was sitting on a green velvet couch in a formal, pale yellow living room. A big-brimmed black hat hid most of her face. Ralph the Talking Dog hid the rest. Candice clung to the big black Labradoodle as if she were a shipwreck survivor. She was so hidden by the hat and the shadows that she seemed lost in grief.

Honey was the interviewer. Her dyed blond hair glowed under the bright TV lights, but she kept her voice soft and respectful. "How are you, Mrs. Manning?" she asked.

Candice dabbed at what Josie thought were her eyes—it was hard to see her face—and said, "I'm heartbroken, Honey, and I know poor Ralph misses Bob, too."

"What?" Josie said. "Frank told us that Ralph didn't get along with Bob. He really was Candice's dog."

Candice's mournful tone matched Honey's. "I know Ralph will miss him. So will I. But we have a duty to carry on for Bob's sake in this empty home."

"Bob didn't live with her," Josie said.

"Sh!" Ted said. "Let's watch this."

"My husband took over the small kennel owned by his parents," Candice said, showing a framed black-and-white photo of a flat white building with a BOB'S KENNELS sign.

"But my Bob saw the possibilities. First, he had dog birthday parties with his famous peanut butter cakes."

A few seconds of video showed Bob and four dogs in party hats clustered around a bone-shaped cake. Bob barked out "Happy Birthday" while the dogs howled.

Probably in embarrassment, Josie thought.

"Then Bob came up with his day-camp overnight suites with themes, like his Pup-anesian Getaway."

In the next video clip, a puzzled boxer lounged in a rattan peacock chair while Bob fanned the dog with a palm leaf. The kennel walls were painted with blue ocean waves. Bowls of food and water were sheltered under a miniature tiki hut.

"And Bob's playtime was famous," his new widow said.

More video of Bob and the dogs chasing balls in the day-care yard. Then Bob tried—and failed—to run after a yellow pup into a giant red exercise tube. His fat body wouldn't fit. Josie felt embarrassed for the dead man.

Candice continued her weepy narration: "But he was best known for his quirky commercials and his special friendship with Ralph the Talking Dog."

Channel Seven ran the amateurish thirty-second spot ending with Bob saying, *"Don't take my word for it. Ask Ralph the Talking Dog. Ralph, how is life for the poor pups who don't go to Uncle Bob's?"*

"Ruff!" Ralph said.

Candice burst into tears. "You all know how much he loved dogs," she said, her voice wobbly. "I'm dedicating my life to his legacy of love."

Honey Butcher nodded and said, "That's an amazing tribute to your late husband, Mrs. Manning."

"It sure is," Josie said. "There's not a word of truth in it."

Chapter 13

"Mom!" Amelia called. "There's a moving truck unloading furniture next door. We're getting new neighbors."

Josie ran to the front window and discreetly held back the curtain for a better look. The sunny morning was perfect for moving. She and Amelia watched two burly movers unload a sleek navy couch and carry it inside the house.

Next, the movers struggled with a plumply padded dark recliner. The front door was open, and Josie thought she saw a shadowy woman hovering near the entrance, but she couldn't tell anything about her, not even her hair color.

"I hope our new neighbors are a couple our age," Josie said. "It would be fun to have them over for barbecues."

"Maybe the new neighbor is a single lady, like Betty was," Amelia said. "Rain, the woman who lived there before Betty, was single, too. Maybe the house attracts only single women."

"I think this woman is married," Josie said. "That's a stylish couch, but the clunky recliner is definitely a guy chair."

"Mom, that's so sexist," Amelia said.

"Really?" Josie said. "Who heads for our recliner most often?"

"Ted," Amelia said.

"I rest my case," Josie said.

"I hope they have a boy my age," Amelia said.

"Not a girl?" Josie asked.

"I've got lots of girlfriends at school," Amelia said. "I'd like a boy next door." She giggled.

Josie felt uneasy. There it was, that boy-crazy talk. Amelia was twelve, after all. And I'm overreacting, Josie decided.

"They might have a son," she said. "Isn't that an air-hockey table on the truck, behind some end tables? Unless I'm being sexist again, that's something boys like. And we're going to be late. Grab your backpack and let's go."

Amelia nearly fell off the front steps trying to check out the furniture crammed into the big yellow moving truck. Josie herded her into the car and waved to Cordelia Madison, the bronze-skinned college professor who lived in the house on the other side.

"Are you mystery-shopping today?" Amelia asked. She was in a chatty mood. Josie was relieved. She never knew if their trip to school was going to be sullen silence or nonstop chatter.

"Alyce and I are going today," Josie said. "We're taking her Chihuahua, Bruiser, to another dog day-care place. Bruiser gets half a day at Bow-Wow Heaven."

"Does that place have anything to do with the rapper Bow Wow and his song 'Heaven'?" Amelia asked.

"Nope," Josie said. "No connection to Snoop Dogg, either. Bow-Wow Heaven is supposed to be as big as Uncle Bob's, without the corny commercials."

Josie turned into the curved drive of Barrington School and parked. Amelia hopped out and waved to her friends Palmer and Emma. Josie thought her daughter looked stylish in her camel skinny jeans and beige turtleneck. Her two friends, red-haired Palmer and brunette Emma, had a coltish beauty. The awkward tween Barrington boys looked like big-pawed pups in polo shirts.

Fasten your seatbelt, she thought as she cautiously pulled out of the school drive. You're in for a rough ride in the next few years.

Morning traffic clogged the roads to Alyce Bohannon's West County home. She was an unlikely best friend for Josie. Alyce was a full-time homemaker with a lawyer husband and a toddler son. They lived in a Tudor McMansion with a half-timbered garage in the Estates at Wood Winds.

Wood Winds was no cookie-cutter subdivision. The spacious lots on the rolling hills had everything from a Tuscan villa to a French château. By Josie's standards, Alyce was well-off. But the two women had met on a civic beautification committee and hit it off instantly.

Alyce went on Josie's mystery-shopping expeditions like a sociologist eager to study a fascinating tribe.

Josie waved to the guard at the subdivision gate and smiled when she reached Alyce's sprawling home. Her blond friend was outside on her thick green lawn, watching chubby-cheeked Justin chase the Chihuahua with unsteady steps.

"Boozer!" he shrieked with delight.

"Brooo-zer," his mother said, rolling the first *R*.

"Boozer!" Justin said, and squealed the name. "Boozer!" His solo walk ended abruptly when he landed on his bottom on the grass. Justin reached out and hugged the little dog.

Alyce waved to Josie, scooped up her son, kissed his duck's fluff of pale hair, and carried him inside to his nanny. Bruiser trotted at her side. She was back out in a few minutes with a big blue purse and the little dog on a red leash.

Alyce was a curvy woman with porcelain white skin and round blue eyes. They couldn't hide a fierce intelligence and curiosity.

"Morning, Alyce and Boozer," Josie said.

"Hey there," her friend said. "Justin's having a little trouble with that *R*. I keep hoping he'll get the hang of it soon. Where are we taking Bruiser?"

"Bow-Wow Heaven," Josie said. "The one in North County, near the airport. I looked at it on the Internet. It seems more upscale than Uncle Bob's."

"You saw that he died last night," Alyce said.

"Saw! I found him," Josie said. "He was still alive, but just barely. The paramedics thought he'd been poisoned by mushrooms."

Josie told her dramatic story, then said, "I didn't realize Bob had died until we turned on the ten o'clock news."

"You'd think the President had died," Alyce said. "Every time I turn on the TV, I get another video of Uncle Bob and Ralph the Talking Dog. Poor man. What an obituary."

"Don't feel too sorry for him," Josie said. "Ted and two of Bob's employees filed complaints against him for animal abuse. Dear Uncle Bob kicked an old Pomeranian and broke her leg."

Alyce winced and held Bruiser tighter. "That story never made the news," she said, scratching the dog's big brown ears.

"There's the Bow-Wow Heaven sign," Josie said, ten minutes later. A smiling brown pup was wagging its tail on a fluffy white cloud.

But the building was far from heavenly. It was in a dreary brown-brick strip mall. The dog day-care center was wedged between a nail salon and a chiropractor's office. The big plate-glass windows were smudged and dirty.

"This doesn't look anything like the cheerful dog day-care place on the Web site," Josie said. "It's supposed to have green lawns and an outdoor play area."

They were surrounded by acres of potholed parking lot. A few clumps of yellowing grass struggled to survive in a parking strip.

"I don't like the look of this place," Alyce said. "I'm putting Bruiser in my purse. He'll keep quiet."

Josie quickly checked her mystery-shopping list. Bow-Wow Heaven had already flunked two questions: *Is the exterior neat and clean? Are the grounds pleasantly landscaped?*

They could hear a chorus of dog barks before they reached the building.

Inside, the lobby was scuffed beige tile with drab beige walls. Two women staffers were talking to each other and didn't look up when Alyce and Josie entered. One had metal piercings in her lips, ears, and nose and tribal tattoos on her arms. The other had girlish pigtail braids and pink lipstick. Both wore white shorts, sneakers, and blue Bow-Wow Heaven polo shirts.

Josie drummed her fingers on the counter. They'd failed the next question: *Were you greeted with a smile?*

Finally, Ms. Pigtail stopped talking and said, "Hi, can I help you?"

"I'm thinking of bringing my dog here for day care," Josie said. "I'd like a tour."

"Uh, okay," Ms. Pigtail said. "I can show you around. Follow me."

She led them through a beige doorway into a white-tiled kennel area. Two rows of caged canines barked frantically. The kennel smelled unpleasantly of wet dog. Josie saw waste in the cages. Each kennel had a bowl of water, but no toys, food, or beds.

Alyce wrinkled her nose and slid her hand into her big purse, as if to reassure Bruiser. The brown Chihuahua made no sound.

"Day-care dogs each get their own private suite," Ms. Pigtail said, pointing at the dreary cages. "Supervised play is extra."

They followed her down a beige hallway and she pointed to a closed door.

"Our groomer's in there," Ms. Pigtail said.

"In a closed room where visitors can't see her," Alyce said to Josie. The bored yaps of the dogs covered her comment.

Ms. Pigtail opened a yellow door and said, "This is our supervised play room." The narrow, windowless cinder-block room had the charm of a broom closet. Painted the depressing green of a hospital corridor, the playroom had no toys, decorations—or dogs.

"Today's sunny, so the dogs are in supervised play outside," Ms. Pigtail said.

"Can we see that play area?" Josie asked.

"Go out the front door and around the back," Ms. Pigtail said. They were back at the lobby and she sat down behind the counter.

"Do you have a brochure with your prices?" Josie asked.

"The prices are on our Web site," Ms. Pigtail said.

"Yes, but I'd like a brochure," Josie said.

The dog day-care center had racked up an impressive list of failures: The kennel was dirty. Ms. Pigtail didn't ask what kind of dog Josie had, describe the available services, or give Josie a printed price list.

"Wait a minute. I'll see if I can find one," Ms. Pigtail said, and disappeared behind a door marked MANAGER.

While Josie and Alyce waited, they watched a muscular twentysomething man in gym shorts with TRAINER on his shirt supervise a golden retriever trotting on a tread-mill.

"That golden has a pretty coat," Josie said. "But she doesn't look overweight."

"She's not," the trainer said. "The treadmill builds confidence."

Ms. Pigtail was back with the brochure and the price list. Josie was startled to see that treadmill training started at almost three hundred dollars. The private suites—those barren, dirty kennels—were twenty-five bucks a day.

"Thanks," Josie said. "We'll go look at the supervised play area."

None of the staffers seemed to notice when the two women left. Josie and Alyce walked toward the back of the building. They didn't see the acres of grass the Web site promised. The grounds were more cracked asphalt, faded to light gray.

Josie held up her brochure, which showed pugs, poodles, and Labradors romping on lush green grass, shaded by massive trees.

"Where are the wide lawns and trees on this brochure?" Josie asked.

"At some other dog day-care center," Alyce said.

They were behind the building now. Josie and Alyce heard barking from inside a fenced area the size of a Dumpster enclosure.

Alyce, who at five ten was four inches taller than Josie, stood on the concrete curb surrounding the fence and peeked over the top.

"What do you see?" Josie asked.

"Lots of dogs," Alyce said. "Five big ones—two Labs, a sheepdog, a collie, and a Great Dane—and six small ones. Those look like two miniature poodles, a Yorkie, a Chihuahua, a pug, and a Maltese.

"All the dogs are penned up in that little area. A chain-link fence separates the little dogs from the big ones. There's barely room for the big dogs to move, much less play. And nobody's out here with them.

"I've seen enough," Alyce said. "Let's go."

"Uh, step back carefully," Josie said. "Walk straight back. Don't move your foot to the right."

Alyce followed Josie's instructions and narrowly missed a huge dog pile.

"Sorry, Josie," Alyce said. "I am not leaving my dog here. Bruiser isn't going to this heaven."

Chapter 14

"What was that place, Dickens for dogs?" Alyce asked once she was back in Josie's car. "I've never seen such a hellhole. How can anyone leave a dog there?"

Bruiser poked his round, big-eared dome out of Alyce's purse. She lifted the spindly Chihuahua out of the bag, settled him on her lap, and scratched his chin.

"Maybe the pet owners never see it," Josie said as she pulled out of the parking spot. The gray asphalt lot seemed to go on forever. "Bow-Wow Heaven has free pickup and delivery service for day-care dogs. I bet the dog owners don't bother checking the place out. The Web site is beautiful. Pet owners look at it online, call, give the staff their credit card number, and ship their dogs off for the day."

"But won't the dogs let their people know they're unhappy?" Alyce said.

"The pets are returned at night, when the owners get home from work," Josie said. "A stressed, tired dog will sleep a lot, but the owners may think their pets are worn-out from playing."

Alyce shook her head. "We say people treat their dogs like children, but these fur kids are getting a raw deal."

Josie's car hit a pothole with a loud *chunk!* "Alyce, I'm so sorry I dragged you into this," she said. "You don't have to go mystery-shopping with me Friday."

"Why? I enjoy going undercover," Alyce said. "And Bruiser wasn't hurt. He slept in my purse." She scratched his ear and he whimpered with happiness.

"Let me make it up to you, anyway," Josie said. "Let me take you to lunch."

"Thanks, but I need to get home," Alyce said. "I'm on the planning committee for the Christmas party for Jake's firm. We're supposed to choose the caterer."

"You cook so well, you could be a caterer," Josie said.

"But I don't want to," Alyce said. "I like cooking for pleasure. I like being a homemaker."

Josie pulled out of the lot and looked in her rearview mirror. "I hope that's the last I see of Bow-Wow Heaven," she said.

"Amen," Alyce said.

"How much is that so-called supervised playtime?" Josie asked.

Alyce studied the price list. "Day care is twenty-five dollars a day, but you can buy a monthly pass for five hundred bucks. Supervised playtime is an extra ten dollars a day."

"What a racket," Josie said, "penning those poor dogs into that cramped space and calling it playtime. And so much for that attentive staff the brochure claims Bow-Wow Heaven has. I never felt so invisible in my life as I did there. I had to practically reach over the counter and grab that staffer by the shirt to get waited on."

"My mother used to say the only thing more invisible than one housewife was two," Alyce said. "That was true this morning. I'm glad you take your mystery-shopping duties seriously, Josie. I think they're important."

"It's up to me to protect Mrs. Minivan," Josie said.

"And that's me, even if I don't drive one?" Alyce asked.

"That's my name for all the anonymous American shoppers. Women like us drive the nation's economy, but we're secretly laughed at, dissed, and dismissed in the stores that are supposed to serve us. Well, I'm Mrs. Minivan's personal representative, and I'm going to fight to make sure she's treated right."

"And her dogs," Alyce said.

Josie was getting wound up now. "When I finish this report, there's no way Bow-Wow Heaven will ever be a Certified Pet Care Center."

"Good," Alyce said. "It doesn't deserve to be one. But you don't seem worried about Mr. Minivan."

"Amelia told me I was sexist this morning," Josie said. "But I don't think men have the same problems that we do getting waited on. When I'm out with Ted, store clerks fall all over themselves to help him."

"Ted's a looker," Alyce said. "But I agree. When my Jake goes into a place, he never has to flag down the staff for service. I figured he had that lawyer's air of command."

"Nope, it's the Y chromosome," Josie said. "Even Frank, my mother's sixtysomething renter, gets more respect than we do, and he's retired. Doubly retired now. Frank quit his job at Uncle Bob's yesterday to protest Bob's treatment of that little dog with the broken leg."

"He's a good man," Alyce said. "And a good match for your mother. Do you think she's serious about him?"

Josie didn't want to tell her friend about Frank's struggle with alcohol. She knew Alyce would never look at him the same way. Josie certainly didn't.

"Mom's being cautious," she said.

"Smart," Alyce said. "My aunt married a man when she was nearly seventy. No prenup or anything. He cleaned out her savings and left her for a younger woman."

"Sad," Josie said.

She took the winding back road to Alyce's subdivision, where rich farmland was rapidly yielding to crops of oversized homes. The white limestone cliffs burned with fall color.

"Your neighborhood looks beautiful," Josie said. She turned onto the drive for the Estates at Wood Winds and the gate guard waved them through. She heard the drone of leaf blowers and saw a lawn crew manicuring a nearly perfect yard.

"It's been a gorgeous fall," Alyce said. "Do you want to come inside while I drop off Bruiser?"

"No, I'll check my messages and then leave," Josie said, reaching for her cell phone. She patted Bruiser and waved good-bye.

"I'll stop by your place about seven Friday morning," Alyce said. "Then we can go mystery-shopping with Festus."

But she was barely through the kitchen door when Alyce ran back outside. "Hurry, Josie! Come in. There's been a development in the Uncle Bob murder case."

Josie dropped her phone in her purse and raced into Alyce's kitchen, where a potato chip commercial was on the small counter TV.

"Channel Seven said it would be back with the news after the commercial," Alyce said.

With that, the noon news returned with a blaring, flashy JUST ONE STATION logo. Honey Butcher gazed into the camera as if announcing that a world war had broken out. "Channel Seven has learned that Robert Jarvis Manning, known to St. Louisans as Uncle Bob, beloved owner of Uncle Bob's Doggy Day Camp, was poisoned," she said.

"Paramedics had suspected poison when they found Uncle Bob unconscious in his office and alerted the Summerdale police. Originally, the unusual mushrooms were thought to be poisonous, but they turned out to be cremini mushrooms and oyster mushrooms, police sources said.

"However, an analysis of the rest of the salad showed that it contained a quantity of deadly azalea leaves as part of a so-called spring mix of various types of greens."

"What?" Josie said. "I didn't know azaleas were poisonous."

"Oh yes," Alyce said. "We didn't let the landscaper use them in our yard because of the neighborhood children."

Honey Butcher continued. "Azaleas are a member of the deadly rhododendron family. Azaleas and rhododendrons are ornamental shrubs, grown for their bright flowers and attractive foliage. They have potentially toxic leaves and flowers. Even the honey from their flowers can be poisonous."

"I had no idea. I've never heard of azalea poisoning," Josie said.

As if in response to her comment, Honey Butcher said, "Poisoning by azalea leaves is rare because they contain a resin which burns the mouth. Usually, that's enough to stop most people from eating the leaves. But police say the victim had been to the dentist that morning and may not have been aware of the burning sensation because his mouth had been numbed."

Now a shifty-eyed police spokesman, who looked like talking on camera was torture, said, "The azalea leaves were introduced into the victim's salad and he ate a considerable quantity."

Honey was back on camera. "The symptoms of azalea poisoning include nausea, vomiting, abdominal upset, and low blood pressure," she said. "The receptionist at Uncle Bob's Doggy Day Camp gave us this exclusive interview."

A weepy, red-eyed Beverly appeared on-screen, a crumpled tissue clutched in her hand. "Uncle Bob believed organic food was always the best, for himself and his dogs." She brushed her brown bangs out of her eyes.

"That's why he served only organic treats at his day camp and ate only organic meat and salad. He had the same lunch every day—a spring mix salad and a Niman Ranch steak. He came back from the dentist with his mouth still numb, but he was hungry. I told him—"

She stopped and wiped her eyes. "I told him to go ahead and eat. I could hear his stomach growling. He had to handle a personnel matter first, and then he had his lunch."

"I wonder if that 'personnel matter' was his fight with Frank Hyzy," Josie said, and prayed that Bev wouldn't go into details.

She didn't.

"After the employee left Uncle Bob's office and shut the door, Bob didn't come out for the rest of the afternoon. I assumed he didn't feel well and was napping after lunch."

Josie relaxed. Bev had left out any mention of the slammed door, and that Frank had quit after a bitter quarrel.

Honey asked, "Did you find the, uh . . ." Bev's face started to crumple and Honey quickly changed her question to, "Did you find Uncle Bob?"

"No," Bev said. "But I called 911. A customer found him."

"That's me," Josie said. "Thank goodness she didn't mention my name."

"Where did Bob keep his salad at work?" Honey asked.

"In the staff refrigerator," Bev said. "In the kitchen. We all keep our lunches there. We've never had any problems, except when a camp counselor ate my piece of chocolate cake three weeks ago, and he didn't get sick or anything."

"Did anyone touch Uncle Bob's salad on that fatal day?" Honey asked.

"Honey seems to be channeling Mike Wallace," Josie said. "Since when did that blond bit of fluff become an investigative reporter?"

"Josie!" Alyce said. "Quiet, please!"

"Only his wife, Candice, opened his salad," Bev told Honey. "But that's because she brought Bob his favorite mushrooms. The police already said they weren't poisonous."

"But anyone could have walked into your kitchen and mixed some azalea leaves into his salad," Honey said. "What about the staff?"

"We don't want to lose our jobs," Bev said. "That's what we're worried about now. We don't know what's going to happen here without Uncle Bob."

"The customers could get into the kitchen, too, couldn't they?" Honey said.

"But they wouldn't," Bev said. "All the customers loved Uncle Bob."

Josie knew that wasn't true. But she wondered about Honey's questions. Had the TV reporter stumbled onto the killer's trail?

Chapter 15

"Mom, Mom, wait till you see my new dress," Amelia said, eyes shining, as she climbed out of Priscilla Lindell's polished black Mercedes in their driveway that evening. She held her plastic dress bag as if she were carrying a treasure.

Josie felt a tiny pang of envy. She'd wanted to go on this shopping expedition, just the two of them. Instead, Amelia shopped with her new friend Palmer and the girl's mother, Priscilla.

"It is so cool," Palmer said, drawing the words out with the reverence usually saved for the Grand Canyon. "I saw it, and I said, like, oh my God, this is pretty. And Amelia can wear coral. It turns my red hair orange."

"But you look better in green," Amelia said.

Josie tuned out the girls' discussion, leaned into Priscilla's open window, and said, "Thanks for doing this. I hope Amelia wasn't too much trouble."

"Your daughter is a delight," Priscilla said. "I drank coffee and read a magazine while the girls shopped. They showed me their choices. You're going to be pleasantly surprised."

"Come in for coffee," Josie said.

"Thank you, but we need to get home for dinner," Priscilla said. "It's almost six o'clock."

Priscilla's speech was formal and slightly old-fashioned, like the woman herself. She was ten years older than Josie and wore a hunter green knit pantsuit with gold buttons.

"The party starts at seven," Priscilla said. "Gifford and I will pick up Amelia at six forty-five, so the girls will arrive after it starts."

"Good idea," Josie said. "It's always awkward to be the first ones at a party."

"Thank you for agreeing to pick up the girls," Priscilla said. "Giff is on the road so much, we don't get many nights out alone. Palmer, time to go."

Josie and Amelia waved good-bye and walked into the house. Josie loved the details of their two-story brick cottage: the gabled windows, art glass, and arched antique front door, with its wrought-iron hinges. Inside, maple woodwork and elm floors warmed the house, along with the living room fireplace. Today those details would only be in much grander homes.

"Can I show you the dress, Mom?" Amelia asked.

The dress, Josie thought. As if it were the only dress in the world. "Can't wait to see it," she said.

Amelia looked out the front window. "The moving truck is gone," she said. "Are the new neighbors all moved in?"

"The truck left half an hour ago," Josie said. "But nobody's living there yet. I got a good look at the woman supervising the move. She's a brunette about my age. So is the man who picked her up. I think they're married. I didn't see any kids."

"Oh," Amelia said. Josie heard her disappointment. "What kind of car was the dude driving?"

"Bright red," Josie said.

Amelia looked interested.

"A red Honda Civic," Josie said.

"Borrring," Amelia said.

"Not boring," Josie said. "Friendly and easy to live

next to. That car tells me they'll make good neighbors, and the color says they'll be fun."

She saw Amelia's scornful face and thought of the locket her mother had given her: *Always my daughter, now too my friend.* Would she and Amelia become friends some day?

Josie hoped so. Right now she didn't want to argue. Someday, when Amelia was older, she'd understand what Josie was saying.

Instead, Josie changed the subject. "Hey," she said. "Let's see that dress."

"I'll go try it on," Amelia said. "But I'll need new shoes. My coral flats are scuffed."

"Why go matchy-matchy? What about that turquoise pair I bought you?" Josie said. "They're new. You can borrow my turquoise bracelet, too."

"Cool," Amelia said.

She was back in a few minutes, wearing a coral lace A-line with a soft ribbon sash. The vibrant color brought out the red highlights in her daughter's dark hair and the green in her hazel eyes. Josie caught a glimpse of the dramatic-looking woman Amelia was becoming and gulped back her tears.

"What's the matter?" Amelia said. "Don't you like it?"

"I love it," Josie said, getting control of herself. "I was just thinking how grown-up you look."

Those were exactly the right words. Amelia's face was sunshine bright. "The shoes work, too, don't they?" she said.

"They're perfect," Josie said. "The dress is perfect."

"Forty-two dollars," Amelia said. "And it's washable."

"Even better," Josie said.

They heard a car park in the drive, door thuds, and a soft *woof!* The back gate slammed; then there were footsteps on the deck stairs.

"Ted's home," Amelia said. "I can't wait for him to see it."

"Don't let the animals snag that lace," Josie said, rushing into the kitchen to avoid a fashion disaster. She caught the pets as they charged through the door. Josie picked up Marmalade and grabbed Festus by the collar.

"Aw, he won't jump on me," Amelia said.

"He'll slobber on that lace," Josie said.

"Hey, what's happening?" Ted asked. His hair was mussed and his shirt wrinkled after a long day at the clinic.

"This is my new party dress," Amelia said.

Ted whistled. "Very sophisticated."

Josie smiled at her husband. He'd said exactly what Amelia wanted to hear. The girl blushed with pleasure.

"Run upstairs and change," Josie said. "You don't want to get chicken on your new dress."

"Is that what smells so good?" Ted said.

"Chicken and dumplings," Josie said, kissing her husband. "I love you."

"Even though I smell like dog hair?" he said, kissing her back.

"I'll love you even more after you shower," she said.

She fed the animals, then gave dinner a final check. Ted and Amelia loved the Wolf stove in their newly renovated kitchen. Josie thought the stove was overcomplicated, but she'd bought it secondhand and knew it was her shopping triumph. If her two favorite cooks were happy with it, then she was, too.

In the dining room, Amelia talked nonstop about the party and shopping with Palmer. After dinner, she helped clean up without complaint. Amelia was eager to escape to her room. There she texted her friends and sent photos of her dress until Josie reminded her it was bedtime.

"Ted's taking you to school Friday," Josie said. "I have an early mystery-shopping assignment."

"Yay!" Amelia said. She loved riding in Ted's tangerine '68 Mustang. "His car is way cooler than a Beemer or a Mercedes."

Ted and Josie carried their evening drinks downstairs to the family room, and she snuggled next to her husband on the couch. The TV was on low, but Josie was focused on Ted.

"Amelia likes it when you drive her to school," Josie said. "She says your Mustang is 'way cooler' than the mom-mobiles."

"Kids say 'cool' now?" Ted said.

"It's back in—this week," Josie said. "Her new party dress is also cool."

"That first grown-up party is a big deal for a girl, huh?" Ted said.

"It is for Amelia. I hope it lives up to her expectations," Josie said. "I haven't seen her this excited since she still believed in Santa Claus. Do you remember your first grown-up party?"

"I remember how much I didn't want to go," he said. "My mother made me wear a scratchy suit and a tie. I hung out with the other guys and left early. I was too young to appreciate girls then. After that, I went to a few parties, but they were scary, especially the dances. The boys stood on one side and the girls talked to each other and then disappeared into the bathroom in flocks. Why do they do that?"

"To talk about the boys," Josie said. "I bet you were adorable." She ran her fingers through his thick brown hair. "You still are. You smell nice. The door is closed and Amelia can't hear us down here." She unbuttoned his shirt, and soon their clothes were tossed on the floor, the rug, and the coffee table.

Their lovemaking was sweet, urgent, newlywed sex.

Afterward, when Josie was buttoning her shirt, she saw Honey Butcher on the Channel Seven news. The interview with the weeping Beverly, the dog day-care receptionist, was running again.

"Turn up the sound," Josie said. "Let's see if there's more on the Uncle Bob murder."

The camera was panning across blooming azalea bushes with pink, purple, and white flowers like masses of ruffles. Josie heard a man's voice say, "Poisoning by these beautiful plants is rare, but it does happen."

Now Honey was back on the screen, solemnly announcing, "The funeral for Robert Jarvis Manning, St. Louis's own Uncle Bob, will be private, but friends are invited to a public reception afterward at Uncle Bob's Doggy Day Camp from ten a.m. to two p.m. Monday."

A photo of Uncle Bob leered over her shoulder. "Don't they have any serious photos of Uncle Bob?" Josie asked.

"I've never seen a serious photo of him," Ted said. "It's like he doesn't exist outside of his business. They've never showed photos of his wedding, his childhood, his education, or his wife."

"Candice gave one interview yesterday, right after Bob died," Josie said, "and even then we could hardly see her face. There's a lot missing from this story besides photos."

"Like what?" Ted asked.

"Frank told me the staff didn't like Bob," Josie said, "but Beverly wept on TV."

"Maybe she's afraid she'll lose her job if the place closes," Ted said. "Good jobs are hard to find. Who wants to be seen attacking a dead victim? I bet the whole staff is afraid to say anything bad about him."

"Bob's portrayed as a real animal lover," Josie said. "But he broke that little dog's leg. I'd think Sharon, Angel's owner, would say something."

"Not if she's planning to sue the day-care center," Ted said. "Her lawyer would tell her to keep quiet. I bet the lawyer waits until several months after Bob's death. It won't help Sharon's case if she spoke up now. The timing is bad."

"Uncle Bob and his wife were estranged," Josie said. "Frank told me they didn't live together. But the TV stories never mention that."

"I can see why," Ted said. "They're busy making him into a local saint. They'll keep quiet about the couple's marital problems out of respect for Bob and his widow."

"Then why did Candice bring him mushrooms for lunch?" Josie said. "I know the police said they weren't poisoned, but angry wives don't give their husbands gifts—especially expensive little extras for lunch."

"Maybe," Ted said, "she also took him some organic azalea leaves for his salad."

Chapter 16

Josie woke up with a bad feeling Thursday. Something terrible was going to happen. She knew it.

You're being ridiculous, she told herself. But no matter how hard she tried, Josie couldn't get rid of that uneasy feeling.

She knew Ted was safely at the clinic. He'd called her shortly after he got to work. She'd dropped Amelia off at school and made sure that her daughter was inside. Then Josie called her mother.

"Is everything okay, Mom?" Josie asked.

"Of course," Jane said. "Frank's here. We're having coffee and cake in the kitchen."

Josie mentally checked those sentences for any hidden stress, but her mother sounded cheerful.

"Why don't you join us?" Jane said.

"Well," Josie began.

"I know—you've got a ton of work to do," Jane said. "You always do. But I made your favorite: pineapple upside-down cake."

"With the pineapple rings on top?" Josie said.

"And a cherry in each one, the way you like it," Jane said. "Come by and help us eat it."

"Hm," Josie said. "I don't have to mystery-shop until Friday."

"There's an extra cake you can take home to Ted and

Amelia," Jane said. "You'll be saving time by coming here for that cake. You won't have to plan dessert for dinner."

"But don't you want to be alone with Frank?" Josie said.

"I'd like to see my daughter," Jane said, her voice sharp. "I hope you'll honor me with your presence so I can give you a homemade cake."

"Ouch," Josie said. "I'm on my way, Mom. I didn't want to be a third wheel; that's all."

"Frank wants to see you, too," Jane said. That was the only false note Josie caught in her mother's voice.

She drove to Jane's house with a lighter heart, sure all was well with her world. It was another brilliant fall morning, and Mrs. Mueller was outside, pulling weeds in her garden and looking as cheerful as a Russian winter. Mrs. Mueller's dress was a gray sack with flat black buttons up to her wrinkled neck. Her iron-gray hair was sprayed into submission. Even her gardening gloves were gray.

The neighborhood grouch stood up, crossed her arms, and watched Josie park behind Frank's blue Lincoln. Josie made sure her car's bumper was within the Marcus property line. Mrs. M lived under the delusion that she owned the parking spots in front of her home.

"Hi, Mrs. Mueller," Josie said, waving at her. "I'm on my way to see Mom and Frank. They're upstairs. In her kitchen. Alone."

Josie enjoyed teasing the dour woman. Mrs. M had tried to seduce Frank with a steady supply of casseroles after he moved in, but he preferred Jane's charm and soft manners.

Mrs. Mueller snorted and went back to ripping weeds out of her azalea bed.

Josie noticed that Jane's scarred lawn was healing. The new sod seemed to be taking root in the tire tracks gouged into the grass. Soon the damage would disappear, but Josie knew it would be a long time before Jane forgot—and forgave—Frank for that incident.

Josie entered her mother's house without knocking, the way she had for the eleven years she'd lived downstairs in what was now Frank's apartment. She was halfway up the stairs when she heard Frank say, "Please, Jane, won't you go out to dinner with me?" His voice was intense.

"You know I won't drive with you until you've been sober longer, Frank," Jane said.

"But I haven't had a drink since it happened," Frank said.

"It happened a week ago this coming Friday, Frank," Jane said. "That's not very long."

"I'm trying. I really am. Even with all the pressure of working at—and quitting—Uncle Bob's, I still didn't drink."

"I know that, Frank," Jane said. "I do wish you would join AA. They meet at our church."

"I don't need meetings, Jane," he said. "I need something to keep me busy. I need you. You're my reason for staying sober. Every time I thought about hitting the bottle, I saw your sweet face."

Silence. Frank started talking again. "Please go out with me. We can walk to dinner. There are five or six good restaurants only a block away. Say yes. Please."

Josie's face was flaming red. She hadn't meant to eavesdrop on her mother. She really hoped Jane would say yes, though she knew it was risky to date a man with a drinking problem.

Josie didn't believe Frank was a drunk, just a widower who turned to alcohol because he was lonely. But Jane was right to be cautious.

And she'd kill me if she knew I overheard this conversation, she thought.

Josie tiptoed back down the stairs, praying the old

wooden steps wouldn't betray her with a creak or Stuart Little wouldn't realize she was there.

She'd made it to the bottom when she heard Jane say, "All right, Frank. I'll go to dinner with you. But we're walking, not driving."

"Tonight?" he said. It was painful to hear the hope in his voice.

"Friday," Jane said, her voice firm. "I have other plans tonight."

Josie wondered if Jane really did have plans, or if she was following the old-school dating rule she'd taught Josie: A smart woman plays hard to get.

Either way, Josie was relieved that Jane had agreed to have dinner with Frank. She noisily opened the front door, then slammed it shut and yelled, "Yoo-hoo, Mom, it's me. Are you home?"

"Come on upstairs," Jane called.

Woof! Stuart Little said.

Jane and her shih tzu met Josie at the top of the stairs. Jane's face was bright pink. She was wearing her good pale green pantsuit and gold earrings. This had been no casual coffee-and-cake session with Frank, Josie thought.

She followed her mother through the spotless living room, which smelled of lemon polish, into the equally clean kitchen. Jane had a vase of yellow mums on the kitchen table, and the pineapple upside-down cake was on a cut-glass plate. Two big pieces were missing.

Frank was at the table, staring into his coffee cup as if searching for his future in its murky depths. His thick snowy hair was neatly parted and combed, and he wore a long-sleeved blue plaid shirt. He stood when Josie came into the kitchen.

"How are you, Josie?" he asked.

"Fine, Frank, but don't get up." She took the chair next to her mother's.

Jane poured her daughter coffee, then cut another generous slice of cake. She made sure the slice had a pineapple ring with a maraschino cherry in the middle.

Josie smiled at her, then asked, "How have you been, Frank? Have you had any problems with the police since you quit Uncle Bob's?"

"So far, so good," he said. "The police haven't bothered me yet. I've kept in touch with some of the staff, especially little Beverly."

Josie took a bite of her cake.

"She's the receptionist?" Jane asked. "The one who looks like a pug?"

"Mom!" Josie said.

"Well, she does," Jane said. "A very cute pug, but with those eyes and her high voice, she reminds me of a little dog."

"She's a nice young lady," Frank said. "Bev was interviewed by the police the night Bob died. She talked to that Summerdale detective. What's his name? Ray, Reilly?"

"Radley," Josie said. "Radley Dobbs."

"That's the one," Frank said.

"This cake is fabulous, Mom," Josie said.

Jane nodded and said, "So what about this Detective Dobbs, Frank?"

"He interviewed all of Uncle Bob's staff, including Beverly. She told him that I had a fight with Bob after he broke that little dog's leg, and I quit that same day."

"She what?" Jane said. "I thought she was your friend."

"She is," Frank said. "She had to tell the police. Everyone heard that fight. Dobbs would have found out about it eventually. Better he learned about it from a friend. The cops also know I filed an abuse complaint."

"Your so-called friend told him that, too?" Jane said.

"Now, Jane, don't get yourself riled up. I did file a

complaint and I'm proud of it. I'll stand by my decision. I had to quit. I couldn't work for a man who kicked a poor little dog. Nobody there liked Bob."

Jane still looked indignant.

"Why was Beverly crying on TV when Bob died if she didn't like him?" Josie said.

"She's a sensitive person," Frank said. "It was a shock finding him like that."

"I found him," Josie said. "It was terrible, but I didn't cry."

"Well, you're a stronger person, Josie. And you didn't know him. Bev worked with him five days a week. She's a divorced mom with a little girl and she has a mortgage to pay. I think she cried from fear—for herself and her girl. She's afraid she'll lose her job and her house.

"I know you spent a lot of years on your own, but Bev doesn't have a supportive mother like you do. Bev gives me the inside dope on the investigation. She's the one who told me that Bob was poisoned by azalea leaves before that story was on TV."

"Do you think his wife, Candice, could have mixed the poison leaves into his salad when she brought the mushrooms?" Josie said.

"Sure. Anybody could have. The kitchen is wide open. Bob poured so much of that thick ranch dressing on his salad, he probably had no idea what he was eating."

"Bob and his wife didn't get along, right?" Josie said. "I mean, they didn't live together."

"No. I don't know why they split, but he lived in a little efficiency apartment about ten miles away. Candice and Bob kept up appearances for the sake of their business. He had his organic produce delivered to the house. I guess that's why he never changed the delivery address when he moved out. Candice would bring his salad fixings into work with her."

They heard Frank's doorbell ring; then someone pounded on Jane's front door.

Woof! Stuart Little said.

"I'll go see who it is," Josie said.

She opened her mother's front door, and there was Detective Radley Dobbs on the porch, looking like he'd walked off the set of *Mad Men* in his vintage fifties suit with the white shirt and narrow burgundy tie.

"Detective," Josie said.

"Is Franklin Hyzy here?" he asked.

"He's upstairs, talking to Mom," she said.

He pushed past Josie, his handcuff tie tack nearly snagging her sleeve.

Chapter 17

Detective Dobbs pushed past Josie and was up the stairs to the living room. Jane met him at the top.

"Why are you invading my home, Detective?" she asked. Frank stood behind her, hands protectively on Jane's shoulders.

"Your daughter invited me in," he said.

Josie said, "I—," but Dobbs rolled right over her protest before she could finish.

"I could take you to the station for questioning, Mr. Hyzy," he said, "but I'm doing you the courtesy of questioning you here."

"Let's go downstairs to my apartment," Frank said.

"No!" Jane blocked his way. "I think you'd better talk to Franklin here, Detective. In front of witnesses. You can have a seat on the couch."

The detective sank into the soft green couch. Jane pushed Frank firmly into the stiff-backed chair opposite, so he sat slightly higher than the detective. Then she stood protectively behind Frank, one hand on his shoulder, like an old-fashioned wedding photo. She did not offer Dobbs any coffee, a grave breach of her hospitality rule.

Josie admired her mother's quick thinking and stubborn good sense. Jane was a survivor, and she'd watch out for Frank, who looked lost. He kept running his big hands through his silvery white hair until it stood up in spikes. He looked ready to bolt out of his chair.

Detective Dobbs tossed his skinny-brimmed hat on Jane's coffee table. Josie was beginning to hate that hat. She leaned against the kitchen doorway to watch the verbal battle.

"Aren't you going to read Frank his rights?" Jane said.

"I'm not taking him into custody," Detective Dobbs said. "Yet." He shot his French cuffs with the square silver cufflinks. "I want to ask him a few questions; that's all."

Jane frowned but said nothing. She realized she'd pushed Dobbs too far.

"Mr. Hyzy, the staff said you were a new hire at Uncle Bob's Doggy Day Camp," he said. "You came in Saturday, begging for a job. Then you quit Tuesday."

"Yes, I did," Frank said.

"Why quit a job you were so desperate to have? You didn't even last a week." Dobbs was lean but muscular, Josie thought. That gray silk suit with the maroon stripe looks good on him. And this isn't a fashion show.

She saw the sweat beading on Frank's forehead. "I couldn't work there anymore after I realized what kind of person Bob was," he said.

"And what was that?"

"He abused a dog. A Pomeranian named Angel. The dog barely weighed five pounds. She's fifteen, fragile, and incontinent. That's why she peed on Bob's foot. She couldn't help it. Bob got so mad he kicked that tiny dog with his big clodhoppers and broke her leg. Her old bones are brittle."

Frank clenched and unclenched his hands, he was so upset.

"Angel cried, he hurt her so bad. Bob told me to get her out of his sight and take her to the vet, and not the vet the clinic ordinarily uses. I said my daughter worked at the St. Louis Mobo-Pet Clinic in Maplewood, thirty miles away. Bob ordered me to take that poor little dog there, even though she was in pain and there were closer vets. Angel whimpered the whole time."

"Is that the clinic run by Ms. Marcus's husband?" Detective Dobbs said. He's done his homework, Josie thought.

"Yes, and it's a good clinic. Bob wanted me to tell Dr. Ted some crazy story about how Angel had jumped up on a table and had fallen off, but I didn't. Any reputable vet would know the story was a lie. That dog is too arthritic to jump on anything.

"Sure enough, Dr. Ted knew what happened. He said Angel's broken leg was no accident. He asked me how she'd broken it, and I told him. Dr. Ted said that was abuse, and that he'd call the police. His clinic is in the Village of Rock Road. They said they'd contact Summerdale, your jurisdiction."

"I'll have to check," Detective Dobbs said. "Complaints can get lost."

On purpose? Josie wondered.

"Ted also said he'd file an animal-cruelty complaint against Bob with the Humane Society, and he suggested I do the same. And that's exactly what I did."

"Why did you quit?"

"Because I love animals and I couldn't work for someone who hurt them. Bob pretended to love dogs, but he didn't like them at all."

"Did the victim threaten you after you told him you'd filed the cruelty complaint?"

"He said he wouldn't give me a reference," Frank said. "I didn't want one from someone who hurt dogs. I said my complaint would put him out of business and he'd be asking *me* for a reference."

"Were you mad at the victim?"

"Of course," Frank said.

"Was anyone else mad at him?"

"His wife. Candice threw him out of their house and he was living in a cramped one-room apartment. The staff says the couple has a big three-bedroom brick home in Summerdale, and Candice lives there alone with Ralph the Talking Dog."

"When was this? When did his wife throw him out of their home?"

"I don't know. It happened before I was hired. The separation wasn't public knowledge. They pretended to be living together when they were at work."

"Any clients upset with the victim? Lovers? Creditors?"

"I wasn't there long enough to learn much about Bob or his business," Frank said, "but the day camp seemed prosperous. The staff got paid on time. He had plans for an outdoor pool. And he had lots of clients.

"Lovers? I never saw him make a pass at any woman, either a client or a staffer. As for upset clients, I'd imagine the woman whose dog he injured was upset about Angel's so-called accident, but I wasn't there when she picked up her Pomeranian."

I was, Josie thought, but I'm not volunteering anything more unless the detective asks me.

"Let's talk about that," Detective Dobbs said. "Why did you quit Uncle Bob's?"

"Like I said, I couldn't work for him after he hurt that little dog."

"Oh, but you did," Detective Dobbs said. "If I have it right, you came back to the day-care center with the dog the day it was injured and you continued working until closing. Then you went back to work the next morning— after you filed the complaint. Is that correct?"

"That's right," Frank said.

"In fact, you worked the entire morning after Bob hurt the dog."

Josie tensed. This was a trap that could snap closed on both of them. Frank worked that morning because of me, she thought. He stayed at Uncle Bob's to protect Stuart Little until Jane's dog went to Karen, the groomer. I didn't tell Detective Dobbs that I was mystery-shopping Uncle Bob's. If Frank says anything, I'll look like a liar and be drawn into the investigation. If he doesn't say anything, it will look like Frank stayed till lunch to poison Bob.

"You didn't quit work until after one o'clock the next day," Detective Dobbs said. "Why did you stay so long at Uncle Bob's if you couldn't stand it?"

Frank answered without hesitation. "I wanted to tell Bob in person what he did and why I was leaving. I wanted to quit like a man, Detective, not sneak out the back door. Bob was busy that morning showing the facilities to customers, and then he had to go to the dentist. Bob didn't get back to the day-care center until almost one o'clock. That's when I confronted him."

"Where?"

"In his office."

"Were there any witnesses?"

"No, the door was shut. But his office walls are thin. I'm sure some of the staff heard us talking."

"Was the victim in good health?"

"Yes. Bob had had some dental work and his mouth was still numb so he talked a little odd. Other than that, he seemed fine."

"What was his mental state?"

"I don't know," Frank said. "He was Bob. He was a loudmouth and a bully. He said he was busy and asked what I wanted. When I told him, he got angry and threatened me."

"Threatened you how?"

"Bob said he'd fix it so I couldn't work in the business again. I wasn't too worried about that. I took the job because I needed something to do. I'm retired and have enough money to live comfortably."

"Then why did you sell your house in Maplewood?"

"It was too big after my wife died and my daughter moved out. Too big and too lonely. My flat downstairs is the right size."

"Did you want Robert Manning dead?"

"What? No. I'm not sorry he died, but I didn't kill him. I filed a complaint that would seriously damage his business, and then I quit."

"How do you feel about the dog abuse?"

"It's despicable," Frank said. "Anyone who would hurt an innocent animal is the lowest of the low. It's even worse for Bob, a professional, to hurt a harmless old dog."

Detective Dobbs switched subjects so fast, Josie nearly had whiplash following him. "When you entered the victim's office, what was he doing?" he asked.

"Getting ready to eat his lunch."

"Which was?"

"A steak and a salad. He made a big deal about his food being organic."

"Who brought his food?"

"It was brought from his home—his old home, where he lived with his wife," Frank said. "I think Candice brought it into work that day, but I don't know for sure."

"Did he often eat salads and a steak?"

"Every day," Frank said. "The same thing. That's what the staff told me."

"At what time?"

"Between one and two o'clock, most days."

"Did the victim have a regular source for his food?"

"Yes, but I don't know the company's name."

"Who fixed his lunch?"

"Heidi, usually. She's the redhead. She makes the organic dog treats, too. Heidi grilled his steak and made his buttermilk ranch dressing. He poured a ton of that glop on his salad."

"Who put the azalea leaves in his salad?"

"I have no idea."

"Did you know azaleas were poisonous?"

"I don't know anything about azaleas. My wife did the gardening at our house, and I cut the grass. We never had azaleas."

"Why not?"

"My wife said they were too hard to grow in St. Louis and dangerous to children, like castor bean plants. She didn't grow those, either."

"Why were they dangerous for children?"

"Because of the . . ." Frank stopped.

"Because of the what?" Detective Dobbs said.

"Leaves," Frank said. He looked confused.

"Did you kill Robert Manning?"

"Me? No! Where would I get azalea leaves?"

"Off the bushes growing at the edge of this property," the detective said. Josie thought she saw a triumphant smile on his face. "The azaleas belonging to your next-door neighbor, Mrs. Mueller."

"What?" Frank and Jane both said. Josie gripped the doorjamb.

"Mrs. Mueller is a very observant and cooperative citizen," the detective said.

That old troublemaker, Josie thought. She'd waylaid the detective before he got upstairs and filled his ear with poison.

"Mrs. Mueller said you were intoxicated Friday night," Dobbs said, "and you drove your car up onto Mrs. Marcus's lawn. In fact, you nearly mowed down Mrs. Mueller's azaleas. She says Mrs. Marcus refused to press charges."

"There was no reason, Detective," Jane said, her face flaming. "Frank replaced the grass with new sod and no one was hurt. Mrs. Mueller is a busybody. She made a play for Frank from the day he moved in here, but he wasn't interested in her."

"Thank you, Mrs. Marcus," the detective said. "I gather Mr. Hyzy is interested in you."

"We're landlord and tenant," Jane said. "That's all."

But her body language said that was a lie. Jane had both hands on Frank's shoulders, claiming him for herself.

No matter how much Mom protests that she's not interested in Frank, I can see how she really feels, Josie thought, and so can that detective.

"So you had no idea that azaleas—those bushes you nearly ran over—were poison."

"Absolutely not," Frank said.

"Thank you, Mr. Hyzy. That's all. For now."

Chapter 18

"Is this place really for dogs?" Josie asked. "It looks like an estate."

At seven thirty the next morning, Alyce drove through the welcoming wrought-iron gates of Westminster Dog Day Care in Maplewood. The colonial-style sign was so discreet, the place could have been an upscale bed-and-breakfast.

"I'd like to take Ted here for a getaway," Josie said.

"Not sure he'd want to spend a weekend on a leash," Alyce said, and grinned at her friend.

The drive curved gently through a lush green lawn, ending at a gleaming white two-story mansion framed by flaming trees.

"Westminster looks like the Hilton for hounds," Josie said.

"More like Tara for terriers," Alyce said. "Check out the white columns on that porch."

"I keep expecting to hear the theme from *Gone With the Wind*," Josie said. "This is imposing for Maplewood."

"And West County," Alyce said.

"Glad we took your Cadillac Escalade," Josie said. "It fits in better than my old car."

Arf! Festus said from the SUV's rear compartment. His big head popped up, pink tongue hanging out in a doggy smile. The Lab stuck his huge paws on the seat back.

"Festus," Josie said, her voice stern. "Down! Get your paws off the leather seats."

The Lab sat.

"He's so well behaved," Alyce said. "But he can't hurt anything. Justin runs his trucks over those seats. He even dropped a sippy cup of juice on one. They clean up."

"Festus knows better," Josie said.

Alyce parked the SUV between a Porsche Cayenne and a Beemer while Josie checked the questions on her mystery-shopping list again.

"Ready?" Alyce asked.

Josie nodded and the two women strolled down a flagstone path lined with cushiony yellow mums, the Lab straining at his leash. His glossy dark coat shone in the early-morning sun.

"Festus is getting a half day off work," Josie said. "Ted will call if the clinic needs a canine blood transfusion for emergency surgery."

"Poor guy," Alyce said, stroking the dog's soft ears.

"Ted says Festus likes being a donor," Josie said. "He's not afraid of needles and everyone makes a fuss over him. He's paid in treats, but Ted has to really exercise him. Labs have a tendency to put on weight. But this morning, Festus gets treats and fun."

They were on the grand porch, standing under a huge light held by four black chains. The double doors were topped by a graceful fanlight.

"I expect to be greeted by a belle in a hoop skirt," Josie said, and opened the doors. The woman seated behind the maple desk was a belle with a soft Southern accent and blond curls, but she wore a practical navy polo.

"Welcome to Westminster," she said. "My name is Sarah. How may I help you ladies?"

Chalk up one for Westminster, Josie thought. The receptionist greeted us before we were through the door.

"I'd like to drop my Lab off for a morning of day care and then tour the facility," Josie said.

"Certainly," Sarah said. "I'll buzz Mark, our manager. He'll take you on a tour. Meanwhile, let's talk about this handsome gentleman. What's his name?"

Festus sat at the receptionist's feet, tail thumping on the thick Oriental carpet. Sarah fed him a treat.

"Festus," Josie said. "He's a Lab. Here are his papers. He's had all his shots."

"How is he with groups?" Sarah asked.

"He gets along fine with other dogs and people," Josie said, "but we'd like private lessons this visit."

"We have private agility training. If you're hoping to enter your dog in national trials, I'd recommend that." Sarah lowered her voice to confide, "We currently have a mixed-breed Lab–border collie training here for the Westminster Dog Show agility trials."

"The New York show?" Josie asked.

"Yes," Sarah said. "That Westminster lets in mixed breeds now. We're not affiliated with them. Our private agility classes last half an hour. They're forty dollars."

Josie hesitated. "Festus really isn't competing," she said, "unless there's an eating contest."

"It's also fun exercise," Sarah said, looking pointedly at Festus's solid middle.

"He does need a good workout," Josie said. "We'll take it."

"Labs love water," Sarah said. "What about pool time? Fifteen dollars for thirty minutes. Our lap pool has no chlorine or harsh chemicals."

"He'll like that," Josie said.

"Do you want the indoor or outdoor pool?"

"Outdoor," Josie said. "It's a sunny day."

"Good," Sarah said. "We use the indoor pool for rainy

days and recommend it for white dogs or thin-haired and hairless breeds. They sunburn quicker. But our outdoor pool is covered by a UV shade tent. We'll put sunscreen on your dog's ears, nose, belly and groin."

"Which lucky staff member gets to rub sunscreen on a dog's sensitive areas?" Josie asked.

"Nobody. We use a spray specially designed for dogs," Sarah said. Her Southern accent had thickened and Josie wondered if she was annoyed by the flippant remark. "We use the only FDA-compliant sunscreen on our dogs."

"My vet said any brand of sunscreen that's safe for babies is safe for my Chihuahua," Alyce said.

"True," Sarah said. "But this sunscreen is designed for dogs. It's safe if Festus tries to lick it off, and it's water-repellent."

"Sign him up for pool time," Josie said.

"How about individual playtime?" Sarah asked. "It's six dollars for fifteen minutes."

"We'll take half an hour," Josie said.

"That's an hour and a half workout," Alyce said. "Shouldn't our guy have some fun?"

"He can hang out in the playroom," Sarah said. "Our counselors supervise the dogs, and any troublemakers are removed."

"Festus is a lover, not a fighter," Josie said. On cue, he slurped her hand.

"Then he'll like the playroom," Sarah said. "It has dog-friendly 'people' furniture, a fireplace, and a forty-two-inch flat-screen TV."

"What do dogs watch?" Josie asked.

"We'll turn on your dog's favorite show," Sarah said.

"Festus likes to watch TV with the family, but he doesn't have a favorite show," Josie said.

"Then we have DogTV, the channel designed for dogs. They like to watch other dogs playing in the snow, romping, riding in cars. They love watching letter carriers. DogTV will help Festus relax."

Festus was resting his head on his paws, snoring.

"I don't think relaxation is his problem," Josie said.

"Other dogs find DogTV stimulating," Sarah said.

"But I've heard some experts say that dogs don't see TV the way we do," Alyce said. "Canines see TV at a faster frame rate than humans, so dogs see the individual frames in the TV show and the dark space between them."

"I've heard that, too," Sarah said. "It's true on old-school TVs. But we have the newest LCD screen and the refresh rate is faster. It's perfect for canine viewing. Festus can hang out in the playroom for free."

"Sounds good," Josie said. "And he deserves a treat after his workout."

"How about a pizza biscuit?"

"Uh, pizza is a problem," Josie said. "He has a bad habit of poking his nose into our pizza boxes at home and eating leftover pizza. He's been banished outside for pizza snitching more than once."

"Oh, these aren't real pizzas," Sarah said. "They're pizza dog biscuits. The dough is peanut-butter flavored, and the yogurt icing makes it look like a slice of pizza, decorated with pepperoni and green peppers. It's two-fifty a slice."

"He'll take a slice," Josie said.

"Any ice cream, truffles, or organic biscuits?" Sarah asked.

"That would undo the exercise," Josie said. "But if he's swimming slathered with sunscreen, he should probably have a bath."

"A shampoo with milk-bath conditioner, cologne, breath freshener, nose and pad cream, and a paw massage is forty dollars. Would you like a pawdicure?"

"No, his nails are okay," Josie said.

"A twenty-minute massage? It's only fifteen dollars."

"Well, sure, he can have that," Josie said.

"Would he be interested in a private ball-chasing session? He'll get his own monogrammed tennis ball."

"Thanks, but we've scheduled enough exercise," Josie said.

"A car ride? All doggies wear seat belts and take a scenic tour of Forest Park."

"No, he rides with my husband every day," Josie said. "I think that's it for this visit."

"When would you like to pick him up?" Sarah asked.

"Noon," Josie said.

"Come on, big fella," Sarah said to Festus. "You have a busy morning ahead of you. Josie and Alyce, let me introduce you to Mark, who'll take you on a tour of Westminster."

Mark, pink faced, chunky, and muscular, looked like a high school gym teacher. He had a deep voice and a serious manner, and he proudly showed them the highlights of Westminster.

"Downstairs we have our cageless boarding suites," Mark said. "Each has a fenced private yard with grass. Rooms also have water fountains and are cleaned daily.

"The beds are designed for dogs and have orthopedic mattresses to support their hips and shoulders. We have sizes for big, small, and medium dogs. The covers are washable and changed after every guest."

Each dog suite is about the size of Amelia's bedroom, Josie thought.

One looked like a hunting lodge with pine log walls, a fake deer head over a fireplace, and a plaid dog bed.

"Very popular with Labradors, beagles, and other outdoorsy dogs," Mark said.

Josie didn't dare look at Alyce.

Another room was done in white and gold with a crystal chandelier. An extra-large dog bed nestled under a sheer white canopy. "This is our honeymoon suite," Mark said. "We're booked for weddings through July."

After they looked at a pink princess suite and a seaside suite with its own beach, Mark took them into a white room with stained-glass windows and a statue of St. Francis of Assisi, the patron saint of animals.

"This is our nondenominational chapel for ceremonies, including bark mitzvahs," he said.

Josie wondered how St. Francis felt presiding over a bark mitzvah and if Jewish people found the idea offensive. She looked at Mark to avoid Alyce's eyes.

"When your pet crosses the rainbow bridge, we offer caring and dignified funerals, as well as grief counseling." Mark pointed to two stacks of small white cloth and dark wood caskets behind a screen.

Alyce shuddered. "I can't look at those," she said. "They remind me of children's coffins."

"Let's go into the playroom," Mark said, and quickly steered them into what looked like a suburban great room. Two shih tzus were watching Animal Planet, while a boxer snored on an oversized plaid couch.

"I wonder if he's allowed to do that at home," Alyce said.

"Snore?" Mark asked.

"Sleep on the couch," Alyce said.

Outside, Mark showed them two grassy fenced play areas, each about half an acre. "That one is for big dogs," he said. A golden retriever and a Border collie were catching Frisbees.

"This yard is for small dogs." A miniature apricot poodle and a white Maltese romped on the grass.

"Both play areas have UV sunshades, and that's new sod," he said. "Those yellow umbrella tables along the edge are for dog owners who like to watch their pets playing."

Josie and Alyce admired the sleek, granite-edged rectangular pool from a distance. They could see Festus paddling in the water and didn't want to disturb him. Mark walked them through the restaurant-grade kitchen, where one chef prepared gourmet dog treats while another iced pizzas with colored yogurt icing.

They were back in the lobby again. Josie noticed it smelled pleasantly of cinnamon.

"Well," Mark said, "what do you think?"

"I'm impressed," Josie said. "You aren't the first day-care center we've toured. One—a very well-known one—was dirty, and there was dog waste in the cages and on the grounds."

"Unacceptable," Mark said. "We have two staffers each shift who do nothing but clean the grounds and the inside. Cleanup is a full-time job."

He pointed to a young man trundling a cleanup cart bristling with a broom, a rake, a shovel, and a big trash can. "That's Kevin's job."

Josie and Alyce thanked Mark and made it back to Alyce's SUV, where they collapsed into giggles. "I couldn't believe that dog wedding and the honeymoon suite," Josie said. "Did you check out the overdone decor?"

"I almost asked him if it was doggy style," Alyce said, and they laughed so hard they had tears in their eyes.

"My sides hurt from laughing," Alyce said. "I wish I could be with you when you pick up Festus at noon, but I'm not sure I could keep a straight face. What a difference from that horrible Bow-Wow Heaven."

"And Uncle Bob's," Josie said. "I wonder what will happen to his empire. Detective Dobbs was at Mom's yesterday and grilled Frank. That rotten Mrs. Mueller told the police that . . ."

Josie stopped. She still didn't want to tell Alyce that Frank had been drinking and drove into her mother's yard.

"Uh, Frank knew she had azalea bushes growing on the property line between her house and Mom's."

"That woman!" Alyce said. "She's been a problem since you were a kid. You don't think Frank killed Uncle Bob, do you?"

"Of course not," Josie said.

"Well, I'd be tempted to poison someone who hurt a little dog."

"I think Frank would punch out Bob, but I can't see him doing anything sneaky, like poisoning him. Ted thinks the killer is Bob's wife, Candice. But that detective has it in for Frank. I'm afraid he'll arrest him any minute."

"What do you want to do?" Alyce said.

"Uncle Bob's funeral is Monday morning. It's private. But his wife is holding a public reception afterward from ten a.m. to two p.m. at the day-care center. I want to go. I can talk to the staff and the customers. Maybe I can find out something that will change Detective Dobbs's mind."

"Everyone will want to talk to you," Alyce said. "You found Bob, and they'll want to hear the gory details. But you'll need the support of your loyal friend."

"See you Monday morning," Josie said.

Chapter 19

Josie was still worried about Frank. She called her mother as soon as she got home from Westminster, the decadent dog day-care center.

"Has Detective Dobbs given Frank any more trouble?" Josie asked.

"He hasn't been back," Jane said. "Frank left home at ten this morning, as soon as the stores opened, dressed in a nice blue suit and tie. He's looking for another job. He promised me he would."

And Frank's just your tenant, Josie thought. No romance there at all. So why do you seem so starry-eyed, Mom?

"I hope Frank looks for a lawyer, too," Josie said.

"Nonsense," Jane said. "A lawyer is a waste of money."

"Frank nearly talked himself into jail yesterday," Josie said. "He told Detective Dobbs that he didn't know anything about azaleas and in the next breath said his wife refused to have those plants in their yard because they were dangerous for children."

"He forgot, Josie," Jane said. "He'd had that conversation with his wife thirty years ago."

"He picked a heck of a time to remember it," Josie said. "Frank needs a good defense attorney. Like Renzo Fischer. At least give Frank his name."

"I'm not giving Frank anything more to worry about,"

Jane said. "He has enough on his plate. Frank's car had barely turned the corner when Mrs. Mueller had the nerve to knock on my door. She must have been watching my house, waiting for him to leave.

"There she was, wearing that gray eyesore. I wouldn't take out the trash in that rag. She tried to come inside, but I wouldn't let her.

" 'You're not welcome,' I told her.

"Mrs. Mueller said, 'I don't know why you're mad at me, Jane. I simply did my duty as a citizen.' So self-righteous.

" 'Duty!' I said. 'Spreading gossip is a sin, not a duty.'

" 'Those were facts, not gossip,' she said. 'At least I don't rent to drunks.'

"That did it! I looked her right in the eye and said, 'Get off my porch and out of my yard. And stay out. You're as poisonous as your plants!' I slammed the door in her face before she could say another word."

Josie heard her mother's triumph. Jane had given the interfering old bat a piece of her mind. Once, Jane and Mrs. M had been best friends—as long as Jane did what her neighbor wanted. But it wasn't an equal friendship. Jane never called Mrs. M by her first name.

"Which dog day-care place did you mystery-shop today?" Jane asked, abruptly changing the subject.

"Westminster in Maplewood," Josie said. "Alyce and I could hardly keep a straight face. You wouldn't believe the luxuries they lavish on dogs, including indoor and outdoor pools, even a honeymoon suite."

"Why would dogs need a honeymoon?" Jane said.

"To celebrate their wedding, of course," Josie said.

"They're dogs, not dolls," Jane said.

"I wonder if those pampered pets would really rather kick back with some kibble and snooze on the porch," Josie said. "Ted and Amelia send their thanks for the cake. We scarfed it down at dinner last night.

"Today's the big day for Amelia. Her first grown-up party. I want to make sure her outfit is ready. If the police give Frank any trouble, let me know, night or day."

Josie hung up, wishing her mother would convince Frank to call a lawyer. He'd hire one if Jane asked him. Josie was sure he'd be arrested any moment.

Nothing I can do about it now, she thought. Instead, she cut the tags off Amelia's new coral dress, then pressed it and laid out her daughter's shoes. Josie put her turquoise bracelet on Amelia's dresser.

Then she cleaned the house until it was time to pick up Festus. Josie dusted and vacuumed, cleaned two of the three bathrooms—Amelia handled her own—and ran up and down the stairs to the laundry room.

Soon she was in the Zen-like state that also cleared her mind.

Who killed Bob? she wondered. Ted believed Candice had murdered her husband. After all, Bob's wife had brought his mushrooms to work. She could have easily garnished his salad with azalea leaves.

Detective Dobbs seemed to suspect Frank, and Jane's renter didn't help when he blurted out why his wife wouldn't grow azaleas in their yard.

But Dobbs wasn't stupid. He'd investigated Frank carefully before he interviewed him at Jane's house.

Josie had watched enough TV to know the wife was the first suspect when a husband was murdered. So why did the police give Candice a pass?

I'll have a lot of questions to ask the guests at Bob's wake, she thought, then glanced at the kitchen clock. Time to pick up Festus—and steal a few moments with Ted at the clinic.

She changed into a fresh white blouse, combed her shiny brown hair, and added lipstick. She was ready to back out of the drive when their new neighbor's red Honda Civic pulled into the driveway next door. Josie still didn't get a good look at the man at the wheel, but the woman getting out was taller than Josie—maybe five-nine—and curvy, with fluffy brown hair.

Dressed in old jeans and a blue T-shirt, she carried a scrub bucket bulging with cleaning supplies, and a new mop. I bet I know how you're spending the afternoon, Josie thought.

The woman saluted the man with her mop. He tapped the horn and waved good-bye. I think I might like these neighbors, Josie decided.

At Westminster Dog Day Care, the princely pup palace, Josie was glad she was sitting down when she saw the bill for Festus. A morning of doggy indulgences was more than her electric bill. She hoped the mystery-shopping client wouldn't object, but they had to know what high-end dog day care cost.

The ebony Lab looked like he'd been steam cleaned. He trotted proudly on his leash, glowing with health and dog spa products, a jaunty blue bandana around his neck. Josie thought his doggy cologne was too strong, but she was happy to see him.

So was the staff at the St. Louis Mobo-Pet Clinic. Kathy, the receptionist, welcomed Festus back to the clinic as if he'd been gone for a year. While Festus was collecting hugs and scratches, Josie ran down the hall to see Ted in his office.

"Our new neighbor is working at the house next door," she said. "I'd like to have a barbecue this weekend for her and her family. Pork steaks, burgers, and hot dogs, if you'll do the barbecuing."

"Sounds like fun," Ted said, "and a good way to meet our new neighbors."

"You don't have to do all the cooking. I have mostac-cioli in the freezer," she said, pronouncing the Italian noodle dish "musk-a-cholee," like a local.

"Let's invite our neighbors on the other side, Wil and Cordelia," Ted said.

"Definitely," Josie said. "I'll take the newcomers some beef stew as a welcome gift when I get back home."

"Thanks to Amelia's cooking lessons, we're never short of food," Ted said.

"Thanks to my chef, who's always willing to teach her more about cooking," she said.

They shared a lingering kiss until Kathy cleared her throat discreetly, then tapped on Ted's office door. "Your next appointment is here, Dr. Ted," she said.

At home, Josie carried the covered dish of stew to her new neighbor's house. The woman who answered the door looked like she'd been wrestling rabid dust bunnies. She had cobwebs in her hair and a dark smudge on one cheek. Her hazel eyes were tired, but she greeted Josie with a forthright smile.

"Laura June Tracy," she said, pulling off a yellow cleaning glove and shaking Josie's hand. "Laura for short. Follow me to the kitchen and grab a chair. I've been working for hours, and I'm due for a rest. And that smells like beef stew."

"My mom's recipe," Josie said. She didn't add *made by my daughter*.

The Tracy home had the same floor plan as Josie's house, with powder blue carpeting in the living room instead of hardwood floors. Laura led Josie through towers of cardboard boxes to the kitchen.

She put the casserole into the fridge and said, "You saved us from another night of pizza. This is our first official night in our new home. Coffee?"

"No, thanks," Josie said. "I wanted to invite you and your family to a barbecue at our place tomorrow night."

"We'd love to," she said. "We moved to Maplewood because my husband's company transferred him here from the DC area. Clete sells computer systems to businesses."

"What do you do?"

"I just got a job here. I'm assistant manager at the Maplewood Shoe Boutique."

"Love their shoes," Josie said. "Do you get a discount?"

"I do, but right now I'm trying to keep CJ—our son, Clete Junior—in shoes. That boy grows so fast, one pair doesn't get a chance to wear out before he needs a bigger size."

"Where will he go to school?" Josie asked.

"He's in school now. Maplewood. We've been living in a residence hotel since September so CJ could start the school year here. He's fourteen."

"Two years older than my daughter, Amelia," Josie said.

Amelia will be thrilled, she thought. Josie wasn't sure if this was a blessing or a curse. The two women chatted about kids, husbands, and moving. Josie avoided mentioning her job, in case she had to mystery-shop Laura's store.

By the time she left Laura's to pick up Amelia, Josie felt like her new neighbor could become a friend.

At Barrington School, Amelia usually took her time getting to the car. Today, she sprinted out of the building as if Miss Apple, the head of school, had fired a starter's pistol. Amelia tossed her backpack in the car and said, "Hurry, Mom. I only have two hours to get dressed."

Josie took the fastest way home while Amelia texted Palmer about how she should wear her hair: up, down, ponytail, ballerina bun, loose, or side parted?

Josie thought Amelia's hair looked fine the way it was, but she was only a mom. The girls debated the subject as if the fate of future generations depended on Amelia's hairdo.

At home, Amelia raced upstairs, trailed by her cat pal, Harry. Josie heard the shower, then the blow dryer, then music—probably One Direction.

At six, Ted came home with Marmalade the cat and the spiffy, sweet-smelling Festus.

"Today's the big day. How are Amelia's party preparations?" he asked, kissing Josie hello. She handed him a beer and a bowl of pretzels and poured herself a glass of wine. They made themselves comfortable in the living room.

"Priscilla and Palmer are due in fifteen minutes," Josie said. "I'd better see if she needs help."

Amelia's door was shut. Josie knocked on it and said, "It's six fifteen. Can I get you anything?"

"I'm fine," Amelia said.

"Can I come in?" Josie asked.

"No!" Amelia shouted. Josie retreated downstairs to sit next to Ted on the couch.

Ten minutes later, Amelia came shyly downstairs, Harry at her heels. The setting sun gave her coral lace dress an ethereal glow. She'd piled her hair artfully on her head, showing off her long, graceful neck.

Ted whistled. Josie gulped back the tears she knew would annoy her daughter and managed, "Beautiful."

"You like it?" Amelia asked.

"I love it," Josie said.

Harry had climbed onto the couch and started to spring to his favorite perch on Amelia's shoulder. Josie caught the cat in midleap. "Oh no," she said. "Claws and lace don't mix."

Amelia gravely scratched her cat's ears, a princess granting a favorite's wish.

Josie heard a car in the drive and said, "Palmer and Priscilla are here. We'll pick you up at nine, honey, but if you want to leave earlier, call."

"Palmer!" Amelia said, running out the door. "You look so cool." Each word was a separate sentence. The two girls squealed and giggled. Palmer flipped her long hair and Amelia twisted a stray lock.

"I thought they wanted to go to the party," Josie said. "Why are they hanging out on our porch?"

"I think the reason is leaning against the fence next door," Ted said, and grinned.

Josie saw a tall, muscular teen with thick brown hair and boy-band good looks. "You've solved the mystery," she said. "That's CJ, the boy next door."

Priscilla Lindell leaned out of her car window and called, "Palmer and Amelia, we should be leaving."

The girls ran off in a flurry of giggles and good-byes.

Josie started sniffling once the car was out of sight. "Hey," Ted said. "She'll have a good time. She's as beautiful as her mother."

"But she's so young," Josie said. "I don't want her hurt or disappointed."

"When those disappointments do come," he said, "we'll both be here for her. But tonight she'll have fun. Let me fix you an omelet."

When her cell phone rang at 8:07, Josie pounced on it.

"Mom!" Amelia was crying.

"Honey, what's wrong?" Josie said.

"Mom," Amelia said between sobs. "Palmer and I wanna come home. Now."

"We're on our way. We'll pick you up at the Rivingtons' home."

"No!" Amelia said. "Not the house. Meet us a block down the street, toward Lindbergh."

"Okay, honey. Stay on the phone. Ted and I are leaving now. He'll drive. Keep talking to us."

Chapter 20

"Amelia, honey, Ted and I are in his car," Josie said. "We'll be there in fifteen minutes. Are you and Palmer safe? The police can get there quicker."

"No! Not the police," Amelia said. "If you call the police, I'll die. We're fine. We're at Oakleigh Heights Road and Ramsland Terrace. Under a streetlight."

Amelia sounded calmer now. The hiccuping sobs had stopped.

"Tell me what happened," Josie said. "I have the phone on speaker so Ted can hear."

"Palmer and I went to the party." Amelia's voice was still shaky. "A bunch of kids were there already. Kate has this really big house—three stories and an entertainment center on the lower level."

Josie guessed that was the basement.

"About thirty kids were in the great room and the living room. Maybe half were from school. The rest were friends of Kate's older brother, Ridley. He's a freshman in college. The older boys were drinking beer, and the girls wanted Captain and Coke."

Josie knew that Captain and Coke was Coca-Cola and spiced Captain Morgan rum, a drink for girls who didn't like alcohol. Older boys joked that Captain was a date-rape drug.

Josie tried to control her fury. "There was booze at the party? I thought Kate's parents are home."

"They are," Amelia said, "but they went upstairs to their room so we could have a good time."

Josie was afraid to say anything, she was so angry.

"The DJ had terror wrists, Mom. He was playing a killer mix and we were dancing and stuff and I met this really cute older man named Matt."

"How old?" Josie said. She was seething but trying to hide her anger.

"Nineteen," Amelia said.

"Did you tell Matt you were twelve?"

"Uh," Amelia said. "I don't think so.

"Matt wanted to get me a drink, and I said I just wanted Coke, and we were talking, and he asked if I wanted to see the entertainment center downstairs. It's like a really cool private movie theater. So I went downstairs with Matt. It was dark in the room, and at first I couldn't see and then I saw this boy and girl in the corner, and he had his pants unzipped and she was on her knees and ..."

Amelia stopped. Josie heard her daughter's tears and her heart twisted.

"Matt wanted me to do that to him, Mom, and I said no, and he said it was okay, it wouldn't hurt, and it wasn't real sex."

Josie fought to keep quiet and let her daughter talk.

"I started crying and ran up the stairs, and this other older dude was trying to kiss Palmer, and she was trying to get away. She saw me, and I took her arm, and he spilled his beer on her new dress, but we got away and ran out the front door and called you."

"Thank God," Josie said.

"You're not mad, are you, Mom?" Amelia said in a small voice.

"No, sweetheart, I'm not mad." At you, Josie thought.

But when I get my hands on Kate's parents, I'll rip them a new one.

She looked at Ted and he whispered, "After we pick up the girls, we'll stop at Kate's house."

Josie nodded.

"What, Mom?" Amelia said.

"We're turning off Lindbergh onto Oakleigh Heights," Josie said. "We're almost there. Hang on, honey."

Now all the houses were mansions with vast lawns and professional landscaping. The streets were smooth S curves and the streetlights were wrought iron.

Ted slowly cruised up the winding road, and Josie saw Amelia and Palmer huddled under the ornate black streetlight at Ramsland. They could hear the pounding party music, and cars were parked haphazardly on the neighboring lawns. Josie figured they belonged to the older students at the party.

The girls' party splendor was spoiled. Palmer's red hair hung limp and her green dress was wrinkled and stained. Amelia had a dark stain on her skirt and her dark hair spilled out of her updo.

The girls spotted Ted's orange Mustang and waved like castaways on a desert island.

Ted stopped and Josie ran out and wrapped both girls in her arms. They sobbed on her shoulders. Palmer smelled like apple shampoo and stale spilled beer.

Amelia shook with fear. "We're sorry, we're sorry, we're sorry," she sobbed as her tears washed away the last of the party glow.

"You didn't do anything wrong, sweetheart," Josie said. "Neither one of you. You left the party and that took courage. I'm proud of you both. Let's get in the car."

Josie pulled back her passenger seat so the girls could climb into the backseat and gave them each a packet of tissues. She'd expected tears.

"Ted!" Amelia said as Ted drove up Oakleigh. "Why are you going forward? Lindbergh is back that way."

"Your mother and I have some business first," Ted said. He parked the Mustang across the Rivingtons' drive, blocking it. Waves of music pounded his car like surf.

"You're going in there," Amelia said. "We're ruined." She hung her head and wept harder.

"We'll be right out," Josie said. She and Ted slammed their doors and marched toward the Rivingtons' slate-roofed colonial. Josie saw a young boy and a long-haired girl coupling behind the manicured bushes at the edge of the lawn and averted her eyes. A pale blond boy was throwing up in the flower bed and a drunken girl wept in a wrought-iron chair. Her long blond hair hid her face.

The grass was strewn with beer bottles, red plastic cups, and cigarette butts. Josie saw a red-eyed swarm of cigarettes at the side of the house.

The front door was wide open and the party inside was an extension of the bacchanalia on the lawn. The twig wreath on the red door looked forlorn surrounded by the drunken, dancing horde.

Ted and Josie found a pale red-haired boy on the front doormat. "That's Jared," said a giggling girl in pink. "He's asleep." She had to shout above the din.

Ted bent down and checked the boy's pulse, then saw the pool of vomit near his head. "Give me a tissue, Josie," he said. He wrapped his fingers in the tissue and ran it inside the boy's mouth to make sure his airway wasn't blocked.

"Ew," the blonde said. "That's gross."

Ted lifted one of Jared's eyelids. The boy's pupil was a pinpoint.

"Jared isn't asleep," Ted said. "He's unconscious. I think he may be in an alcohol or drug coma."

He turned the boy on his side and commanded the blonde, "Get me some couch pillows."

The girl looked confused, so Josie ran to the closest couch and came back with six white silk pillows. Ted positioned the boy so he wouldn't choke if he was sick again, then brought out his cell phone.

"Are you calling the police?" the girl asked, eyes wide with fear.

"No, 911," Ted said. "He needs an ambulance."

"I better go," the girl said, while Ted talked on the phone.

"Jared needs your help. Please stay with him," Josie said.

"We only hooked up, like, once or twice," the girl said, and stepped over Jared toward the door. "I gotta get home."

"The ambulance is on its way," Ted said. "We have to shut down this party, but we can't leave Jared alone."

Josie stopped an elfin brunette in a red bubble skirt trying to get past them. "I need your help," she shouted. "What's your name?"

"Halley," the girl yelled back. "That's Jared. He falls asleep at parties."

"Jared is seriously ill," Josie said. "He may die. Do you know what he took? Was it pills? Alcohol?"

"Well . . ." Halley hesitated.

"Halley, we're not going to tell anyone and get you in trouble," Josie said. "We're trying to save Jared. What did he take?"

"He was slamming Captain and Coke, and dudes started saying it was a chick drink. So he dropped in some pills he stole from his mother and said, 'Real men play pill roulette.'"

"What kind of pills?" Josie asked.

"I don't know. His mom, she can't sleep at night since his dad split. Ammy, Ambie, something like that."

"Ambien?" Ted said.

"That's it."

"Pink or white?" Ted said.

"White. He took five or six."

"Damn," Ted said. "That's the higher dose. Do you have his parents' number?"

"His mother's number is in his cell phone." Halley pawed Jared until she pulled out his cell phone, then flipped through his contacts. "That's his mom," she said. "Six, six, six. That's for the devil or something."

Josie took the phone, called up the number, and keyed it into her own cell phone. When a woman answered, she said, "This is Josie Marcus. We believe your son Jared has ingested pills and alcohol at the Rivingtons' party. My husband found him passed out and the ambulance is on the way. You may want to meet your son at the ER. Yes, we believe he'll be taken to the Ladue Health Center.

"Here's my number, but we'll be leaving shortly. I'm so sorry. This party is out of control. We have to shut it down before anyone else gets hurt."

"Stay with Jared," Ted told Halley. "We have to see these so-called chaperones." He was angry, and Josie loved him for it. She felt battered by the heavy bass of the music.

Ted and Josie stepped over a young couple in the throes of passion on the bottom stair and marched upstairs and down a wide marble hall to the white double doors of the master bedroom. They didn't knock. Ted flung open the doors and they saw a sitting room bigger than their living room.

The forest green room held a charming domestic scene: A woman who had to be Eve Rivington was needlepointing, and a man, presumably Simon, was reading *The Economist*. Both sat in matching plaid wing chairs.

Josie had no idea how the couple could concentrate with the noise raging below. The walls vibrated and the delicate cups rattled in the flowered tea set between their chairs.

Eve and Simon may not have been from St. Louis, but they looked like a certain breed of old-money rich. Eve's hair was straight, gray, and parted down the middle, her face was makeup-free, and she wore a dowdy navy boiled-wool jacket sprinkled with autumn leaves. Simon had neat gray hair, faded blue eyes, a blue button-down shirt, and khakis.

They didn't even look up when Ted and Josie entered. Ted stalked over to Simon, pulled the magazine out of his hands, and said, "Do you know what's going on downstairs?"

"Huh?" Simon said, and pulled out his earplugs. "Who are you and how dare you enter my sitting room?"

"I'm Ted Scottsmeyer. My twelve-year-old daughter was nearly assaulted at this party. Couples are having sex on your lawn and all over your house. Some sleaze wanted oral sex with my girl."

Simon shrugged and waved his hands to dismiss the subject. "That's just kids, playing around. They can't get pregnant."

"That pair on your steps sure can," Josie said. "And you can get STDs from oral sex."

Eve pulled out her earplugs and abandoned her needlepoint.

"What happens in my home is none of your business," Simon said.

"The hell it isn't," Ted said. "My daughter and her friend called us crying and afraid. They wanted to go home."

"So take them," Simon said. "No one's forcing them to stay."

"There's underage drinking in this house," Josie said.

"Better that the children drink safely in homes," Eve said. "If they drink somewhere else, they could get hurt."

"Oh yeah?" Ted said. "What about that poor kid passed out downstairs? I called an ambulance for him."

"You what?" Simon said. "In my home? Sir, you have exceeded the bounds of your authority."

"So sue me," Ted said. "My wife and I are leaving now. And if I'm not mistaken, that's the sound of a siren. The ambulance is coming up your road."

Ted moved aside the heavy velvet curtains and looked out the window.

"I believe the police may be not far behind it. Have fun explaining this supervised party to the police and that boy's mother. His name is Jared, by the way."

Ted and Josie ran down the stairs. The party was still in full swing, and the first floor smelled like rum, beer, and vomit. The music was so loud Josie felt like she'd walked into a wall. Her head hurt.

Ted checked on Jared, who was lying on his side, barely breathing. "Jared," he said. "Can you hear me?"

Halley was crying.

Jared did not respond, but now the paramedics charged through the door with a stretcher. "I'm the one who called," Ted said. "I came here to get my daughter out of here. The homeowners are sitting on their duffs upstairs, wearing earplugs. This boy, Jared, was drinking Captain and Coke and took five or six white sleeping tablets, possibly Ambien."

"His mother will meet you at the Ladue Health Center ER," Josie said.

The paramedics worked on Jared. Josie caught a few phrases, including "pump his stomach" and "intubate."

Suddenly, the music stopped. The quiet was deafening. The DJ threw his equipment into cases as partygoers in various stages of undress and intoxication ran for the front door, but it was blocked by the paramedics and Jared's stretcher. Others sprinted for the back and side entrances.

Ted pushed Josie past the stretcher, and she winced at

Jared's gray, sweating face. They ran down the sidewalk and jumped into the Mustang.

Ted did a squealing U-ey before Josie even buckled her seat belt, and they were out on Lindbergh as two police cars roared up Oakleigh Terrace.

Only then did Amelia ask, "What happened inside?" Palmer was huddled with her friend. Josie told them, while Ted drove.

"Palmer, we're taking you home, honey, but I want to call your mother to make sure someone is at your house. We're almost there."

Josie talked with Priscilla and gave her a quick version of what happened. "Palmer is fine," Josie said. "She's shaken and she needs TLC. We're turning down your street now."

Palmer lived in a prim gray Victorian frosted with white gingerbread trim and spiced with black shutters and a lavender-blue door.

Priscilla was in the driveway, wearing a blue jacket, her blond hair perfect. Palmer climbed out of the car shakily and said, "Mommy!" Priscilla wrapped her arms around her daughter.

"We'll talk later," Josie promised, and climbed into the backseat with Amelia. "Are you hurt?" she asked.

"Just scared, but I'm okay," Amelia said, then burst into tears. Josie hugged her daughter and rocked her.

"I got Coke on my new dress," Amelia said, sniffling.

"It's washable," Josie said. "You were smart to buy a washable dress. I'll fix it when we get home. I'm so proud of you. You were so brave, to walk out of that party. The other girls didn't."

Josie hugged her daughter, smoothed her rumpled hair, and kissed her. "I'm so proud of you," she said again, but Amelia was already asleep.

Chapter 21

"Josie, I know it's six in the morning, but can you come over right away?" Jane's phone call woke her up.

Even half-asleep, Josie heard the urgency in her mother's voice. She dragged herself out of her deep Saturday slumber and said, "Mom, what's wrong? Are you hurt?"

"It's not me," Jane said, her voice low and quick. "It's Frank. The police are parked outside. They're at Mrs. Mueller's house right now, but I'm afraid they'll be here next. A police officer is on my front porch and another one is parked in the alley at the back gate. We're surrounded!"

Josie fought back a giggle at the idea of her law-abiding mother surrounded by cops like a fugitive, and reached for her jeans. "I'm getting dressed now, Mom," she said. "I'll be at your house in ten minutes."

"Make it fifteen, Josie. You don't want a ticket. The police are everywhere."

Josie washed her face, ran a brush through her hair, and decided that would have to do.

Ted was awake now. "Who called?" he asked, rubbing his eyes.

"Mom," Josie said. "She's afraid the police are coming after Frank. I'd told her to call anytime, day or night."

She slipped on her flats and grabbed her purse.

"Wait! I'll go with you," Ted said.

"No, please, stay home. I need you here with Amelia. I don't want her to wake up alone after last night. Besides, somebody has to feed the animals. I'll call if I need you."

Josie admired her husband's curly brown sleep-rumpled hair and muscular shoulders. She kissed him and wished they could go back to bed for sleepy Saturday love. But Jane needed her.

On the way down the hall, Josie looked in on her daughter. Amelia was asleep in her purple bedroom, one arm around her cat, Harry. Festus and Marmalade were sprawled across the foot of the bed. The big dark Lab and the orange tabby left Amelia penned into a space the size of a baby's crib.

Amelia's coral party dress hung on her closet door. The stain had come out. Josie had made sure of that before she went to bed last night. She'd washed and ironed the lace dress, finishing after midnight. Now the dress was as good as new, but Josie was worried about the damage to her daughter.

Amelia had stood up to her classmates and left the party. Through no fault of her own, her brave move brought the police and the ambulance. Josie thought Ted's arrival at the Rivington house had probably saved Jared, but the partygoers would blame Amelia for shutting down their fun. Kids could be cruel.

But Amelia isn't alone, she told herself. Ted and I will help her. But how much can we help her in the closed tween society?

She'd worry about that later. Right now, Josie had to help her mother.

Ten minutes later, she was at Jane's flat. A dark blue Summerdale patrol car was parked in front of her mother's house.

Behind it, a shiny navy Crown Victoria screamed "unmarked police car." The car's big, square trunk intruded into Mrs. Mueller's imaginary territory, the parking place in front of her home.

Josie saw the old woman waving her flabby arms and yelling at Detective Dobbs. Surely Mrs. M wasn't chewing out a police detective for parking in "her" spot.

Josie parked her car across the street and strolled over, hoping to eavesdrop on the conversation. Even on a Saturday morning, the Summerdale detective wore a retro suit. This one was brown with an understated windowpane grid. That blasted skinny-brimmed hat was cocked at a jaunty angle.

She hoped Mrs. M's lurid hot pink peony-patterned housedress hurt his eyes as much as it hurt hers. Mrs. Mueller's steely hair looked like it was held in place by Super Glue. A brisk fall breeze sent a swirl of autumn leaves down the street, but Mrs. M's coiffure stayed rock steady.

"What do you mean you had to take the leaves from my azaleas?" Mrs. M shouted, and probably not for the first time. Her face was red with indignation.

Dobbs took a deep breath as if hoping it might help him keep his temper, and said, "As I explained, we need the leaves from your plants for DNA analysis." His tone was even and clipped. Josie thought his teeth were gritted.

"Why are you wasting my tax money on expensive DNA tests?" Mrs. M shrieked. Her voice was so shrill, Josie expected the neighborhood dogs to howl. "Of course that man killed Uncle Bob. Franklin Hyzy is a drunk. Look what he did to Jane Marcus's lawn."

She waved her arms at Jane's yard. Unfortunately for Mrs. Mueller, that gesture didn't have the impact she wanted. The sod was taking root and colorful leaves hid most of the damage.

Dobbs tugged on his hat brim and said, "Your tax money won't be used for the DNA test, Mrs. Mueller. We're the Summerdale police. You live in Maplewood."

"I don't like my azaleas in a police investigation," she said, and crossed her arms.

"May I remind you, Mrs. Mueller, that you approached us as a citizen doing her duty. You were eager to tell us why you believed Franklin Hyzy was a suspect. You even signed a statement this morning. So why balk at losing a few azalea leaves? You can't even see where they were clipped from the bushes."

"It's just a waste; that's all," Mrs. M said. "A waste of time and effort when the answer is obvious."

"To a civilian." Detective Dobbs made it clear that a civilian was not his equal. "A good police investigation requires proof, and I do the best, Mrs. Mueller."

"What will the neighbors think with the police crawling all over my yard?"

"I'm sure they couldn't possibly think anything bad of you. Good day, ma'am."

Josie hurried up the walkway to her mother's porch before Dobbs caught her listening in. She smiled at the burly young officer guarding Frank's front door and knocked on her mother's door.

Jane didn't call down for Josie to come inside, and after her embarrassing but unintentional eavesdropping on her mother's stairs, Josie didn't dare let herself in.

While Josie waited for Jane to answer her door, Dobbs followed her up the stairs and tipped his hat. Josie rather liked that old-fashioned gesture, even if she didn't care for the detective.

The detective pulled a sheaf of white paper out of his elegantly tailored brown jacket and knocked on Frank's door. Jane's tenant answered after the first knock.

"Mr. Franklin Hyzy," Dobbs said, "I have a search warrant here for your home and your computer."

That's when Jane opened her front door. The blood drained from her face as she heard Dobbs.

Josie hurried inside and Jane shut the door. They tried

to hear what was going on, but the plaster walls in the old building were too thick. Josie was shocked by how frail her mother seemed. Jane's hands trembled and she sagged against the wall. She looked washed-out and tired.

"Let's go upstairs, Mom," Josie said. "I could use some coffee." She let her mother lean on her and Jane accepted the unspoken help.

"Of course you can, dear. I'm sorry I dragged you out at this hour."

"I'm always here for you, Mom. You know that."

Stuart Little greeted them upstairs. Josie scratched the curly-haired dog. Jane's flat was as spotless as always, but the perfume of fresh coffee made Josie's stomach growl.

"How about if I make you French toast?" Jane said.

"Yum. A real Saturday breakfast. Give me some coffee to go and I'll walk the dog for you."

Stuart pattered down the stairs, eager to go outside. Josie didn't see Mrs. M. She must be inside, Josie thought, watching from an upstairs window.

Stuart tugged on his leash. He wanted to water Mrs. M's precious azaleas. Josie wondered if the old woman would come screaming out of her home if he did. She decided she had police protection and gave the dog his freedom.

She watched the young cop carry Frank's clunky old computer tower, then three cardboard boxes, to his patrol car. By the time Stuart's walk was finished, the Summerdale patrol car and Dobbs's Crown Vic were both gone.

Back at Jane's flat, Josie savored her mother's French toast, delicately spiced with cinnamon and nutmeg. Jane even produced a jug of real maple syrup.

"Mom, isn't it time for Frank to get a lawyer?"

Jane set her face in that stubborn look Josie knew so well, thrusting her jaw out like a bulldog. "I'm not meddling in that man's business, Josie. The police aren't going to arrest him because they aren't going to find anything," she said. "Besides, they're testing Mrs. Mueller's azaleas for DNA."

"DNA tests for people can take two weeks or more," Josie said. "Who knows how long plant testing will take?"

"I don't want to discuss it," Jane said, nearly freezing Josie's coffee.

Subject closed, Josie thought. Move on.

"Ted and I are giving a barbecue for our new neighbors tonight," she said. "The Tracys have moved here from the DC area."

"Good idea," Jane said. "You want to get off on the right foot with your neighbors. I'm stuck living next to You Know Who."

And living above Mr. Right, Josie thought.

"So how was Amelia's big night?" Jane asked.

"Horrible," Josie said, and told Jane about the party from hell.

"That's so sad," Jane said. "Really, what were those parents thinking?" She glanced at her kitchen clock. "It's nine o'clock already. Go home to your girl. She needs you."

"She hardly talks to me anymore," Josie said, though that wasn't entirely true. She and Amelia had discussed the party and the plans for tonight's barbecue.

"Then let her cook for the barbecue while you and Ted get the house and yard ready," Jane said. "She loves that, and it will keep her mind off what happened."

Jane removed Josie's empty coffee cup, kissed her, and said, "Now go. Shoo! I love you."

Back home at Fresno Court, Josie slipped in quietly through the kitchen door and saw Ted and Amelia eating breakfast in the dining room. Amelia looked more pale than usual. She was carefully spreading grape jelly on her toast so all four corners were covered and laughing at Ted's latest story about his clinic patients. Josie leaned in the kitchen doorway and watched them.

"The cat's name really is Jaspurr?" Amelia asked.

"Yep. *P-U-R-R*," Ted said. "And he's a champ at purring, louder than any cat I've heard. Lots of thick yellow fur. Big fellow, too. Yesterday he tipped the scale at 27.4 pounds. He's on a diet now. Belongs to Mike and Maria Kight.

"Jaspurr is a rescue cat and famous for nearly ordering a pay-per-view movie."

"How'd he do that?" Amelia asked.

"He was rolling around on the TV Dish remote and Maria caught him when he was one click away."

"What movie?" Amelia asked.

"Some thriller. Definitely not kitty porn."

Josie burst out laughing.

"Good morning, gorgeous," Ted said. "How's Jane?"

"Worried," Josie said. "The police served Frank with a search warrant and Mrs. M was busy stirring up trouble." She poured herself a cup of coffee and sat down.

"Did Frank get a lawyer?" Ted asked.

"Mom says he doesn't need one. I think that's a mistake. How are you this morning, Amelia?"

"Fine," Amelia said, shortly.

Uh-oh, Josie thought. "I need your help for the party tonight," she said. "Will you bake a cake and some brownies? I'll give the house a lick and a promise and shop for the drinks."

"I'll clean up the yard," Ted said.

The day passed in a blur of work. Soon it was seven o'clock, and the guests were arriving. Laura Tracy brought three-bean salad and her husband, Clete, gave Ted a six-pack of Schlafly's Pale Ale.

"I like your local brewery," he said.

Clete and Laura looked like a well-matched pair. Both had brown hair and were the same height. Clete had a boyish, good-humored face and a cute snub nose. The Tracys took the house tour and admired the new deck. Josie fixed strawberry margaritas for her and Laura.

Fourteen-year-old CJ hung back shyly until Amelia brought out her iPad. Soon the two of them were sitting on the deck exploring its electronic wonders. Amelia was a bit giggly, but Josie hoped that was nervousness at having a cute boy all to herself.

The neighbors on the other side, Cordelia and Wilner Madison, arrived next. Cordelia was a professor of Victorian literature at City University and a dark beauty.

Josie thought she looked like an Egyptian queen with her dark hair and brown eyes. Her husband, Wil, was a large, rather portly salesman with coffee-colored skin and broad, muscular shoulders. Josie wondered if he'd been an athlete in school.

Cordelia brought a good bottle of wine and a tray of exquisite appetizers, including cheese tartlets, artichokes in puff pastry, veal pâté, and "pigs in a blanket," Cordelia said, half apologizing. "Wil insisted on those."

"Beer food!" Ted said, and popped one in his mouth.

By the time the barbecue was served, the party was in full swing. Everyone praised the food, and Amelia turned pink with pleasure when her desserts were unanimously declared delicious.

After the table was cleared, Amelia and handsome CJ retreated to the living room with the pets and the iPad. Outside on the deck, the drinks were renewed and Josie told the adults about the Rivingtons' wild party and Ted's rescue.

"How is the boy?" Laura asked.

"Jared is still in a coma in intensive care," Josie said. "I talked with his mother this afternoon. The doctors don't know if there's going to be brain damage. His father was driving back from Chicago."

Cordelia, the college professor, was the only grown-up who wasn't shocked. "I encounter this all the time at City

University," she said. "A lot of parents say, 'The kids are going to be drinking anyway, so they might as well do it here at home and not drive.'

"When you mix middle schoolers with college students, you're asking for trouble. The girls get drunk and have sex and then the permissive parents are shocked when their daughters become pregnant.

"Josie, you should commend your daughter for walking out of that party. She's a young woman of character."

"I'm worried about her," Josie said. "I'm afraid the students at school will turn on her."

"She'll survive," Cordelia said. "Young Jared might not be so lucky."

Chapter 22

Warm fall sunlight spilled through Ted and Josie's bedroom window, and a light breeze scented with spicy fall leaves gently ruffled the bed skirt. It was ten o'clock on a lazy Sunday.

"A perfect morning," Josie said, and sighed.

"After a perfect evening," Ted said. He traced his finger lightly along her profile and kissed her eyes, then her chin, then her lips.

"I love how you look when you wake up, all sleepy and sloe-eyed," he said.

"And for once, we have the morning to ourselves," Josie said. "Amelia is downstairs in the family room watching an Animal Planet show to research a term paper on bears. She won't be back upstairs until at least eleven."

"And she can't hear us in the basement," Ted said, "so let's . . ."

Josie's cell phone rang. She reluctantly reached over and checked the display. "It's Mom," she said. "I have to take this. Sorry."

They were both sorry when Jane said, "Josie, please come over, right now. That Detective Dobbs is back. Frank's in trouble."

"What happened?"

"We were walking back from church, just rounding

the corner onto our street, when I saw the police at my house. That Detective Dobbs's dark blue car was parked outside behind Frank's car, and a Summerdale patrol car was right behind it. The patrol car has a cage in the back—for prisoners! I think that detective is going to arrest Frank."

Josie bit back the "I told you so" she wanted to say. That wouldn't help anything.

"Since Frank's car is in front of the house, the police must think he's home," Jane said. "I pulled Frank out of sight and we went up the street to Manchester. We're having breakfast at Tiffany's."

"Good move, Mom," Josie said.

Tiffany's Original Diner was an old-school twenty-four-hour diner that served awesome grease. Everything cooked on the grill was bacon flavored, whether customers ordered it or not. Josie thought bacon belonged on all diner food.

"Josie, we got two seats together at the counter," Jane said.

"On a Sunday morning? That's a minor miracle, Mom."

"I don't want to keep talking about this on my cell phone," Jane said. "Can you come here? Please?"

"On my way."

Once again, Josie scrambled into her clothes while she explained to Ted why she had to leave. She kissed him quickly, said, "To be continued," and ran for her car.

Next door, Clete and his son, CJ, were working in their yard. CJ was raking leaves in the side yard, wearing iPod earbuds, while his father raked and bagged the leaves in the front yard. Clete seemed to be filling the leaf bags with gold.

Josie waved to them as she backed out of her driveway.

I am lucky to have good neighbors on both sides, she thought. That wasn't always the case. I'd stupidly offended

Cordelia when I first moved in and she was kind enough to forgive my blunder.

Fifteen minutes later, Josie was parked near Tiffany's Original Diner. That stretch of Manchester Road was Maplewood's downtown. The two-story flat-fronted red-brick shopping district was lined with quirky restaurants and stores, from Airedale Antics for pet lovers, to Kakao Chocolate, to the Book House.

Tiffany's smelled of lightly fried grease and coffee. The layout was classic diner: a long, narrow room with a counter and red-vinyl-and-chrome stools. All the seats were filled and more hungry people were waiting.

Josie saw Frank and Jane on the last two seats at the far end, and they waved her over. The couple was dressed for church. Jane wore an orange pantsuit and matching pillbox hat. Frank looked professorial in a tweed jacket with patches on the elbows and a brown tie.

Josie hugged her mother and caught a pleasant whiff of Estée Lauder, Jane's favorite perfume. Frank got up to give Josie his seat, but she refused. "Thanks, Frank. Finish your breakfast. I'll just have coffee."

Stephanie, the waitress, poured her a cup, and Josie stood next to her mother. Frank was chowing down on toast, fried eggs, and hash browns. Jane picked at her scrambled eggs. Josie guessed her mother was too worried to eat.

"The waitress is really nice," Jane said. "Frank and I decided to grab breakfast while we figure out what to do."

"I can't think of a better place to be on the lam than Tiffany's," Josie said, "but it's time to take some serious steps. Frank, you think you're going to be arrested?"

"I know it. I'm in trouble," he said.

The all-night eatery was the sort of offbeat place where diners could say that without raising too many eyebrows. Liquor bottles were lined up over the cash register, and a sign read YOU CAN'T DRINK ALL DAY IF YOU DON'T START IN THE MORNING!

"Yesterday Mom said there was nothing in your computer to worry about," Josie said.

"Well, there is," Frank said. He'd abandoned his nearly empty plate. "I told Jane what I did on our way to church."

Please don't confess, Josie thought. Uncle Bob was an awful man, but you're too good a person to lose your freedom for killing him.

"After Jane, uh, found me on the lawn," Frank said.

You mean, after you passed out in your car, Josie thought, which you'd driven over the curb and onto the lawn, tearing a path through the grass.

"And she helped me inside," he said.

Because you were too drunk to walk, Josie thought, but waited patiently for his next set of euphemisms.

"I fell asleep."

Passed out again, she thought.

"I woke up later and Googled those bushes I nearly ran down."

"You mean the azaleas?" Josie asked.

"Yes," Frank said. "Those. I was wandering around on the Internet, the way you do, and I found a site that named azaleas as one of the top ten poisonous plants. Then I found another site, and soon I was reading a whole bunch of stuff about how they were poison. I had no idea they were such bad news."

"They are poisonous," Josie said. "But I heard that people don't usually eat the leaves because they burn your mouth."

"I read that, too," Frank said. "There was an online article about that."

"So that information is part of your computer's search history," Josie said.

"I guess it is," Frank said. "I never thought of that."

"But you didn't know that Bob had a dentist appointment on Monday," Josie said.

"Oh, we all knew that," Frank said. "He was such a

baby about dental work. He whined about the pain to the staff and even the customers. He was worried he couldn't eat afterward. He even told us that he checked with the dentist's office to see if he could eat lunch after his appointment. The dentist said yes, as soon as the numbness wore off, he could have his lunch. But he didn't wait. Bob was so greedy, he ate as soon as he could."

And died, because his mouth was still too numb to detect the azalea poison, Josie thought.

"Frank, this is not good," she said. "I've watched enough TV to know that the police now have motive, means, and opportunity for you."

"Josie doesn't get her knowledge just from television," Jane said. "She's helped solve several cases. She's a natural detective."

"Thanks, Mom," Josie said. "But Frank has to understand why he's in serious trouble. Not only do the police have three good reasons to arrest you, but you lied to them when you said you didn't know azaleas were poisonous."

"I didn't lie," Frank said. "I forgot. I was, uh, indisposed when I did that Internet search."

"Frank, you weren't indisposed," Josie said. "You'd been drinking."

Jane looked shocked by Josie's blunt comment, but Frank hung his head.

"You're right, Josie. I had been drinking. But it's not my fault."

Josie, who'd dated an alcoholic, knew that admitting a drinking problem was the first step to recovery. Frank wasn't taking that step.

"Frank," she said, "we don't have time for excuses. The police could arrest you any moment."

"How are they going to find him?" Jane said. "We're here at the diner."

"Which has big plate-glass windows, Mom," Josie said. "Dobbs is a seasoned detective. Your car is in the garage and Frank's is parked in front of your flat. Nobody's answering the door.

I'm sure Mrs. Mueller will volunteer that she saw Frank and you leave in time for church at nine, and you were wearing a hat. Neither one of you is dressed for a hike. When the cops figure out you're not at church, they'll start checking the shops and restaurants along Manchester. I expect them anytime. Frank, you need to call Renzo Fisher. Now."

"Won't a lawyer cost extra on a Sunday?" Jane asked.

"We're beyond that, Mom," Josie said. She didn't add, *If you'd listened to me, Frank could have called the lawyer earlier this week.* Instead she said, "Frank needs help."

"She's right," Frank said. "I'm not a young man. How long do you think I'll last in jail? I have some savings and a CD, Jane. I can afford a lawyer."

"I still have Renzo's cell phone number," Josie said. "From when he helped Mom's friend Tillie."

Josie called the lawyer before Jane could object. Renzo answered on the first ring. His Texas twang had been tuned up.

"Of course I remember you, darlin'. I'm not so old I'd forget a pretty little gal like you. You must be in trouble if you're calling me on a Sunday morning."

"I'm not, but my Mom's friend Franklin Hyzy may be arrested for murder any minute." She quickly outlined Frank's dilemma.

"Lucky for you, I'm at my office in Clayton," Renzo said. "I can be there in ten minutes. Tell Frank to stay put and if the police get there before I do, he's not to say a word." Renzo hung up.

Josie relayed Renzo's instructions and said, "You're in good hands, Frank. Your lawyer looks a little different, but he's good."

"He's short," Jane said. "Small but mighty, I say." She'd perked up a little once the lawyer issue was settled.

The waitress poured them another round of coffee and Frank paid the bill. He was leaving a generous tip when Josie saw Detective Dobbs march through the door, accompanied by two uniformed officers.

His Sunday suit was a subdued gray stripe, but there was nothing subtle about his actions. He walked straight back to where Frank sat. Every eye in the restaurant was focused on Dobbs.

"Franklin Hyzy," he said, "I'm arresting you for the first-degree murder of Robert Jarvis Manning. You have the right to remain silent."

Frank looked incapable of speech. The entire diner was watching the drama. Josie saw several forks hovering in midair.

"Anything you say will be used against you in court," Dobbs said. "You have the right to consult with an attorney and to have that attorney present during questioning, and if you cannot afford an attorney, one will be provided at no cost to represent you. Do you understand, Mr. Dobbs?"

The officers moved in and cuffed Frank.

"Hold on, there! That's my client you're manhandling!" a man shouted.

Josie looked up and saw Renzo Fischer standing in the doorway of the long, narrow diner. He looked like a sheriff in an old-time cowboy movie.

Renzo wore a white Stetson, a blue Western-cut shirt with pearl buttons, and a turquoise bolo tie. His black ostrich-skin boots added two inches to his sawed-off stature, but his presence filled the room.

"This man is my client," the lawyer said. "Don't say a word, Mr. Hyzy."

Frank was led off in handcuffs while Jane wept on Josie's shoulder.

Chapter 23

Josie was restless and uneasy. After a week of brilliant sunshine, she woke up this Monday morning to a cold, relentless rain. She dropped Amelia off at Barrington School and watched her daughter lope through the slashing storm.

She was worried. This was Amelia's first day at school after that disastrous party. She feared her daughter was facing a chilly reception from her classmates.

Back at home, Josie had about an hour before Alyce picked her up for Uncle Bob's memorial service at ten o'clock. His private funeral was this morning.

Josie threw in a load of laundry and caught the last of the local TV news.

Channel Seven was covering Bob's funeral. Honey Butcher, the TV anchor, wore a raincoat as gray as the day and talked in the subdued voice usually reserved for state occasions. Somehow, the damp weather didn't wilt her hair.

She'd staked out a spot next to a marble Victorian angel. "Robert Jarvis Manning—known to the city as Uncle Bob—is being laid to rest in Bellefontaine Cemetery," Honey said, "and it's a sad day in St. Louis."

The camera panned to an artistic shot of rain tears running down the weathered stone angel's face.

"Uncle Bob's widow, Candice Manning, and Ralph

the Talking Dog are at the graveside, along with many of Uncle Bob's employees."

Damp mourners holding big black umbrellas clustered around the silver casket. Candice's head was bowed, her face sheltered by her big-brimmed black hat. Josie picked out Beverly, the receptionist, dabbing her eyes with a white handkerchief.

Karen, the groomer, stared stoically at the flower-covered casket, as if waiting for the burial to be over.

Heidi, the gourmet treat maker, looked vampiric on this gloomy day. Her skin was corpse pale against her black coat and her damp red hair was a river of blood. She seemed at home among the tombstones.

Josie was relieved Honey didn't mention the Uncle Bob's ex-employee now in jail. How was Mom doing after Frank's humiliating arrest? Josie wondered. She turned off the TV and called her mother.

"I tossed and turned all night," Jane said. "This morning, Frank was arraigned for first-degree murder. He's all over the news. He's innocent, Josie. He really is."

"I know, Mom, but he's done some foolish things that don't look good."

"Josie, you have to help him."

"I'm working on it," she said. "Alyce and I are going to Uncle Bob's memorial. But Renzo, his lawyer, has a private investigator on his staff, Mom. A trained professional."

"A PI can't find out what you can. People like you. They talk to you."

"I'll do my best," Josie said.

She dressed warmly for Uncle Bob's memorial in a dark raincoat, sweater, and wool pants. When Alyce pulled into her drive, Josie ran out to meet her friend.

"I'm sorry Frank is all over the media," Alyce said as soon as Josie was buckled in.

"Me, too," Josie said. "Mom's taking it hard."

Alyce sneezed.

"Bless you," Josie said. "Are you coming down with a cold?"

"It's not coming," Alyce said, "it's here." Now Josie noticed her friend's red nose and flattened blond hair.

"Do you feel well enough to drive?" Josie asked.

"It's just a cold," Alyce said. "I got it from Justin. Did you see Bob's funeral on TV this morning?"

"Live coverage," Josie said. "If you can have live shots of a funeral. Some of my primary targets were at the burial. Bob's widow, Candice, was the mysterious woman in the black hat. Three women staffers were there, too."

"Does Vampira, the pale woman with the long red hair, work at Uncle Bob's?" Alyce asked.

"Yes. Her name is Heidi. Frank said her duties included fixing Bob's lunches and making the organic dog treats."

"She looks familiar, and I've never taken Bruiser to Uncle Bob's."

"Maybe she was in a commercial," Josie said.

"You know she wasn't," Alyce said. "No human but Bob ever appeared in those."

Alyce could hardly find a parking spot at Uncle Bob's Doggy Day Camp. She and Josie ran through the slicing rain for the porch. This time, Josie didn't hear the familiar chorus of barking dogs. The red front door had a huge color photo of Bob draped in black, grinning at the mourners.

"That's creepy," Alyce said. "Bob looks like he's happy to be dead."

"Somebody's happy he's dead," Josie said.

Inside, they were hit with a wall of sound and the smell of wet wool and mothballs. The reception desk had been transformed into a buffet table with a coffee urn. Next to it was a portable bar, and Josie recognized a male camp counselor serving jug wine and soft drinks.

An endless reel of Uncle Bob commercials played on a big-screen TV.

"I'll pay my respects to Candice," Josie shouted into Alyce's ear, "then circulate among the staff and customers."

"I'll head toward Vampira," Alyce said, "and see why she seems familiar. Maybe if I hear her voice, it will trigger my memory. Get me when you're ready to leave."

Josie gently pushed through the crowd and joined a line of people offering condolences to Candice. That wide-brimmed hat overwhelmed the tiny bird-boned woman, as if she was overshadowed by grief. But as Josie got closer, she realized no one, not even the widow, seemed sad.

A beige-haired woman with a matching raincoat asked Candice the question Josie didn't dare. "Are you going to keep the business open?" Ms. Beige said.

"I don't know yet," Candice said. "I'm torn between selling the day camp and keeping it going. Bob was the public face of the business."

Suddenly, the public memorial service made sense, Josie thought. This was a real estate showing. The day camp's customers crammed into the lobby were living proof of its huge client base.

Ms. Beige patted Candice's hand and moved toward the buffet. Josie was next. "I'm so sorry for your loss," she said. "I was the person who found Bob in his office."

She expected Candice to ask for details about how Josie had discovered Bob and about the rescue effort, or possibly thank her for finding her dying husband. But Candice seemed oblivious. Is she numbed by grief, on tranquilizers, or simply indifferent to her husband's death? Josie wondered. The couple was separated, but they were still married.

"So nice of you to come," Candice said vaguely.

"Your husband has so many friends," Josie said. "We could hardly find a spot in the parking lot."

"Everyone loved Bob's commercials," Candice said. Not Bob, Josie thought. His commercials. His widow could be discussing a stranger.

"Are you a regular customer?" Candice asked.

"I brought my mother's dog in Monday for playtime and pampering," Josie said. "Your groomer, Karen, made Stuart Little look so cute."

"Karen has the touch," Candice said. "What breed is Stuart?"

"A shih tzu," Josie said.

"Do you know they're called lion dogs because shih tzus resemble the king of beasts?"

"They do?" Josie said. To her, Stuart looked more like a toy than a ferocious killer.

Candice continued spouting shih tzu facts. "Tibetan monks used to call them Snow Lion Dogs. They considered shih tzus holy because they guarded the Imperial Palace."

Candice was coming alive now that she was discussing dogs—at least from what Josie could tell. The widow's small face was shadowed by her vast, gloomy hat.

"I didn't know that," Josie said.

"They're an ancient dog breed, according to DNA studies," Candice said. "They have a close genetic relationship to wolves."

"Stuart looks like he has a close genetic relationship to a teddy bear," Josie said.

"Being related to wolves is a good thing," Candice said. "They mate for life."

Josie thought she was looking wistfully at one of the endless Uncle Bob commercials, but she couldn't tell. That overpowering hat was in the way.

"We could learn a lot from wolves," Candice said.

The man behind Josie loudly cleared his throat and she realized she'd been monopolizing Candice.

"Uh, yes," she said. "Well, I'd better get going."

That was weird, she thought. Candice has no interest in or sympathy for her late husband, but she turns into Animal Planet when I mention Mom's dog.

Josie was cruising toward the buffet when she bumped into Karen, the groomer. "I saw you on TV today," Josie said. "At Bob's funeral. It must have been cold."

"In more ways than one," Karen said. "You're a friend of Frank's, aren't you?"

"He's my mom's renter," Josie said. "He didn't like Bob." She stopped, afraid she was saying too much.

"I didn't, either," Karen said. "I don't think Frank killed him. We need to talk."

"Definitely," Josie said. "It's noisy here. Is there a quiet room we can duck into?"

"I'd rather not. Especially with his wife and two of his girlfriends here. They could wander in on us."

"Two?" Josie said.

"Oh yes. Bob was quite the hound. Where do you live?"

"Maplewood," Josie said.

"Near my favorite coffeehouse. How about if I meet you at Foundation Grounds on Manchester at twelve thirty this afternoon?"

"As long as I'm free by three o'clock," Josie said. "I have to pick up my daughter at school."

"I have to leave at one thirty. See you there," Karen said, and was soon swallowed by the crowd.

Josie spotted Alyce by the buffet table, sipping a cup of coffee. "Ready to go?" her friend asked.

"Definitely," Josie said.

"We need to talk," Alyce said as they ran through the rain to her SUV.

"Let's go to Flaco's Cocina for an early lunch," Josie said. "My treat."

Flaco's Cocina was more Miami than Missouri. The colorful art and tropical colors were extra-cheerful on a rainy Monday. The waitress quickly brought their fish tacos. Josie ordered a peach-jalapeño margarita, but Alyce stuck with coffee.

"I'll take a rain check," she said. "Alcohol doesn't mix well with cold medicine. I saw you talking to Bob's widow. What did you learn?"

"She's not overcome with grief; that's for sure," Josie said. "I told her I found Bob, but she seemed barely interested. I'd at least want to know if my husband had suffered. She was more interested in talking about Mom's shih tzu."

She recounted the conversation and Alyce said, "That's bizarre. But I have more news. I know who Vampira is. As soon as I saw her up close, I recognized her. She's Annabelle Lee Cody."

"Who?" Josie said. "Frank said her name was Heidi."

"I think she changed it," Alyce said. "I would if I was known as the Persimmon Creek Slayer."

"What?" Josie put down her fork.

"Don't you recall the story? It made the national news. Her looks are so striking—that pale skin and dark red hair—I knew who she was once I got close.

"I'm guessing she's maybe eighteen now," Alyce said. "When she was fourteen or fifteen, she lived in Persimmon Creek, Missouri."

"Is that in the Ozarks?"

"It is. A little mountain town, population one hundred and eight. Heidi—I'll use her current name—was suspected of killing her parents. They drank a lot and one night their trailer caught on fire. Heidi made it out, but her parents died. The investigators said the fire was arson and the parents' bedroom door was jammed. The case never went to trial."

"Why do you remember it?" Josie asked.

"I was pregnant at the time and jittery. You know how you get. I wondered how any child could kill her own parents. From what I gather, those two deserved it, but the story still scared me. Double patricide left an indelible impression."

"But you don't believe your baby, Justin, is capable of murder, do you?" Josie said.

"Not for a minute. The first time I saw my boy, I fell in love and all my fears vanished. But I remembered that scary story. I think she changed her name to Heidi and moved to St. Louis."

"She seems meek as a mouse," Josie said. "Why would she kill Uncle Bob?"

"Guess you'll have to find out," Alyce said. "But be careful. She's already gotten away with murder. Twice."

Chapter 24

"Karen, who killed Uncle Bob?" Josie asked.

The dog groomer was a generously proportioned woman with shiny chin-length brown hair, green eyes, and small, pretty hands with pink-painted nails.

Karen and Josie had scored a table by the window at Foundation Grounds in downtown Maplewood Monday afternoon. The rain had finally stopped and the sun-splashed coffeehouse smelled like fresh coffee and warm pastry.

They both ordered the organic pear tart and coffee. Josie felt virtuous because she passed up the honey cardamom latte for a cup of black free-trade coffee.

"Who killed Bob?" Karen said. "That's easy. Heidi."

Josie saw no hesitation, doubt, or any sign of second thoughts.

"Heidi?" she said. "The redhead who works at Uncle Bob's, right?"

"You know any other Heidis?"

"Why would she kill Bob?"

"Because he ended their affair."

Whoa. Josie was so startled she nearly spilled her coffee. "Bob dumped Heidi?" Josie couldn't hide her surprise.

"I told you he was a hound," Karen said.

"But he's at least fifty-five and, uh . . ." Josie didn't want to say "fat" and insult Karen.

"He's fat, old, and disgusting," Karen said. "And if you're worried about using that particular F-word around me, I'm a woman of size and proud of it."

"But Heidi's so young. She's what? Seventeen, eighteen?"

"She just turned eighteen last month," Karen said, and took another bite of pear tart. "We had a party for her at work."

"And she's pretty," Josie said. "Well, not conventionally pretty, but certainly striking."

"Heidi could be smokin' if she had some confidence and went to the right stylist. But she's shy and a little bit country."

"Why would she fall for a man three times her age?" Josie said.

"Like I said, Heidi's naive. She was impressed that a big-time celebrity was interested in her."

"Bob?" Josie said. "He's a joke."

"Not to Heidi," Karen said. "Bob gave Heidi her first taste of the good life. He took her to fancy restaurants with wine lists and white tablecloths, sent her red roses, and maybe gave her money. At least, I think he did. After they hooked up, she bought lots of new clothes and a black Neon. She was as proud of that little car as if it were a Mercedes. She was dazzled by his sophistication."

"Bob," Josie said, still trying to convince herself.

"She wasn't the first woman Bob had an affair with— or the last."

"How do you know they were seeing each other?"

"Honey, they were doing more than seeing," Karen said. "Bob used to take his women into his office to 'talk,' but his walls weren't soundproof. We knew what was going on. I think Bob was worried his wife would find out.

Candice would have had to be blind and deaf not to know.

"I'm not judging Heidi," Karen said. "I didn't care that she had a fling with Bob. She's a hard worker, keeps to herself, and she's quiet."

"That sounds like the kind of interview the serial killer's neighbors give to reporters after he's caught," Josie said. "Which reminds me, where is Heidi from?"

"She grew up in Branson, the big Ozark tourist town," Karen said.

"A guest at Bob's memorial reception thought she recognized Heidi as the Persimmon Creek Slayer," Josie said.

Karen looked blank, then said, "Wait! Was she the teenager who locked her drunken parents in their trailer and then set it on fire?"

"That's her," Josie said. "At least, the person at the reception thinks so. Heidi was never arrested or convicted of any crime."

"She must have changed her name when she moved," Karen said. "It would make sense that she'd want to get out of a wide spot in the road like Persimmon Creek and hide in the big city. And St. Louis would be big to her."

"Maybe the woman who said that was wrong," Josie said.

"No, it makes sense," Karen said. "For someone who supposedly grew up in Branson, Heidi knew nothing about the place.

"My family used to vacation there every summer. I'd been to Branson so often I could find my way around town without a map. But Heidi didn't know any of the big performers' names. I thought maybe she couldn't afford to go to their shows.

"When I asked her about the Shepherd of the Hills theater, Heidi had never heard of it. It's impossible to live in Branson and not know about the Shepherd of the

Hills. That novel and its spinoffs practically created the local tourist industry.

"Heidi said one other thing that seems odd now," Karen said. "I found her crying in the kitchen and asked what was wrong. She said Bob didn't want to see her anymore, and she cried on my shoulder. She said he was the first man she'd ever truly loved and she didn't care that his apartment was small, because his heart was big."

"Poor thing. She really was in love with him," Josie said.

"That's what I thought. Heidi told me, 'He misses his big house, but I'm used to small spaces. I grew up in a trailer. I'd be happy to share anyplace with him, but he didn't want me anymore.'"

"But there are trailers in Branson," Josie said.

"Yes, but Heidi told me she grew up in a white farmhouse. I think she let part of her real past slip."

"How long did Bob's affair with Heidi last?" Josie asked.

"About three or four months. Then she started hinting about marriage. Bob didn't want to lose his wife."

"Why not?" Josie said. "Candice didn't seem to care about him."

"And he didn't love her," Karen said. "That part of the marriage was over. They didn't even seem to like each other. But Candice adored dogs."

"I could tell," Josie said. "At Bob's funeral, she was more interested in discussing my mom's shih tzu than her late husband."

Karen thoughtfully sipped her coffee and said, "Candice knew his secret: Bob didn't like dogs, but he loved being a celebrity. Ralph the Talking Dog is really Candice's pet. That dog couldn't stand Bob. Those commercials took forever to tape because Ralph would snap and growl at Bob. Candice was on the sidelines, soothing the dog with scratches and treats, begging him to cooperate."

"Why did Bob quit taking women to his office and rent an apartment?"

"Bob's affairs were so flagrant, even he realized he'd have to cool it. That's when he rented a closet-sized efficiency. It was a rathole with a crummy plaid couch that folded out into a bed."

"Did you go there?" Josie asked.

"What? Do I look stupid? Do you really think I'd let someone like Bob near me?" Her face was pink with anger.

"I'm sorry," Josie said.

Karen looked like a hen with ruffled feathers. She drained her drink and scraped up the last crumbs of her pastry with her fork.

Josie finally broke the punishing silence with, "May I buy you another pear tart?"

"I'd love one," she said. "And a latte."

Josie came back with another tart and drinks for both of them. Karen seemed to accept them as an apology. "Here's why I know what Bob's apartment looks like. It's run by my mom's friend Myrtle Billings. We call her Aunt Myrt. You know how St. Louisans make people they like into honorary family members. Aunt Myrt thought I might want to rent the place because it was cheap, but it was too run-down and dreary. One furnished room with a view of the parking lot. Instead, Bob took it. It's all he could afford and Heidi didn't seem to mind it."

"Why did Bob drop Heidi?" Josie asked.

"He started seeing Sharon, Angel's owner."

"You're joking," Josie said. "He broke her dog's leg."

"I'm sure that's what ended their affair," Karen said, "if it wasn't over already. Sharon told me she was suing him for hurting her dog. I promised to testify, and Aunt Myrt agreed, too. So will Frank."

"If he's out of jail," Josie said. "Why would your aunt Myrt testify?"

"Because she saw Bob break the dog's leg."

"I thought the so-called accident happened at the day camp."

"It happened at Bob's apartment, but I told everyone I saw him kick Angel. Bob knew I knew what really happened to that little dog, and I made it clear Aunt Myrt was testifying against him. It was my way of keeping him in line until I quit the place."

"So how did it happen?"

"Aunt Myrt keeps an eye on Bob's place," Karen said.

And an ear, Josie thought. Bob must be more entertaining than a TV soap.

"Aunt Myrt said Sharon stopped by Bob's apartment before she went into work and brought Angel with her. She was afraid she'd be late for her job. After she and Bob had their fun, Sharon threw on her clothes and told Bob to pack up Angel in her caddy and take her in for day care. Then she left.

"Angel was cranky. She didn't like Bob and ran out the door. Bob chased the dog, but it wasn't much of a chase. Angel can't run very fast. Aunt Myrt was watching from the doorway and laughing at Bob. He caught the dog and she peed on his shoe. That's when he kicked Angel.

"Aunt Myrt heard the poor thing howl. Bob picked up the dog and pretended nothing had happened. Aunt Myrt called me and gave me a heads-up. Wouldn't you know it? That sneaky Bob brought in Angel, took her to the senior center, and pretended nothing was wrong. I could hear her crying down the hall.

"I threatened him and he made Frank take the dog to a vet clinic."

"Is there any way I can talk to Aunt Myrt?"

"Sure, she loves to talk."

Josie saw the apartment manager as a slightly less rabid Mrs. Mueller.

"When?" Karen asked.

"How about after I talk to you?"

"I'll call her now and set it up."

While Karen called Myrt, Josie tried to take in all the new information Karen had given her. Karen interrupted Josie's roiling thoughts with, "Myrt says you can stop by tomorrow morning, about eleven o'clock. Will that work?"

"Perfect," Josie said, and got the address and directions.

"You'll love Myrt," Karen said when she hung up. She looked at her watch. "I'm going to have to leave soon. What else?"

"I don't understand why Sharon brought Angel back for day care after Bob hurt her dog."

"She had no choice," Karen said. "Angel is old and set in her ways. She howled until she was back with her dog pals. We promised Sharon we'd protect her little Pomeranian and Bob wouldn't get near her."

"Why did Sharon have an affair with Bob anyway? He was repulsive," Josie said.

"Hey, you didn't see me lining up to be one of his ladies," Karen said. "Sharon was single, bored, and thought Bob was a 'hoot'—her words. She didn't much care for Candice and I think she enjoyed sneaking around with Bob behind his wife's back.

"Don't underestimate the thrill some people get from adultery. It can be addictive. Sometimes I think the slipping around is more of a turn-on than the sex.

"And Sharon got one king-sized thrill. Candice followed Bob to his little love nest and caught them in the act."

"Bob gave his wife a key to his hideaway?"

"Oh no," Karen said. "But Bob left his keys lying

around their house. Candice was suspicious, made a copy of the newest key, and walked in on the cheaters.

"Aunt Myrt heard the fight—and it was a doozy."

The walls to Bob's apartment had ears, Josie thought, and they belonged to Aunt Myrt. I can't wait to talk to that woman.

"Candice forced Bob to move out of their big house and into that cramped apartment. She threatened to tell his customers he didn't like dogs. Bob was worried she'd divorce him and he'd lose his business—and his place in the limelight."

"Pathetic," Josie said. "Are you going to stay on at Uncle Bob's?"

"No, I'm going to Westminster. They've been after me for months. When Bob kicked that poor dog, that was the last straw. I turned in my notice that day. Candice asked me to stay but I told her I'm gone for good."

"Do you think Candice will sell Uncle Bob's?"

"That's my guess. I've never met such a shy person. She doesn't even like going out in the lobby and greeting customers, much less making public appearances. She's the exact opposite of Bob."

"Did you tell Detective Dobbs about Bob's affair with Sharon?"

"Yes. I also told the detective about Heidi. You'd think he'd have her fingerprints if she was the Persimmon Creek Slayer."

"Maybe not," Josie said. "Heidi was a young teen and she was never arrested or charged with a crime. Aren't juvenile records sealed?"

"Well, Detective Dobbs is convinced that Frank is guilty," Karen said. "I said Frank would never kill anyone, even someone as obnoxious as Bob. The detective said I sounded awfully confident when I'd only known Frank three days."

"What about Candice?" Josie said. "She'll benefit the most from Bob's death. Why wasn't she arrested?"

"She has an alibi," Karen said. "Heidi said she was in the day-care kitchen when Candice brought in Bob's organic mushrooms. Heidi watched Candice wash and slice them while she mixed Bob's salad dressing."

"I'm not quite sure that's an alibi," Josie said. "The salad was made hours before Bob's death."

"But Candice left after she fixed his salad," Karen said. "Wc saw her go. She went shopping and she had the receipts to prove it."

"Still," Josie said. "Are Heidi and Candice both saying there were no azalea leaves in the salad at that time?"

"That's right," Karen said. "Beverly saw Bob's wife come into work. They talked for a bit and she showed Bev the mushrooms. Candice didn't have any other salad greens with her. Candice put the salad in the fridge when she finished slicing the mushrooms, according to Heidi, and it stayed there until Heidi served Bob his lunch."

"I don't know," Josie said.

"Well, it was enough for Detective Dobbs," Karen said. She sounded almost resentful.

"So Heidi is Candice's alibi—and vice versa."

"Yep," Karen said. "Nice, isn't it? We've got a real killer alibiing the woman who has the second-best reason to kill Bob."

Chapter 25

Josie was so excited, even her cell phone's speed dial wasn't fast enough for her. As soon as Alyce answered, Josie said, "I know who killed Uncle Bob."

"Are you okay, Josie?" Alyce said. "You sound kind of . . ."

"Excited," Josie interrupted her friend. "I just finished talking to Karen the dog groomer. You were right. Heidi killed Bob."

"I didn't say that," Alyce said, and suddenly Josie was reminded that Alyce was a lawyer's wife. "I said I thought she might be Annabelle Lee Cody, who was suspected in the arson murders of her parents."

"Well, now she's giving my other prime suspect an alibi for Bob's murder," Josie said. "Heidi told the police that Candice brought the mushrooms for Bob's salad into the day-care kitchen. She watched Candice prepare the 'shrooms while Heidi made Bob's buttermilk ranch dressing. Heidi claimed Candice never had any azalea leaves with her. I'm sure she didn't—because Heidi had them."

"Whoa, back up," Alyce said. "Why would Heidi want to kill Bob?"

"Because he dumped her. He was a hound. Heidi was in love with him and he left her for another woman. She's Candice's alibi. Heidi could have poisoned Bob's salad. The police never looked at his murder from that angle."

"How do you know?" Alyce said.

"Because they arrested Frank," Josie said. "That's why I want you to go with me tomorrow so I can question Heidi."

Alyce hesitated, then said, "What are you going to say to Heidi, Josie? I can see the scene now: You stroll into Uncle Bob's Doggy Day Camp and say, 'Hey there, Heidi. You got away with murder in Persimmon Creek, Missouri. Now you're in St. Louis and Bob, the man you wanted to marry, left you. Guess what? He turned up dead, too. Did you kill him?'

"Heidi will break down immediately. 'Oh, stop your relentless grilling, Ms. Mystery Shopper,' she'll say. 'Please. I can't take it anymore. I confess. I did it, and I'm glad. Now lock me up.'"

Josie was so hurt by her friend's mockery, she didn't answer. The silence stretched until Josie said, "I wasn't planning to do it quite that way."

Alyce heard the hurt in her voice. "I'm sorry, Josie," she said. "I sounded like a real witch. But talking to Heidi is risky. How will you get her to talk?"

"I'm good at getting people to talk," Josie said. Alyce's words still stung.

"Yes, you are," Alyce said, sounding contrite. "But Heidi isn't an ordinary person. If she's the Persimmon Creek Slayer, she killed her parents when she was a teenager. The police must have interrogated her many times, but she didn't break down. She stayed strong even in the glare of the national media spotlight. Why would she cave now?"

"I just thought . . ." Josie's voice trailed off and she shrugged, though Alyce couldn't see that. "I guess it was a lame idea. I've been mainlining sugar and caffeine for almost two hours. I wasn't thinking clearly."

"If you do talk to Heidi, you need an excuse," Alyce said. "Something that sounds plausible, so you can safely walk away."

"I could say my mom's dog really liked her organic biscuits and I want to buy more," Josie said. "That's true."

"Except they're for sale in Uncle Bob's gift shop," Alyce said.

"Oh. Right," Josie said. "Wait! I know! I can say that Ted's clinic wants to sell the dog biscuits and ask Heidi to bake some for him."

"And what if Heidi buys your story and starts making organic biscuits for Ted?" Alyce said.

"Then I'm going to be stuck with a whole lot of dog biscuits. Ted can give them away. But it's worth a try. I can see if there are any azaleas near Heidi's place, too."

"So what if there are, Josie? Azaleas grow all over St. Louis. Frank's in jail accused of murder, and your mom doesn't have any azaleas."

"They're growing right next door, along her property line," Josie said. What's wrong with my friend? she wondered. She must be cranky from that cold.

"But azaleas aren't locked in a cage," Alyce said. "The killer could pull off a deadly handful and nobody would even notice. Those plants are everywhere.

"The Missouri Botanical Garden in South City has a huge azalea display in the spring. Garden shops sell them. Late spring and early fall are supposed to be good times to plant azalea bushes.

"If I wanted to murder someone, I'd buy an azalea at Home Depot, pick off the leaves, drop them in the salad, and throw away the plant. Then there would be no plant DNA to connect me to the murder."

"Oh." Josie could feel her sugar-and-caffeine high disappearing, along with her optimism. "Well, I still want to talk to Heidi. Will you go with me?" she said in a small voice.

"No, Josie. She's dangerous. You've been lucky so far. No, more than lucky. Smart. You have a knack for investigation. I'm not discounting your skill, but you shouldn't go up against someone as deadly as Heidi. You have Ted and your daughter to think about. Not to mention your own safety."

"What about if I talk to someone safe, like Angel's owner, Sharon? First thing tomorrow morning."

"Um, Josie, I'm not feeling so good in the mornings."

"Your cold is that bad?"

"It's not a cold," Alyce said. "I couldn't keep anything down this morning but 7Up and soda crackers."

"You have the flu?"

"Not exactly. But I do have to be careful." Alyce sounded too cheerful for someone who was ailing.

Slowly, the light dawned on Josie. A queasy stomach in the morning. No alcohol at lunch. "Alyce! You're pregnant! Congratulations!"

"We've been trying for some time," Alyce said, and Josie heard her smile for sure. "I'd love to have a little girl and give Justin a little sister to play with."

Josie instantly forgave her friend.

"I just got the news from my ob-gyn when I got home," Alyce said. "You're the first person I've told, besides Jake. I wanted to tell him over dinner tonight, but I was so thrilled I couldn't wait. I called him at the office. He told me not to cook. We're going out to celebrate."

"I can't wait to give you a baby shower," Josie said. "Amelia will love being an honorary aunt. Can I tell her?"

"It's early yet," Alyce said. "I'm not expecting any difficulty, but . . ."

"I understand," Josie said. "If it's a girl, we'll have such fun shopping for clothes. And the little boys' clothes are supercute, too. But it's time for me to pick up my girl at school."

Josie had traded her somber wool for a crisp white shirt, jeans, and strappy red sandals. After the rain, the world looked freshly cleaned.

She celebrated Alyce's good news and her own progress on Frank's case until she got to Barrington School. When Miss Apple, the head of school, called Amelia's name, her daughter ran for the car, tossed in her backpack, and said, "Hurry, Mom!" as if she were pursued by demons.

Josie didn't react fast enough.

"Let's go, Mom! Don't just sit there."

Josie saw a cluster of students around the luxury cars belonging to the parents of the mean girls. She thought she caught the words "snitch" and "rat." She definitely heard loud squeaks.

Josie pulled out of the school's circular drive, narrowly missing the bumper of a blue Beemer. The scrawny blonde driving it gave Josie a pained smile. She thought the girl in the front seat sneered at them, but the encounter was so brief, Josie wasn't sure.

Amelia was. "That's Zoe's mom," Amelia said, and Josie heard the agony in her daughter's voice.

Zoe Delgado, a class troublemaker, Josie thought. Yep, I read that girl's expression right. It was a sneer.

"What's wrong?" Josie said. "What did Zoe and her nasty friends say to you?"

"Nothing," Amelia said.

"I can tell by your voice the mean girls have been tormenting you. They called you a snitch, didn't they? They were at the Rivingtons' party."

"If I say anything, you'll turn around and yell at Miss Apple, and that will make it worse," Amelia said. "Then I really will be a snitch."

"I promise not to do anything until we talk to Ted first," Josie said. "We'll decide together, okay?"

Amelia believes Ted is more reasonable, Josie thought. Maybe we do need a second opinion for this case.

"Promise?" Amelia asked.

"Pinkie swear," Josie said, "though we'll have to wait till we get to a stoplight to seal the deal."

"Okay, I'll tell you. Everyone at school knew what happened at the party, and they blamed me."

"But it was Ted who stopped the party, and he saved Jared."

"Mom! Are you going to listen?"

Josie shut up.

"Jared doesn't count. He doesn't go to our school. He goes to Rove." That was the local public school. Miss Apple and the more stuck-up Barrington students considered Rove School socially inferior. "He was there because he hangs with Kate's brother.

"Zoe said because I ruined a good party, she was having a pimps-and-hos party on Friday night. She invited everyone but me and my friends—Palmer, Emma, and Bailey. In the cafeteria, she stopped by our table and said, 'Snitches, bitches, and rats aren't welcome at cool parties.'

"I said, 'I don't want to go.'"

"Good for you," Josie said. She knew what Amelia's defiant answer must have cost her. "I'm afraid I already know, but what's a pimps-and-hos party?"

"The guys dress like, you know, pimps. Flashy suits, long coats, rapper bling. Gotta have sunglasses, a pocketful of fake money, and a cigar. The girls wear booty shorts, *lots* of makeup, microminis, halters, and dress, like, you know, hos."

"You mean prostitutes?" Josie said.

"That's what I said."

"No, you said 'ho.' 'Ho' is a mispronunciation of the word 'whore.' It means a loose woman, and I don't want you using it. If you wanted to go to that party, I wouldn't let you."

"Why not?"

"Because it's sexist and racist. It's wrong on so many levels, I can't begin to list all the reasons why I wouldn't let you go to a party like that."

She drove into their charmed circle, Fresno Court, and parked under the red-and-gold canopy of fall leaves. Josie waved at her neighbor, Cordelia. The college professor was picking up a newspaper on her lawn.

"What would Cordelia and Wil think of that party?" Josie said. At home, Amelia was subdued. She took her cat pal Harry up to her room and texted her friends. Josie called Ted at work and explained what had happened. "I'm worried about Amelia," she said.

"I was afraid of that," he said. "I've got just the antidote."

"What?"

"It's a surprise. You'll both have to wait."

Chapter 26

"Ted, are you sure we can afford this?" Josie whispered to her husband. She hoped he couldn't hear her fear, but she was worried.

Ted was waiting for Amelia to come back downstairs so he could give her his surprise. It was also a surprise for Josie, and once Ted told her exactly what it was, she was stunned by the cost.

Ted had come home from the clinic at six o'clock, bursting through the kitchen door with his animal entourage, Marmalade and Festus.

Josie was fixing chicken fajitas for dinner. She had the electric skillet on to warm the tortillas. The kitchen was scented with the marinade, heavy with lime juice, garlic, and cilantro. The peppers and onions were already grilled. As soon as she added the chicken, dinner would be ready.

"Hey, gorgeous, where's Amelia?" Ted said, kissing her hello.

"In her room," Josie said. "She's been subdued since she got home from school."

"Wait till she sees what I have," Ted said. "She'll be recharged immediately." He winked at Josie.

"Amelia," Ted called. "I have a surprise for you."

Amelia flew downstairs and into the kitchen. "What? What?" she said, jumping up and down as if she were eight instead of twelve. "I love surprises. I— Harry! No!"

Josie winced at Amelia's ear-piercing shriek, then saw the reason for it. Harry the cat was slinking along the countertop toward the four grilled chicken breasts ready to be sliced into fajita strips on the cutting board.

Amelia scooped up her cat and ran up the stairs, carrying Harry under her arm like a football. His tail and ears drooped. He was caught and looking at jail time in Amelia's purple bathroom.

Josie heard Amelia say, "Bad boy! Bad! Stay there," followed by a slammed door.

In the midst of the cat confusion, Ted had told Josie about Amelia's surprise. Josie wished she'd been sitting down—or her husband had discussed it with her first.

"But those tickets are nearly sold out," Josie said. "That concert is all Amelia's talked about on the drive to and from school. She told me tickets are two hundred fifty dollars each—and those are only the medium-priced ones."

"Close," Ted said. "They're exactly $251.46. I got four, so that's $1,005.84."

Josie felt the blood drain from her face. Panic made her voice higher than usual. "There's no way I can afford that, Ted. Mystery-shopping jobs are getting scarce. I barely made enough for her new party dress."

"I don't expect you to buy them," he said.

"But you've got your loans for the clinic remodeling and we have the house payment, and the utilities are going up—"

Ted stopped Josie in midsentence with a kiss. "Trust me," he said. "This will be worth it when we see the look on Amelia's face."

"I want to see the look on her face when there's no money for groceries," Josie said.

"I'd never do that. Both my girls will enjoy this surprise. I promise." He gave her a hug and another kiss. They broke apart when they heard Amelia pounding down the stairs. A slim tween girl in a hurry could sound like a water buffalo.

"Sorry," Amelia said. "I don't know what got into Harry. He usually doesn't do that."

"It didn't affect your surprise," Ted said, and grinned. "Ta-da!" He pulled four tickets out of his shirt pocket and handed them to her.

Amelia's hazel eyes grew wide. "*O. M. G.* This is beyond cool," she said. "Tickets to One Direction. My fav band. Front and center, lower balcony. I thought this concert was sold out."

"Not for you," Ted said. "You can take three friends."

"Palmer, Emma, and Bailey won't believe this," Amelia said. "Thank you! Thank you." She threw her arms around Ted.

Josie smiled to see Amelia so happy—she was back, enthusiasm restored, a shine to her eyes.

"I'm calling them now," Amelia said.

"Call?" Josie said. "On the phone?"

For Amelia's age-group, a phone call was as formal as an engraved invitation.

"I want to hear them when they get the news," she said. "They're going to the coolest concert in St. Louis."

"Texting can't convey a good squee," Josie said.

"Tell your friends I'll be their chauffeur," Ted said. "Their parents can call my cell and we'll work out the times."

"I will," Amelia shouted, already on her way to her room.

"Wow!" Josie said. "She's a new woman. And where did you snag the city's hottest tween tickets?"

"They're a favor from David, one of my clients who works for a ticket agency. He said if I ever needed tickets to any show or concert, all I had to do was call him. He thought I'd want to take you to a musical or maybe a hot adult concert, like Sting. David was surprised when I asked for four tickets to One Direction, but he made sure Amelia got good seats."

"Why did David do that for you?"

"He thinks I saved his boxer's life. Any competent vet could have saved Killian, but I cashed in that favor."

"Thank you," Josie said. She hugged Ted, then picked clumps of brown dog hair off her white shirt.

"Shower time for me," Ted said.

"Dinner's served when you're ready," Josie said.

But Ted's cell phone rang before he could make it upstairs. "Devlin Michael Novak," Ted said. "You're Bailey's father, Amelia's friend. How are you?"

Ted didn't have to put his cell phone on speaker. Josie could hear the lawyer's booming courtroom voice. "It's Mick, remember? That was damn nice of you, getting One Dimension tickets for the girls."

"One Direction," Ted said.

"Right. My girl's been moping around since those mean little twits said she and her friends weren't invited to that party. When Amelia called her about the tickets, it's the first time I've seen Bailey smile since she came home from school. Let me reimburse you for Bailey's ticket."

"No, thanks, my treat," Ted said.

"I figured you'd say that," Mick said. "I've hired a limo so the girls can go in style. You can leave your chauffeur's uniform at home."

"That's incredible," Ted said. "The girls will love it."

"Show starts at seven. How about if we pick up Amelia at five fifteen?"

"She'll be ready and waiting," Ted said.

At dinner, Josie could have served Amelia a bowl of cat food for all the attention she paid to her fajitas. She was busy talking about the five band members in One Direction—Harry Styles, Louis Tomlinson, Niall Horan, Zayn Malik, and Liam Payne.

"They're all over social media," Amelia said. "We can follow One D on Twitter, Instagram, and Vine."

"Vine?" Josie said. "What's that?"

"It's short videos—about six seconds. Harry Styles has this really cool video on Vine where he does this funny thing with a coatrack and pretends like he's hung up. First time I saw it, I thought, 'Wow! How cute is he?' There's another video of Niall dancing with socks on his hands and boxers on his head. It's so cool."

"They sound like the Beatles fifty years later," Ted said.

"Harry said that in an interview," Amelia said. She was now on a first-name basis with Harry Styles.

"One D has, like, millions of screaming fans, and Harry said they weren't in the same league as the Beatles music-wise, but fame-wise, One Direction is probably bigger."

"Sounds like Harry has his head on straight," Josie said.

"It's totally cool that Harry said that. Even though he's rich and famous, he's, like, humble."

"And cute," Josie said.

"Did you hear the Beatles when they played in St. Louis, Mom?"

"That was 1966, honey," Josie said. "I wasn't born yet. Some of Grandma's friends were at that concert in the old Busch Stadium."

And couldn't hear a word the Beatles sang, thanks to all the screaming fangirls, Josie thought. She wondered if Amelia would be able to hear One D but said nothing. She didn't want to be Buzzkill Mom.

Amelia ran back upstairs after dinner, this time to text her friends. Josie was touched that her daughter made a special trip downstairs at bedtime to thank Ted again for the tickets.

Chapter 27

Tuesday morning was as sunny as Amelia's mood. She dressed with extra care and was ready for school early. She couldn't wait to spread the word about the One Direction tickets.

"Who cares about a dumb house party when me and my friends have real tickets to a hot concert and a limo?" she said.

After Josie dropped off Amelia at Barrington, she switched back to detective mode. She wanted to talk to Sharon Pancera, the woman who owned the Pomeranian with the broken leg. Then she'd meet Myrtle, Karen's honorary aunt.

Josie knew she wasn't doing anything rash. Sharon was suing Uncle Bob's Doggy Day Camp. She'd get her revenge against Bob's beloved business that way— although it would be his wife, Candice, who'd pay if Sharon won the suit. Josie wondered if Sharon would enjoy that payback after Candice caught her in bed with Bob.

Sharon lived about two blocks from Uncle Bob's on a main South County road, Gravois, pronounced "GRA-voy" in fractured St. Louis French. Thanks to Karen the groomer, Josie knew that Sharon worked at the Fenway Department Store in South County Center.

Josie was relieved when Sharon answered her phone that morning. "Ms. Pancera, my name is Josie Marcus.

My husband is Ted Scottsmeyer. He's the veterinarian who treated your dog, Angel, after the accident at Uncle Bob's."

"It wasn't an accident," Sharon said sharply.

"That's what I understand," Josie said. "Could I talk to you about it this morning? In person?"

"I saw you at the day camp the day Bob got sick," Sharon said. "You found him, didn't you?"

"Yes," Josie said.

"I hope he suffered," Sharon said, not bothering to hide her spite. "I hope he was hurting ten times worse than my girl. My regular vet says your husband did a good job with Angel.

"I have to be at the mall at eleven, but if you want to come by for coffee, I could talk for half an hour."

She gave Josie her address and added, "I'm in Unit 2 on the first floor."

"How about if I swing by Federhofer's Bakery for German chocolate muffins first?" Josie said.

"Then you're really welcome," Sharon said.

Federhofer's was an old German bakery with a landmark neon sign of a chef holding a birthday cake. Inside, the air was sweetened with warm sugar. Josie bought four giant muffins, thickly iced and topped with chocolate shavings—two for Sharon and two for Aunt Myrtle. Most people knew the city's German-Americans ruled the beer industry, but they also created scrumptious sweets.

Sharon lived in a drab four-unit redbrick shoe box between two small ranch houses. Josie hurried up the cracked sidewalk. She checked the straggly shrubbery huddled against the foundation but saw no azalea bushes.

The lobby needed a good cleaning. A cracked gold-framed mirror hung over a chipped black lacquer table piled with take-out menus. Free newspapers were stacked on a black straight-back chair. A dusty silk plant drooped next to the elevator, and a faded golf umbrella was abandoned by the door.

Josie knocked on Unit 2's door and heard Angel yapping. Sharon answered, all angles and elbows. Her black-and-white dress made her look like a walking geometry illustration.

She welcomed Josie and her luscious German chocolate pastries. Angel was in a heavily padded dog bed, her leg still uncomfortably encased in metal.

"Poor little girl," Josie said. "How's she feeling?"

"Restless and cranky," Sharon said.

Josie followed Sharon to the coffee-scented kitchen. The room was a cheerful blue with well-polished oak cabinets. Sharon had done her best to brighten up the apartment.

Josie took a seat at the oak kitchen table. Sharon poured two mugs of coffee and gave Josie a muffin on a flowered plate, a napkin, and a fork. Josie's first bite of muffin was an incredible sugar rush.

"Mrs. Meyer next door will look after Angel when I'm at work," Sharon said. "Uncle Bob's is closed for the rest of the week. Angel misses her little friends, Pepper and Baby. That's the only reason I took her back there after what Bob did.

"I'm going to contact both dogs' owners and see if they'll switch to Westminster."

"I took our dog there," Josie said. "It seems well run."

"I shouldn't be going back to Uncle Bob's, not when I'm suing the place." Sharon bit into the muffin and moaned, "These muffins are better than sex."

Sex with Bob, Josie wondered, or sex with a good man? She steered her wandering mind back to the subject. "Have you filed your suit yet?"

"My lawyer wants to wait until the whole murder mess calms down. I'm glad the cops arrested Bob's killer, Franklin Hyzy."

Josie wasn't, but she couldn't say that.

"That will speed up the process," Sharon said. "Once that old man is convicted, we can sue. Although if Frank Hyzy killed Bob because he hurt my dog, that man should get a medal."

"Did you know Bob had a cruel streak?" Josie asked. About half her muffin had disappeared.

"Of course not," Sharon said. "I wouldn't send my dog to a monster. I didn't think Bob had much contact with the dogs. The big secret was he didn't like animals. I mainly dealt with the staff, and they were supernice."

"They told me Angel is a great favorite," Josie said.

"They like my dog," Sharon said. "I'm not sure they like me. I guess they told you I was stupid enough to have a fling with Bob."

"Really?" Josie said, pretending she didn't know.

"Bob didn't look like much," Sharon said, "but he was good for some laughs. It was over long before he hurt my dog."

She checked the kitchen clock. "It's time for me to leave for work," Sharon said. "Thank you for the fabulous muffins."

Josie followed Sharon outside and watched her climb into a seventies beater the size of a spare room with a coat hanger antenna. How does she afford gas for that guzzler? Josie wondered, as she watched her drive off in the rattling machine.

Josie was back in her car when she realized Sharon had admitted to an affair with Bob. No, she'd volunteered it—to a near stranger. But she'd neglected to mention that Bob was married and his wife had caught them in the act. She also hadn't mentioned Aunt Myrtle and her testimony.

What was that about? Josie wondered.

She was about to find out.

Aunt Myrtle ran Shady Rest Apartment Homes, about

ten minutes away. Josie thought the name belonged on a cemetery. The Shady Rest was a dead nineteen fifties motel, each unit converted into a separate apartment. The sun-faded cinder-block walls used to be peppermint pink. Now they had scabrous gray patches, like grave mold. There wasn't a tree, bush, or blade of grass on the property, just aging gray asphalt.

Aunt Myrtle was sweeping the cracked sidewalk. She was a sturdy, muscular woman of about sixty with crinkly permed hair, her lips clamped around a cigarette. She wore a tool belt and an apron and Josie guessed she was both the janitor and the repair person.

"You Josie?" she asked, squinting at her. "I'm Myrt. Karen said to be on the lookout for you about now."

"I brought you muffins from Federhofer's," Josie said.

"Well, didn't you just make my morning. Come into my apartment and let's talk. I've got a pot of coffee on."

Myrt lived in two tiny rooms with white walls and red tile floors. The couch was covered with a chenille throw, and there was a vase of silk flowers on the TV set. The rooms smelled of smoke and lemon air freshener.

Myrt ground out her cigarette in a big tin ashtray. Josie sat at a small brass dinette while Myrt poured mugs of coffee and put the muffins on red saucers with swift, efficient movements. Then she sat across from Josie.

"So you want to know about Uncle Bob, St. Louis's sweetheart," she said. "He's dead and I'm glad."

"Who do you think killed him?" Josie asked.

"His wife shoulda murdered him," Myrt said. "I would have. She caught the cheating hound in bed with a customer. Right here. But I don't think Candice killed him. I liked her and felt sorry for her, stuck with that man. Some women don't think they deserve better.

"Didn't feel sorry for that Sharon, though, sneaking around with another woman's husband. I never did see Bob's attraction."

"Me, either," Josie said.

"I'll say this, though—the ladies liked him. Is there a shortage of men that women chased a pudgy old guy like him? It's a mystery; that's all I can say. Must be those phee-romes the scientists talk about. That Sharon was too thin, but what do I know? She did the deed with Bob until she found out he kicked her dog and broke its little leg."

"Did he abuse Angel here?"

"Right out on the parking lot," Myrt said. "I was sweeping that end of the sidewalk and watched that little Pom run out of his room. Bob ran after the dog, trying to catch her. It was more like a turtle race. Neither one was real fast.

"Bob finally caught Angel and she sprinkled his shoe. I liked to died laughing, but he kicked her with those big old shoes. You had to have a heart of stone to ignore that dog's cries, and Bob did.

"He drove off with Angel and I figured he was heading for the day-care center—it's two minutes away. I let Karen know what was up. Sure enough, Bob dropped Angel in her usual room and was going to ignore her injury. But my Karen gave him what-for until he did the right thing. That girl's got spirit."

Josie heard her pride and nodded agreement. "Do you think Sharon killed Bob?"

"The Stick Woman? No, she wanted money. She didn't believe Bob's lie about Angel jumping up and falling off a table. Not for a minute. Karen had clued her in and she came roaring over here.

"Sharon and Bob had a big fight at his place. I was sweeping the sidewalk by his room"—Josie suspected Bob's sidewalk was very clean—"and I couldn't help overhearing some of their conversation.

"Sharon said she'd sue him for every last dime. He laughed and said she'd better get a good lawyer because there was no way she could ever collect a nickel. He said he'd paid all Angel's vet bills.

"Sharon said that Angel had suffered and the whole city would know Uncle Bob—she said his name real sarcastic-like—Uncle Bob hurt her dog. Bob said she had no room to talk when she was the poster child for dog abuse."

"Do you know what he meant by that?" Josie said.

"Not a clue," Myrt said. "She slammed his door and yelled, 'I'll see you in court. And the jury will give me at least half a million.' Bob laughed again and said, 'You ain't gotta chance, sweetie.' But I think that's what she's going to do—sue Bob. Well, sue his estate, now that he's dead.

"I saw where that older man who worked at Uncle Bob's, Franklin somebody, was arrested for killing Bob. He's attractive. I could understand ladies chasing him. But Franklin didn't look like a killer. Not to me.

"No, you ask me, Heidi killed Bob. She had the best reason."

"The tall redhead," Josie said.

"That's her. Very young—way too young for Bob— and she took his attentions seriously. She'd come here all dressed up and they'd go out for steak and lobster, and by the size of that girl, I don't think she had many good dinners before she met Bob. He bought her the cutest black Neon, and nice clothes.

"One night I saw her swanning around the soda machine in a pale green silk negligee, like an old-time movie star. Then Bob dropped her flat, and she came crying to me.

"I brought her in here for some coffee. Sat her right at this table and told her Bob wasn't worth her tears and she'd find someone better. I let her cry herself out and she finally did. Then she got this determined look on her face and said, 'The Lord will smite my enemies. He's done it before and he'll do it again.'"

Josie got a cold feeling, but Myrt kept talking.

"I agreed that religion was a comfort and what goes around comes around. When she left, I thought Heidi was going to straighten up and fly right.

"And then a month later Bob wound up dead, and I wondered if the Lord showed her some azalea bushes."

Chapter 28

"I'm fine, Josie," Frank Hyzy said. "Really."

Frank was lying. Josie could see that. He looked washed-out and wilted through the Plexiglas window in the booth at the St. Louis County Jail.

Josie also knew this was one of many lies told that Tuesday afternoon in the jail's visitor room. At least Frank was trying to make Josie feel better.

But in the two days since he'd been arrested, Frank had aged two years—dog years. He looked as gray as his prison pants and shirt. His big liver-spotted hands trembled slightly when he picked up the phone to talk to her. His voice trembled, too. He was grateful she'd come to see him.

"I know you're innocent, Frank," Josie said. "Nobody believes you killed that man."

"Except the police," Frank said. His fluffy white hair was plastered to his scalp, and he'd lost weight. His physique had slipped from slender to scrawny. Frank needed Jane's steady supply of homemade cakes and pies.

"How is your mother?" he asked.

"Worried about you," Josie said, then realized she'd made the man feel worse.

"I'm sorry I dragged Jane into this," Frank said. "She's a good woman."

Josie heard his unspoken question: Where is Jane?

"You can only have two visitors a week, Frank, and your daughter's already seen you."

"This is hard on Laura, too," he said. His regret and remorse were heartbreaking. It wasn't his fault he was locked in a towering brick jail in downtown Clayton, the county seat.

Josie's hatred of Mrs. Mueller burned brighter. That woman did her best to put Frank in here, she thought. She tried to tamp down her anger. I'm here to help Frank.

"Laura is holding up," Josie said. "She's a good vet and a hard worker. The clinic really needs to hire a fourth vet, so she's swamped with work."

"Good," Frank said. "Laura loves working for your Ted and his partner, Dr. Chris."

"They're keeping her so busy she doesn't have time to brood," Josie said. "Ted, Chris, and the clinic staff are taking good care of her. Mom says she'll visit you this Sunday."

Frank moved restlessly in the uncomfortable plastic chair and looked at his big hands. "We were supposed to go to church this Sunday," he said. "Instead she's seeing me in jail. And I'm told it's one of the busiest days here. The lines will be long."

"She'll be fine, Frank," Josie said.

"But the sort of people she'll have to associate with . . . ," he said.

"What? People like you?" Josie said.

Frank lowered his voice to a whisper and said, "That man next to me has SS tattoos. He's not someone Jane should be near."

"He's behind bars," Josie said. "And Plexiglas. There are guards everywhere. I'm here today because Mom believes I can help you, but don't get your hopes up. She has an exaggerated idea of what I can do. Your lawyer already has an in-house detective. He's a professional."

"Don't underestimate yourself, Josie. Besides, I've already talked to that man, and I wasn't impressed."

"Don't underestimate him," Josie said. "People tend to tell detectives more if they don't feel threatened by them. Some private eyes deliberately cultivate a bumbling image."

"This bird doesn't have much to cultivate," Frank said. "Jane has a lot of faith in Renzo Fischer, but I gotta wonder about a city lawyer who wears a white cowboy hat in downtown Clayton. This isn't Texas."

"Renzo is an old-school defense attorney," Josie said. "He's more like an actor than the younger corporate types. He's colorful and jurors remember him. Renzo calls himself 'the man in the white hat' in his ads, and juries think he defends good guys. That's you, Frank."

Josie glanced at her watch and realized they'd used up fifteen precious minutes of the one-hour visit.

"I saw Sharon, Angel's owner, this morning," she said. "How's that poor little dog?"

"Sharon says her Pom is cranky and restless, and Angel misses her dog pals. Uncle Bob's is closed for the rest of the week. Sharon is trying to get the other two owners of the old dogs who hung out together to move to Westminster Dog Day Care. She doesn't want to go back to Uncle Bob's, especially since she's suing his company."

"I told her I'd testify on her behalf," Frank said, "but now I'm stuck in here."

"I wouldn't feel too bad about that, Frank." Especially since she's waiting until you're convicted so she can file her suit against Uncle Bob's Doggy Day Camp, Josie thought. But Frank didn't need to know that.

"I feel terrible about that dog," he said. "Even if I can't testify, Dr. Ted and Karen the groomer will. They'll both make good witnesses."

"I'm sure they will. I was surprised when Sharon said

she had an affair with Bob. She said he was good for a few laughs."

"A few laughs? See, this is what I don't get about women," Frank said. "Bob was good for a few laughs, all right. He was a joke. A big, fat clown. Sharon's an attractive woman. What did she see in him? Did you find him attractive?"

"No way," Josie said. "Even if I'd spent six months in a lighthouse, I wouldn't have a fling with an oaf like Bob."

"But Sharon did," Frank said. "Why?"

"Beats me," Josie said. "Sharon acted like she had no idea Bob was still married to Candice."

"She knew, all right," Frank said. "Karen told me that Sharon was humiliated when Bob's wife burst in on them in his apartment."

"So that's when Sharon ended the affair?"

"Oh no," Frank said. "As I understand it, they were still going strong right up till the day Bob kicked Angel and broke the dog's leg. Now, I never saw them together, Josie. I'm getting my gossip from Karen. And Karen says when Bob hurt poor Angel, Sharon wanted revenge. She hired a lawyer and said she was suing Bob for all the pain and suffering."

"Angel does look uncomfortable, poor thing," Josie said.

"Yes, she does, but I got the feeling Sharon wasn't talking about her dog," Frank said. "It's like that kick woke up Sharon. Maybe Bob kicked some sense into her. Now Sharon wants payback for her own pain. That's why she's talking about revenge."

"But Bob's dead," Josie said.

"Yes, but his day-care place was his life's work. If she can destroy the one thing Bob cared about, she'll be happy. It won't hurt to get back at Candice, either."

Josie checked her watch again. Less than twenty minutes before their visit was over, and they were playing pop-psychology games, speculating on things they knew nothing about. Time to stop circling the subject, she thought. Here goes.

"Who killed Uncle Bob?" she asked.

Frank looked thoughtful. She could almost see him turning the problem over in his mind, looking at it from every angle.

"I didn't work there long enough to get a feel for the staff or customers," Frank said.

He's dithering, Josie thought. "Then, quick, off the top of your head, say the first name that comes to mind. Who killed Bob?"

"Candice."

"But she's too shy to be the public face of Uncle Bob's," Josie said.

"She is," Frank said. "She doesn't like meeting anyone, not even longtime customers. She's only happy when she's with dogs."

"At Bob's memorial reception, she barely mentioned her husband to me," Josie said. "Candice talked about Mom's shih tzu. She told me that wolves, the ancestors of dogs, were more faithful than people. I didn't mention that cockroaches also mate for life."

"You're right, Josie. But you wanted a quick answer, and there's a lot of anger in that woman. She doesn't like Bob, much less love him. But it wouldn't make sense for her to kill Bob.

"She put up with his shenanigans so she could be with her beloved dogs. Now I'm guessing she's going to have to sell the place."

"I heard that, too," Josie said. "What do you think of Heidi?"

Frank raised his eyebrows. "As the killer? That sweet little redhead? No way."

"One of the women at the memorial service thought

she recognized her. She believes Heidi is actually the Persimmon Creek Slayer, the teen who locked her alcoholic parents in their trailer and set it on fire a couple of years ago. She thinks Heidi changed her name and moved from her little Ozark town to the big city."

"Heidi?" Frank seemed to examine the idea, then reject it. "No, no way. She's too sweet and shy. I called her our little mountain flower."

"Karen said Heidi claimed to be from Branson but knew nothing about the town or its tourist attractions."

"Maybe she didn't live there," Frank said. "But that doesn't explain why Heidi would want to kill Bob."

"She had an affair with him and he dropped her."

"No!" Frank shook his head, as if he could erase an ugly picture in his mind. "He's old enough to be her father."

"Grandfather," Josie said.

"What would a pretty young girl see in that old coot?"

"Karen says he dazzled Heidi with fancy restaurants, flowers, gifts. And she was attracted to his fame."

"A guy who did dog commercials?" Frank said, not bothering to hide his disbelief.

"There's not a lot of fame in Persimmon Creek," Josie said.

"No," Frank said. "I can't see it. I just can't. You might as well say Ralph the Talking Dog killed him. He really hated Bob."

Chapter 29

"What can I do to help Frank, Mom?" Amelia asked.

Josie was trying to pull out of the traffic-clogged drive at Barrington School Wednesday afternoon, carefully steering around the other cars.

She'd expected this trip home would be devoted to the One Direction concert. Ever since Ted had scored the tickets, Amelia had talked of nothing else.

"What?" Josie said. She was so surprised by this unexpected subject she nearly ran into the navy Jaguar in front of her.

"Mom, look out!" Amelia said.

Josie slammed on the brakes and automatically put her arm out in front of Amelia.

"I'm okay, Mom," Amelia said. "You don't have to treat me like a baby."

"I know you're not a baby anymore," Josie said. "But you'll always be my daughter. Protecting you is a mom instinct." Always my daughter, now too my friend, she thought.

"I guess I was surprised that you mentioned Grandma's renter," Josie said.

"Why? Frank's a good dude."

"I know, but you've been kind of wrapped up in the concert lately."

"But now all the important details are settled," Amelia said. "Today at lunch, Palmer and I decided what I would absolutely, positively wear."

"Really?" Josie said. "No more changes?"

"No, this is the coolest one ever. I'm going to wear my coral skinny jeans, that white blouse you bought me, my turquoise scarf, and my new flats. Can I borrow your turquoise bracelet, Mom? Please?"

"Sure," Josie said. "It's never ridden in a limo."

Josie was relieved Amelia had finally decided on her outfit. This was her fourth choice since Ted had brought home the tickets. Amelia had modeled each one for Josie and Ted. Josie thought all the outfits looked good, but Amelia found something wrong with each one.

Her intensity was touching and amusing: Amelia picked out her concert clothes as if the band would see her in the roiling mass of shrieking tween fangirls, abandon the stage, and beg her to go out with them.

Once again, Josie silently thanked Ted for the tickets that had brought her daughter so much happiness. The hurtful pimps-and-hos party was forgotten, and so were the girls throwing it.

"I want to help Frank because you don't seem to be getting anywhere," Amelia said, "and you said jail is making him sick and I know Grandma's worried."

"All true," Josie said. "I'm stalled. I need to know where Frank's coworker Heidi lives, but I can't find her address on the Internet. Frank doesn't know it and neither does her other coworker Karen."

"Karen's the one who groomed Stuart Little?" Amelia asked.

"Right. She told me, 'I think Heidi lives in Affton. But that's the best I can do.' That puts her close to Uncle Bob's and Federhofer's Bakery, but there are a lot of houses and apartments around there.

"That's all I have, and Uncle Bob's is closed until

Monday. I'm spinning my wheels and Frank is fading fast in jail."

"I'll look for your information, Mom," Amelia said. "I'm good at finding things on the Net."

"Yes, you are. Definitely better than me."

"Tell me what I need to do." Amelia fished her iPad out of her backpack and sat up straight like an old-school secretary, ready to take dictation. Josie thought her seriousness was adorable but didn't dare say so.

"First, find out everything you can about a woman currently called Heidi, who works at Uncle Bob's." Josie spelled Heidi's last name. "She just turned eighteen last month."

"What do you mean, currently called?"

"She may have changed her name. Alyce was at Uncle Bob's memorial reception and thinks she recognized Heidi. Alyce believes Heidi is really Annabelle Lee Cody, the Persimmon Creek Slayer."

"Cool," Amelia said.

"Not really," Josie said. "Annabelle is a parent's nightmare. She killed the people who gave birth to her."

"I didn't mean that killing your parents is cool. I like the idea of tracking down a killer."

Josie didn't. *Have I made a mistake dragging Amelia into this project? She's looking for an address on the Internet,* she thought, *so there's no way Heidi could know my daughter is involved.*

"Annabelle's parents must have been pretty bad, huh?" Amelia said.

"That's what Alyce said. At least, they drank a lot and that must have been difficult for a young girl. Alyce said Annabelle lived with her drunken parents in a trailer in a little town in the Ozarks."

"Did they beat her and stuff?" Amelia said.

"I don't know," Josie said. This conversation was making her uneasy. Now I wish I wasn't turning Amelia loose on this gruesome subject, she thought.

"All I know is the family's trailer caught on fire and Annabelle escaped, but her parents were trapped inside. The police suspected she set the fire on purpose, but she was never arrested and charged. She may have changed her name and moved to the big city."

"This is the big city?" Amelia asked.

"It is if you grew up in a town with one hundred eight people. Heidi told her coworkers that she grew up in Branson, Missouri."

"The country music vacation place?"

"That one," Josie said.

"I can check that, too," Amelia said, "and see if Heidi really did live in Branson. There are some amazing free people-finder services online."

"Annabelle is a very distinctive-looking redhead, and so is Heidi. Annabelle's story got a lot of national media three years ago."

"Then there should be photos of her," Amelia said.

"I need you to do two things: Dig up stories about Annabelle and her parents' deaths. Then see if you can find anything about Heidi, especially her current address."

"Do you think Heidi killed Uncle Bob?" Josie asked.

"She's my best suspect."

"Did he drink, too?" Amelia said.

Oh boy, Josie thought. I guess she's old enough for this information. "I was told they had an affair and Bob dropped her."

"Ew. But he's, like, old," Amelia said.

"Exactly," Josie said.

"And he's married," Amelia said. "But I know that doesn't stop people. Zoe's mother has had a bunch of boyfriends and some of them were married. One of the wives came to the house and yelled at her. Zoe was really embarrassed that her mother was such a slut."

"Amelia! It's not right to judge if we don't know the circumstances."

And I put up with people making assumptions about my morals because I was a single mom, Josie thought.

"Well, you wouldn't do that," Amelia said.

"But I'm lucky I'm married to a terrific guy," Josie said. "That's all I know about Heidi and Annabelle."

"I'll start as soon as I get home," Amelia said.

"Don't worry about dinner," Josie said. "I'll make mac and cheese tonight."

"My fav!" Amelia said.

Sadly, mac and cheese was about the only dish Josie made that her daughter liked. Amelia had learned how to cook in self-defense and now enjoyed it. She took over making dinner after school. She definitely had her grandmother's talent, and Ted's lessons had burnished it.

"Uh, you aren't going to put any vegetables in my mac, are you?" Amelia asked.

Josie heard the wariness in her daughter's voice. "That was a onetime thing," she said.

"I never want to find green peas and broccoli in my mac," Amelia said, and shuddered. "That was a dirty trick."

"I know, but I wanted to see if you'd eat your vegetables. It won't happen again. I, Josie Marcus, solemnly swear that I will never, ever put vegetables in any macaroni and cheese again, so help me."

They were stopped at a red light. "That's a pinkie swear," Josie said. Mother and daughter solemnly locked little fingers to seal the deal.

"Maybe that's why Annabelle killed her parents," Amelia said.

I don't like the direction this conversation is taking, Josie thought. Time to change the subject. One Direction was definitely the right direction. "Are you wearing your hair up or down to the concert?"

"Down," Amelia said. "Like it is now, only better. I'll

have time to wash it when I get home Friday night. I can't believe it's the day after tomorrow."

Josie was at Fresno Court. She'd barely put the car in park when Amelia grabbed her backpack and sprinted for the house. She stayed upstairs while Josie started the mac and cheese and fixed a salad.

An hour later, Amelia roared down the stairs, waving a pile of papers, Harry the cat following behind. "I've got it! I've got it! Here are the stories on the Persimmon Creek Slayer."

Josie quickly paged through a stack of black-and-white printouts. The photo of the burned-out trailer was horrific: It had melted and collapsed on itself, like a tin can in a trash fire. The yard was bare dirt with a dying tree and a clothesline with a pair of women's panties on it the size of a parachute.

Another picture showed law enforcement officials combing the wreckage while two body bags were rolled to an ambulance.

A third showed Annabelle and the headline SOLE SUR-VIVOR: HOW DID SHE ESCAPE THE INFERNO?

"That's her," Josie said. "That's Heidi." Her dark hair looked almost black in the photo and her skin was ghost pale, but Josie had no doubt she was looking at a younger Heidi.

"I found her?" Amelia said.

"You certainly did, Detective," Josie said. "That's the same woman who now works at Uncle Bob's under the name Heidi."

"I couldn't find anything about Heidi living in Branson," Amelia said.

"You wouldn't if she never lived there," Josie said.

"I did background checks on both of them. Annabelle was born in Persimmon Creek in Douglas County, Missouri. She went to grade school there but dropped out when she was fourteen."

"That's when her parents died," Josie said.

"She lived with her grandmother, Arabella Taney, until she died two years later. Her obituary said she had cancer."

"So Grandma died of natural causes," Josie said.

"Could Annabelle drop out of school at fourteen?" Amelia said.

"Maybe her grandmother homeschooled her," Josie said.

"Makes sense," Amelia said. "I can guess what the local mean girls would say to her, with her parents dead like that. Mrs. Taney's will was probated and Annabelle inherited about five thousand dollars. Then Annabelle dropped off the radar.

"But six months later, Heidi got a Missouri driver's license and she was in Affton. That's the first time she showed up in any public record. Before that, I couldn't find anything about Heidi in the St. Louis area. No marriage or divorce records."

"She probably never married," Josie said.

"No bankruptcy and no property in her name."

"She might be too young for that."

"And no criminal record."

"That's good," Josie said.

"But I couldn't find any relatives," Amelia said. "No parents, grandparents, or siblings. And, Mom, here's the weird part. There's no birth record for Heidi. Not in the whole state."

"Now, that's odd," Josie said. But she suspected Heidi was really only two years old.

"I did find Heidi's address: 8413 Portman Drive, Apartment 2A."

"Amazing," Josie said.

"And here's a printout of her building from Google Earth."

Josie studied the photo of a neat brick apartment building. It looked a cut above Sharon's depressing residence. Heidi's apartment was well kept, with colonial-style black double doors and a polished brass knocker. The lawn appeared to be perfectly mowed zoysia, the city's favorite grass.

A tall maple shaded the property and well-manicured shrubs grew against the foundation.

Josie stared at those bushes. It was hard to tell in the blurry photo, but they looked like azaleas.

Chapter 30

Rich. Red. Ripe. Real.

Ted presented Josie with a fat bag of tomatoes when he came home that night.

"Ted, these are gorgeous," she said. "And so many. Where did you get them?"

Josie piled the bounty on the kitchen counter and admired her gift. The red tomatoes looked like a decorator accent in her turquoise kitchen.

"They're from Doc Cross," Ted said.

"Is he an MD or a vet?" Josie asked.

"Neither," Ted said. "Doc's an old-school hippie. He really does believe in peace and love and he drives a Magic Bus. Doc grows his own vegetables, and he's proud of his tomatoes."

"He should be," Josie said. "These smell sun warm and they're ripe, not rock hard like those supermarket mutants. Why did he give them to you?"

"I take care of his two basset hounds, Sasha and Daisy. Doc and his wife, Grace, brought the girls in today. Sasha is recovering from pancreatitis. She's doing well on her boiled-chicken-and-rice diet. Still a little snoozy, but she'll recover."

"Is that dangerous?" Josie asked.

"In dogs, it can be fatal. It's often caused by eating

bad, contaminated, or fatty food. We think Sasha may have found a pork roast in a trash can."

"What's wrong with the other dog, Daisy?" Josie asked.

"Nothing, except she's a little overweight. Daisy snagged an entire loaf of whole wheat bread that Grace left unguarded when she was unpacking groceries. Daisy and Sasha go everywhere together."

"It was nice of Doc to give you the tomatoes."

"He says I'm doing him the favor. There are even more on his vines, taunting him."

"I love tomatoes," Josie said, "and I don't like vegetables."

"Technically, they're a fruit," Amelia said. Like her cat, Harry, she had a habit of materializing, especially at dinnertime. "But the Supreme Court says tomatoes are vegetables."

"How do you know that?" Josie said.

"A paper I did for school," she said. "Back in the 1880s, there was a tariff—that's like a tax on imports and exports—to protect American vegetables. A guy imported tomatoes from a Caribbean island, and they were taxed in New York because they were vegetables. There was a big lawsuit that went up to the Supreme Court. A botanist even said that tomatoes were a fruit.

"The Supremes ruled that tomatoes may be a fruit, but we eat them like vegetables, so the foreign tomatoes got taxed."

"You find the most incredible information on the Internet, Amelia," Josie said. "She's been helping me, Ted. Amelia dug up an address in two minutes that I'd spent two days looking for."

Amelia turned pink with pleasure. "I'll do more research for you after dinner," she said. "The mac and cheese is about ready, Ted, and it's my fav."

"Are you saying I should shower so we can eat?" Ted said.

"Yes," Amelia said, pushing him playfully toward the stairs. "I'll feed the animals."

"I'll add some of these tomatoes to the salad," Josie said.

Dinner went quickly. Between bites, Amelia talked about ZabaSearch.com, the free people-finder site she'd used to locate Heidi's hard-to-find address. Then, as Josie expected, the conversation veered off to the One Direction concert and what Amelia was absolutely, positively going to wear. Ted listened patiently. He seemed to enjoy her delight in the concert.

When dinner ended, Amelia said, "Can I be excused, Mom? Please? So I can finish your research?"

"Go ahead," Josie said. "Find out what you can about Uncle Bob's wife, Candice Ellen Manning, and Angel's owner, Sharon Pancera."

Amelia was halfway upstairs, Harry following her, before Josie finished her sentence.

"You're letting Amelia out of her least favorite chore tonight," Ted said.

"Yep, she's serious about that search."

"How do you know?"

"She didn't offer to model the ultimate outfit for us," Josie said, and grinned.

This time, Amelia's search took much longer—until nearly nine o'clock. Ted and Josie were relaxing by the living-room fire with their drinks when Amelia once again roared down the stairs, Harry running after her. She danced around the living room, waving a sheaf of printouts. Harry jumped onto the couch back between Ted and Josie.

"I found them!" Amelia said. "It took some digging, but I found them both! And one is a killer!"

"Who?" Ted and Josie said, like a pair of owls.

"Bob's wife, Candice. Back in 1985, she was the driver in a hit-and-run accident. She was twenty-one and her name was Candy Ostermeyer. She'd been drinking and she ran over a lady named Patti Sue Greenslate."

"What?" Josie said. "Candice killed Miss Patti Sue?"

"Who's that?" Ted said.

"Some local celebrity with a children's show," Amelia said.

"Not some—she was major in St. Louis in the nineteen eighties," Josie said. "I was five years old in 1985, and Miss Patti Sue had *Patti Sue's Panda Party* every afternoon on Channel Seven. I watched it when I got home from kindergarten. I had a stuffed panda named Sparky, and I'd pour him tea and we'd watch TV together."

"Was it like *Sesame Street*?" Ted asked.

"More old-fashioned," Josie said. "Miss Patti Sue read stories and taught letters, numbers, colors, and kids' songs, like the teapot song."

Josie stood up and sang, "I'm a little teapot, short and stout; here is my handle"—she put one hand on her hip—"here is my spout." She held out her other arm, bent and slightly curved. "Tip me over, and pour me out."

Ted laughed. Amelia looked mortified. "Mom, that's so lame. You won't do that in front of Palmer or Emma, will you?"

Josie pretended to think. "I don't know. Maybe you'll like the second verse better. I'll sing it."

"No!" Amelia shouted.

Josie laughed. "Sorry, I got sidetracked. But Miss Patti Sue and her panda party was a big deal for St. Louis kids. We loved her. She had pretty dark hair, a sweet face, and a gentle voice. She never talked down to us. Then one day around Christmastime, she wasn't on TV anymore."

"She was killed December twenty-first as she left the TV station," Amelia said. "At four in the afternoon. Candy was coming home from an office party. She blew through the light, killed Patti Sue, and ran for it, but bystanders got her car's make and model and a partial plate number. The police arrested her that night."

"I asked Mom why my favorite show wasn't on TV the next day," Josie said. "Jane said Miss Patti Sue went away. She never said she'd died.

"I didn't realize it till I was walking past the living room on my way to the bathroom two nights later. Mom was watching the ten o'clock news. A clip from Miss Patti Sue's funeral was on. I saw her coffin piled with stuffed pandas and flowers and screamed. I cried for two days. I hope Candice was punished."

"She got five years in prison for vehicular manslaughter," Amelia said.

"Should have been life," Josie said.

"After Candice got out of jail," Amelia said, "I found only one other thing. Two years later, there's a one-paragraph announcement that she was marrying Robert Jarvis Manning of Summerdale. The story said she was a groomer at Bob's Kennels."

"That was the name of Uncle Bob's business before he inherited it from his father," Josie said. "Some people think Candice is the brains of the operation. But now I know why she stays out of the limelight. She's not shy. Marrying Bob allowed her to change her name.

"But thirtysomething St. Louisans—and their parents— would know she killed our beloved Miss Patti Sue. No wonder she hides her face under those big hats and never wants to meet customers at the day-care center."

"That's all I can find about Candice," Amelia said. "You already saw her TV interview after Uncle Bob died. And here's her address in Summerdale, along with a Google Earth photo of the house."

Candice lived in a handsome white-brick ranch house with black shutters and a black door. The sidewalk was flanked by evergreens trimmed into boxy shapes. Flowering shrubs were massed against the foundation. Josie thought she saw ball-shaped hydrangea blooms and frilly azaleas, but lately, she'd been seeing azaleas everywhere.

"You did amazing work," Josie said.

"I didn't find out much about Sharon Pancera," Amelia said. "She was a high school soccer star. In August 2000, she was on Channel Seven because she locked her Pomeranian in her car when she ran into a drugstore to pick up a prescription."

"Angel would have been about a year old then," Josie said.

"It was a heat wave and a man saw the little dog locked in the car. He called Channel Seven. They were doing a Dog Days of Summer Safety Campaign, and they sent a nearby truck to the scene. The man broke the car window with a tire iron while the TV station taped it. Sharon came screaming out of the drugstore, shouting that she'd only been inside five minutes.

"Her lawyer got the station to apologize and even pay for her broken car window. And that's it, until 2012, when Sharon won an employee-of-the-month award from Fenway's. She works in the lingerie department."

Ted and Josie applauded.

"Excellent work," Josie said. "And now it's bedtime."

Amelia kissed Ted and Josie good night and hoisted Harry onto her shoulder. "One more day," she said. "I can't wait."

"Your daughter is amazing," Ted said, when Amelia was upstairs.

"She really knows her way around the Internet," Josie said. "I can't believe Candice killed Miss Patti Sue. She deserved more punishment than five years in prison."

"Well, she did get life with Uncle Bob," Ted said.

"Not quite," Josie said. "She escaped that sentence. That's why Candice killed her husband."

"Yesterday, you thought Heidi was the killer because Bob dumped her," Ted said.

"But Heidi could move on if she wanted," Josie said. "Candice was trapped. She'd booted Bob out of the house, but she couldn't get rid of him. He knew her secret, and if he ever revealed it, she'd be the most hated woman in St. Louis.

"Killing him was the only way to set herself free."

Chapter 31

"Alyce!" Josie said when she called her friend at nine o'clock Thursday morning. "I know who killed Uncle Bob."

"Heidi," Alyce said. "You told me."

"No," she said, "not her. His wife, Candice."

"You're back to her again?" Alyce said. "You keep seesawing between those two."

"But now I know why Candice did it: She's already a killer. She ran down Miss Patti Sue in a hit-and-run accident in 1985."

"Who's Miss Patti Sue?" Alyce asked.

"St. Louis's answer to *Sesame Street* when I was a kid. Candice served five years for vehicular manslaughter, then worked as a groomer at the kennel owned by Bob's father. I think that's where she met Bob. He built the business after his father died."

"Why would she kill Bob if he was the public face of the business?"

"It's the only way Candice could get free of him," Josie said. "They hated one another. The whole staff knew it. But Uncle Bob knew her secret. She couldn't appear in public because she'd killed a beloved St. Louis celebrity.

"Candice was stuck with an unfaithful hound. She'd managed to force him out of their house into his own apartment, but if she killed him she'd be rid of him for good. Then Candice could sell the business, take the money, and stay out of the public eye."

"Okay," Alyce said, drawing out the word. "But I still don't see why you turned against Heidi as Bob's killer."

"She's young and could be pretty," Josie said. "Candice is fiftysomething and trapped. Heidi can move on."

"But she didn't," Alyce said. "Heidi's still working at Uncle Bob's."

"Maybe she was hoping to get him back," Josie said. "Or quietly looking for another job. Besides, what would Heidi gain by killing Bob?"

"Revenge," Alyce said. "That old toad dumped her for another woman—Angel's owner, Sharon. Now, there's someone with a reason to kill Bob. If he broke Bruiser's leg with a spiteful kick, I'd want to kill him."

"Sharon has her own secrets," Josie said. "Amelia did an online search and found out that Sharon got into a tiff with Channel Seven when Angel was just a puppy. She ran into a store and left her dog locked in her car on a hot summer day. A man broke the car window and Channel Seven taped it. They made a big deal out of it."

"That's terrible," Alyce said.

"Luckily, Angel wasn't hurt," Josie said. "Sharon was smart. She hired a lawyer and the attorney got the TV station to back off. They broadcast an apology and even paid for the broken car window."

"How long ago was that incident?"

"Fourteen years," Josie said.

"Ancient history," Alyce said. "A few days ago, Bob was still having an affair with Sharon. He hurt her dog and she murdered him. Bob died slowly and painfully. Looks like Sharon got revenge."

"No, she *will* get revenge," Josie said. "Legally. Sharon is going to wallop Uncle Bob's Doggy Day Camp in the wallet. She told me she's suing the place. She's already lining up witnesses, including Karen and Ted.

"Sharon needs money, Alyce. She lives in a run-down apartment in Summerdale, works at a department store, and drives an old car. Heaven knows how much she spends on Angel's day care, but that's not cheap.

"A smart lawyer will file a lawsuit before Candice sells Uncle Bob's. The lawyer will know bad publicity could cripple the sale. Candice will settle out of court to avoid it."

"You have good candidates and good theories," Alyce said, "but no proof. How are you going to convince Detective Dobbs that someone else killed Bob?"

"I'm not going to," Josie said. "I'll let Frank's lawyer do it. Amelia dug up a lot of information about Heidi, Sharon, and Candice on the Internet. She even gave me Google Earth photos of their streets. Candice lives on a rich street in Summerdale. Heidi's street is nicely in the middle, and Sharon's is on the skids.

"But they all have one thing in common."

"What?" Alyce said.

"Every neighborhood has its own Mrs. Mueller."

"And how will you find her?" Alyce asked.

"Easy. She'll be watching her neighbors. I'll look for the twitching curtain or the miniblind slat raised by one careful finger—the telltale signs of a snoop at work. Then I'll get her started by saying the women are applying for a new job and I need background information. They'll see it as their duty to tell me everything they know. Then I'll knock on my suspects' doors for a quick chat."

"But the local gossip will see you do that," Alyce said.

"Both Sharon and Heidi live in apartment buildings, and Sharon told me about Mrs. Meyer, her neighbor next door. I can say I'm interviewing more neighbors in their buildings. As for Candice, we're clients of Uncle Bob's. I'll pay my respects for her recent loss."

"Still TSTL, Josie."

"What's that?"

"Too Stupid To Live," Alyce said. "I hate those movies where the woman says, 'Gee, I think I hear a serial killer in the barn. I'm going out to take a look.' Then she goes outside and he hacks her to death with a hatchet. You are not confronting a killer by yourself. You need backup, but I can't leave home at this stage."

"Oh Lord, I was so wrapped up in this investigation," Josie said, "I forgot to ask about you. How are you feeling?"

"Still living on ginger ale and soda crackers," Alyce said. "I'm not doing much cooking. Even the smell of food makes me queasy. Jake doesn't mind that I can't fix his dinner. He brings home take-out from our favorite restaurants. He's ecstatic. So am I. This stage won't last, Josie. It will be over soon.

"But if you insist on this harebrained scheme, you'll make me sick with worry. I can't risk that in my condition."

"Alyce Bohannon! Are you hitting me with the pregnancy card?"

"I'll do whatever I have to if it slaps some sense into you," Alyce said. "You're a mother with a tween daughter. You have a husband. You're not going off on this crazy mission."

"But—"

"The only way I'll allow it is if you take me with you," Alyce said.

"How can I do that?" Josie said.

"Use your cell phone. Call me when you get to the first house and keep your cell phone on in your pocket. That way I can hear what's happening. If there's a problem—if you scream or I hear that you're being threatened, I'll call the police on my landline."

"If I see the local busybody first, she'll be watching me, too. That will make me doubly safe. It could work," Josie said.

"It will have to work," Alyce said. "Otherwise, I'll call

Ted and your mother and you'll have to deal with both of them."

"Deal," Josie said. "I'll start with Heidi, because I have a legit reason to see her. I'll ask if she'll make organic treats for Ted's clinic. Sharon will be next. She doesn't like Candice or Heidi. She'll be more likely to give me the real dirt on them. Then I'll finish with the riskiest choice, Candice. By the time we get to Candice's house, we'll have perfected the monitoring system. It's nine forty. It will take me about half an hour to get to Heidi's apartment. I'll call you when I'm there."

Josie changed into a long-sleeve blue shirt with a button-down pocket, navy pants, and black flats. She threw a handful of sandwich-sized ziplock bags in her purse, in case she came across any azaleas. Picking a couple of azalea leaves for Renzo wouldn't hurt and might help. Then she got a clipboard and a duplicate mystery-shopping questionnaire. She studied herself in the mirror. She looked professional.

It was another gorgeous fall day, sunny and spicy smelling, with a china blue sky. The kind of day where nothing bad could possibly happen. Even the traffic was light on the trip to Heidi's apartment.

Josie dismissed Alyce's fears as the fancies of a pregnant woman. I'm glad my friend cares about me, she thought, but I went through a jittery stage when I was carrying Amelia. I can humor my friend.

Josie turned off Gravois onto Portman Drive, a long, curving street with well-kept apartments and homes shaded by tall old trees. She slowed down until she spotted the huge red-and-gold maple sheltering Heidi's apartment. Josie looked for Heidi's little black Neon. It was parked on the street. Good. Heidi was probably home.

She saw a postal service truck parked three houses up, the mail carrier making deliveries. Otherwise, there was no one on Portman Drive. Josie parked across the street from Heidi's apartment and sat there for two minutes, listening to her car's engine cool and looking for the telltale flutter of curtains or tilt of the blinds that signaled a nosy neighbor was watching.

There it was. The house next door to Heidi's building. The neat one-story brick had a FOR SALE sign with an UNDER CONTRACT sticker. The slat on a miniblind in the front window moved slightly. It was quick, but Josie had learned the subtle signs of spying after years of Mrs. M's surveillance.

Next she called Alyce. "I'm at Heidi's. The local Mrs. M lives next door and her house is for sale. I'm going to knock on her door."

She buttoned her cell phone into her shirt pocket and left her car door unlocked and the keys in the ignition in case she had to make a quick getaway, then picked up her clipboard.

Josie didn't have to knock. A big-boned woman with spiked gray hair met her at the door.

"If you're looking to buy the house, the contract went through this morning," she said.

Josie thought she caught a bit of a country twang in the woman's voice. She was dressed in a no-nonsense outfit: a man's blue shirt, jeans, and walking shoes.

"Actually, I'm not," Josie said. "I wanted to ask you a few questions about your neighbor, Heidi. She's applying for a job with the county and I'm doing a background check on her."

"I figured she'd need a new job after Uncle Bob died," the woman said. "My real estate agent is on her way over to put up a SOLD sign. Even when this house was under contract people tried to buy it."

She sounded proud of that. "Marilyn will be here in about fifteen minutes. Come in and we can talk until she arrives. My name is Trudy. I've never met a private detective before."

You still haven't, Josie thought, and prayed that Trudy wouldn't ask for identification.

Trudy's living room looked as if she was still expecting potential house buyers. The colonial-style furniture was freshly dusted and the blue braided rug was vacuumed. The room smelled of lemon polish and coffee.

"Have a seat on the couch," she said. "Coffee?"

"No, thanks," Josie said. "I have a lot of work to do today. How is Heidi as a neighbor?"

"Quiet. Friendly enough. We're not friends—she's never been in here—but she always waves when she sees me. No loud parties or men over at her place. Not that I've ever seen, anyway. If it wasn't for her past, she'd be the perfect neighbor."

"Her past?" Josie said.

Trudy lowered her voice. "Is this for a job in law enforcement?" she asked.

"I can't say," Josie said.

"Well, it's my duty to tell you what I know."

Shades of Mrs. M, Josie thought.

"My nephew is with the sheriff's office down in Ozark County. Do you remember the Persimmon Creek Slayer?"

"Vaguely," Josie said.

Trudy's voice was eager now, her eyes brighter. She couldn't wait to deliver this gossip bomb.

"About three years ago a trailer caught on fire in the little town of Persimmon Creek. It wasn't in my nephew's county, but everyone in law enforcement down there knew the story. The parents died and the daughter escaped. Their bedroom door was jammed.

"Now, nothing was ever proven, mind you, and no charges were filed, but the local cops were pretty sure the daughter did it. Locked the door on her folks, started the fire, and lit out. They never found any evidence against her, but the local sheriff thought the parents deserved it. They were trash. They drank like fish.

"The investigators found out that poor girl showed up at school with bruises on her arms and legs, but nobody at school reported her abuse. The investigators figured she'd had enough and took matters into her own hands. Probably saved her young life.

"She lived with her grandmother until the old woman died; then the girl left the area. Changed her name from Annabelle Lee Cody to Heidi. My nephew 'bout fell off this porch the first time he saw her. Recognized her right off. Granted, she's been a model citizen, and nothing but nice to me, but I have to tell you I'm relieved to be moving away. It bothered my conscience, selling this house to someone with a double killer next door, but Marilyn—she's my real estate agent—said I'm not required by law to disclose that, especially since Heidi was never arrested."

She looked out the window. "That's Marilyn's car in the drive now."

Josie took the hint. "You've been very helpful," she said, and hurried out the door. She waved to the real estate agent, then waited until Marilyn was inside and Trudy was busy talking to her before she checked in with Alyce.

"I heard it all," her friend said. "My suspicions about Heidi were confirmed. She is Annabelle Lee."

"I'm going in now," Josie said.

"Be careful," Alyce said.

"I will, but Trudy will be at my side in a flash if Heidi tries anything," Josie said.

She buttoned her cell phone back into her shirt pocket again. Then Josie hurried up the sidewalk to Heidi's apartment building, with two fat azalea bushes by the neatly swept front porch. The door was unlocked. The lobby had chic gray walls with a checkerboard floor. The directory said Heidi lived in the first apartment up the stairs.

Josie climbed the curved stairs to the second floor, surprised by how easily she could walk into a well-maintained building. But at the landing, the hall to the second-floor apartments was blocked by a black door with a frosted-glass window. Josie tried the handle.

Locked.

Rats! Josie knocked on the door.

Nothing. She thought she saw some shadowy movement through the frosted window. She froze, then decided it was her imagination.

She was about to knock again when the door swung open.

Heidi, skin pale, red hair flaring, dressed in black, held an eight-inch butcher knife.

Josie screamed.

Chapter 32

The sun gleamed off the knife in Heidi's hand, and Josie backed away.

Heidi looked at her hand and laughed. "I'm sorry," she said. "Did I scare you? We got a stack of free papers delivered and I was trying to cut the plastic strip that holds them together so I could read one."

Josie relaxed. "Scared? No, I wasn't scared, just a little startled." Her voice was still high with fear. "But I'm fine now. Absolutely fine."

She repeated the words so Alyce would hear them.

"You look familiar," Heidi said. "I saw you at Uncle Bob's, didn't I?"

"Yes," Josie said.

"Why are you here?"

Josie watched Heidi put the butcher knife inside a folded newspaper and leave it on the mat by an apartment door.

"Come downstairs with me while I take these papers to the lobby," Heidi said.

Josie followed her down the curved staircase. The sun turned Heidi's hair into dark flame, and her body was willowy in the black T-shirt and tight jeans.

Josie watched her drop the stack of papers on a black marble table in the lobby. She was not going into Heidi's apartment. She didn't like that knife. Annabelle Lee

Cody, possible self-made orphan, had a black car and a dark past.

"I took my mom's dog to Uncle Bob's," Josie said. "A shih tzu, Stuart Little. He loved your treats. My husband owns a vet clinic in Maplewood and sells some pet supplies. I thought your organic cookies would make a good addition."

"Oh, I wish I could," Heidi said. "But those treats are Bob's special recipe and I signed a contract not to disclose the recipe or make treats for any other facility."

"I understand," Josie said, hoping her relief didn't show. "Thanks for considering the idea. I should go. Bye."

She was out the door, quickly pocketing two leaves from the azalea bushes by the door. Josie sprinted for her car and drove to the closest shopping center, where she parked near a dry cleaner, unbuttoned her shirt pocket, and fished out her cell phone. "Alyce," she said, "I'm okay."

"I heard," Alyce said. "You had me worried for a minute. I'm glad I didn't call the cops."

"Me, too," Josie said. "I'm going to Sharon's apartment now."

"I'm confused," Alyce said. "Which one is Sharon?"

"Angel's owner. The skinny lady who had the affair with Bob. She left her dog with him at his apartment at the Shady Rest. That's where Angel got away from him and she peed on his foot when he caught her. Bob kicked Angel and broke her leg. Then he took the dog to the day-care center and tried to pretend she wasn't hurt. Karen the groomer made Uncle Bob get Angel to the vet."

"Right," Alyce said.

"Sharon's hard up for money and wants to sue Bob's estate for half a million bucks. I want to ask her about Heidi and Candice."

"Josie, wait!" Alyce said. "Did you say Bob kicked Angel at his apartment, not at the day-care center?"

"Yes," Josie said. "I've gotta run. I'll drive to Sharon's, talk with the local busybody, then ask Sharon a few questions and go. She's five minutes away."

Josie switched off the phone. A minor fender bender caused a traffic delay and it was closer to ten minutes when she reached Sharon's street. This morning, in the brilliant sunlight, Josie could see that the entire block was slipping. She noticed peeling paint, loose gutters, and lawns that needed raking. One house had lost an ornamental shutter on a front window.

She saw a handful of battered old cars and pickups parked on the street or in driveways, but no sign of Sharon's junker with the coat-hanger antenna.

Josie parked four houses down from Sharon's apartment, in front of the nicest house on the street, a white rambler with green shutters. Its paint was fresh and the lawn was mowed and raked. A safe place to observe the street, she decided.

She turned off her car and sat there, watching. A trash truck rumbled down the street. A stray dog trotted along the sidewalk, inspecting the shrubbery. Then Josie saw it. The ruffled curtains fluttered in the front window of the rambler. White sheers crisscrossed in an old-fashioned style. What were they called? Priscilla curtains. A sweet, homey style.

Maybe the neighbor will invite me in for a soothing chat and a cup of coffee, Josie thought. In her mind, she saw the woman as gray haired and grandmotherly, with a generous build and a flowered apron. Josie could practically smell the cinnamon in her country kitchen. This would be a relaxing interlude after her scary encounter with Heidi.

Josie called her backup. "Alyce," she said, "I'm going to talk to a neighbor four doors down. She's peeking out her curtains. She's the local gossip."

"Be careful," Alyce said.

"Don't worry," Josie said. "She lives in a pretty house with ruffled curtains. She'll be a sweetie. I've got my clipboard and my excuse ready. I'll knock on her door and ask about Sharon."

Josie didn't get a chance to knock. The front door swung open before she was on the porch. A woman shrieked, "What the hell are you doing? I saw you parked out there, talking on your phone. Are you casing the joint?"

"What?" Josie said. Visions of coffee and cinnamon vanished, along with her fantasy of the sweet older woman.

This one had to be at least seventy, and so scrawny Josie wanted to feed her. Her dyed red hair was bristling with curlers and clashed horribly with her magenta satin robe. She held a pancake turner as if she wanted to swat Josie.

"We've had two break-ins on this street this month," Ms. Magenta said. "What are you doing lurking on this street?"

"I, uh, I'm looking for information about your neighbor, Sharon Pancera. She's applying for a job with the county."

"And you want a recommendation from me? Well, you won't get it. She's weird and sneaky. I caught her red-handed."

"What did she do?"

"Tried to steal the leaves off my azalea. That one right there." Ms. Magenta pointed at the trimmed bush near the porch with her pancake turner.

"She was trying to pull off a handful when I caught her. It wasn't even flowering. Azaleas are hard enough to grow. Skinny Minnie was about to help herself to a handful of leaves last week when I chased her away. Told her I'd call the police." She waved the pancake turner.

"You did?" Josie said, hopefully. "What day?"

"What day? Do you think I keep a diary and write,

'Today a crazy woman got it into her head to steal my azalea leaves'?"

"Please," Josie said. "It's important. We need this information to evaluate her for the job."

"It was the same day I won fifty dollars playing bingo at St. Mark's. A week ago Tuesday."

The day Bob was murdered, Josie thought.

"Oh, thank you, thank you," Josie said. "You're sure it was Sharon?"

"Do I look like I'm blind? I know my own neighbor. I chased her away. She's got her own azaleas in her backyard. I told her to take those leaves and she did. She got into her car with a bunch in a ziplock bag."

"That's wonderful," Josie said. Sharon had killed Bob and this neighbor saw her with the poisonous leaves. She had a witness.

"May I have your name and contact information for my report?" Josie asked.

"Certainly. It's Darla Combes. You know the address, and this is my phone number."

She recited it, then said, "Maybe you can tell me what's so wonderful about my azaleas that Sharon wanted them."

"Who knows," Josie said. "But I appreciate your help."

"Don't let her get that job," Ms. Magenta said. "She's a kleptomaniac."

"If you see me on my cell phone, I'm reporting back to my office," Josie said. "Then I'll talk to some neighbors in her apartment building."

And that should get you off my back, Ms. Combes, Josie thought, as she hurried back to her car. She was breathless with excitement when she talked to Alyce.

"Did you hear that? I have the proof and an eyewitness, Alyce. But why would Sharon kill Bob when she was going to make a fortune suing him?"

"She can't sue him," Alyce said. "He's dead."

"But she can sue his estate," Josie said.

"No, I checked the law. Sharon can't sue Uncle Bob's estate because he hurt her dog. Under common law, vicarious liability imposes liability on one person for a tortious act committed by another."

"Huh?" Josie said.

"Sorry. I used to monitor Jake's classes when he was in law school and I can still fall into legal-speak. Bob's widow can say the business isn't liable for Bob's actions because he was performing personal activities outside the tasks of pet day care."

"That's for sure," Josie said.

"I mean," Alyce said, sounding annoyed, "the accident didn't happen at the day-care center, when Sharon could expect her dog would be protected and cared for. Instead, she was late for work after a hookup with Uncle Bob and gave him her dog at his apartment."

"So Sharon can't sue his estate?"

"Under common law, there is no survival of tort actions. I looked this up online. I won't give you the actual case—well, it's right here, I might as well—*DeLong Versus the County of Erie*."

"Alyce!" Josie said. "Speak English, please."

"Sharon can't get that half-million-dollar settlement," Alyce said. "The day-care center has already paid the dog's major vet bills. That's it. Candice might give her a couple thousand to go away, but there's no pot of gold at the end of this lawsuit."

"Then I really need these leaves," Josie said. "It's perfectly safe. I'm not going after Sharon. I'll take the leaves to Renzo Fischer and let him handle the rest of the investigation: He can test them for DNA and his investigator can interview Darla Combes. The azaleas are in the backyard at Sharon's apartment and she's not home. I'm putting you in my pocket and collecting the leaves."

"No!" Alyce cried, but Josie buttoned the phone into

her pocket while Alyce was protesting, and looked again for Sharon's car. No sign of it. She had to get into Sharon's backyard, but an eight-foot privacy fence with a sturdy lock barred the way. The only way into the backyard was through the apartment building's front door, down the hall, and out the back.

The door was open. Josie raced through the dingy lobby into the backyard, a narrow strip of zoysia with a birdbath and azaleas banked against the double garage.

Yes!

Josie pulled off a fat handful of leaves, confident she had the proof that would free Frank. She took a few seconds to label a ziplock with Sharon's name, then stuffed the leaves inside. Time to get out of there.

Josie was about to run when she heard a small dripping noise in the garage. She tiptoed back and looked in the window. She saw a dusty blue Ford Fiesta and Sharon's big square beater, leaking a green puddle like bug's blood.

Uh-oh.

Sharon's home, she thought. She must have arrived when I was talking to her neighbor, Darla. I've got to get out of here, fast.

Josie shoved the bag of azalea leaves into her purse and sprinted up the backyard sidewalk, into the dreary lobby. She ran straight into Sharon, face red with fury, skinny arms fisted on her bony hips.

"What are you doing sneaking around my apartment building?" Sharon said. "And why are you stealing azalea leaves?"

"I wasn't stealing," Josie said, backing around Sharon to get a clear shot at the front door. "I was just borrowing a couple."

"Borrowing, huh?" Sharon held out her thin hand. "Then give them back."

"No!" Josie said, pulling her purse closer. "They're evidence. You killed Uncle Bob."

"They can't be evidence," Sharon said. "He ate the evidence." Sharon doesn't know about plant DNA, Josie thought.

Josie tried an end run around her, but Sharon threw the stack of newspapers at her. Josie dodged them and reached for the abandoned golf umbrella. She opened it as Sharon lobbed the dusty silk plant at her. The plant bounced off the umbrella, causing the ribs to cave in, and the fake plant rolled across the lobby.

Sharon picked up the now empty straight-backed chair and swung it at Josie. She narrowly missed colliding with the chair. Josie closed the crippled umbrella and swatted Sharon with it.

The near miss made Sharon even madder. She swung the heavy chair at Josie's head this time. Josie slid under the table and the chair smashed into the mirror. It shattered into lethal stalactites.

Sharon picked up a long, thin glass icicle and plunged it into Josie's thigh, ripping through her pant leg. Josie spun away, pain burning down her leg. Sharon ignored the cut on her own hand from the glass and stabbed Josie in the upper arm.

Josie screamed and ducked back under the table. "You killed Bob," she said.

"He deserved it," Sharon said, eyes shooting sparks.

From her slender shelter, Josie scoped out the scene. Sharon, blood running down her cut hand, was stalking the lobby and talking to herself—or to Josie. It was hard to tell. Her eyes were wide and crazy and her hair was wild. She clutched the mirror dagger and didn't seem to notice it was slicing her own hand.

"He hurt my baby," Sharon said. "He thought he could get away with paying me two thousand dollars, but that wouldn't even buy me a car. Well, he's dead, and he was in as much pain as my Angel. I only wish he'd suffered longer."

Josie looked frantically for a weapon. The mirror fragments near her hands were too small. The shattered chair was tossed in the opposite corner, next to the plant. The floor was littered with newspapers and tiny mirror fragments. Josie's only available weapon was the broken umbrella.

I have to crawl to the front door, she thought. I hope Alyce has called the police. She thought she heard tires screech and car doors slam. Now was the time to run for freedom.

Josie shot out from under the table while Sharon mumbled to herself, but Angel's owner leaped on her. Josie fell on her back, and Sharon jumped on Josie's chest, pinning her down with her wiry body. She raised the mirror dagger over her head, ready to plunge it into Josie's neck, when two police officers burst through the door.

"Drop it!" one uniform said. "Drop the weapon."

Sharon stared at him defiantly as the second cop grabbed her bloody hand and the dagger shattered on the floor.

Chapter 33

"There they are, officers," Darla Combes howled. "Those two! Trying to kill each other! You caught them red-handed."

Sharon's neighbor in the magenta satin robe, minus the pancake turner, was screeching behind the police officers, her curlers wobbling with outrage.

Josie and Sharon were both red-handed. Sharon's hands were slippery with her own blood, from grasping the mirror dagger. Josie had small cuts on her hands, arms, and back from the broken mirror fragments, and long slashes, one on her arm and the other on her upper thigh. Thanks to her now-ruined pants, her leg wasn't sliced as badly as it could have been.

"They were making such a ruckus, I could hear them next door," Darla said. "That's why I called you."

A frantic Alyce had also called the police, then Renzo Fischer, and finally, Josie's mother. An hour later, Alyce herself arrived at Sharon's apartment, pale with worry, but Josie could also see her pregnant friend was happy.

"Thank you for calling everyone," Josie said.

"I called Ted, too," Alyce said. "The receptionist said he's in emergency surgery, but she'll give him the message as soon as she can."

"I'm fine," Josie said.

"He needs to see for himself," Alyce said. "You look beat up to me."

The responding officers moved the circus outside onto the lawn. It took several hours to sort out what happened. Renzo's arrival helped.

The small lawyer with the white hat, gray suit, and silver bolo tie looked as colorful in South County as he did in downtown Clayton.

"Ms. Marcus is my investigator, Officers," Renzo said. "As an employee, her work product regarding the Franklin Hyzy–Uncle Bob Manning investigation is confidential. I'd like to speak with her a moment."

Josie sat on the bumper of Renzo's black Mercedes and quickly told him what she'd been doing. "I have samples of all the leaves in my purse," she said. "It's somewhere in the lobby of this apartment building."

"Good work," he said. "You are employed as my investigator for now. I'm firing that other one from this case. He was worthless as tits on a bull. You'll be paid his regular rate."

"Wow!" Josie said, and then the yard started spinning. "I feel dizzy." She clung to the edge of the bumper with a gory hand.

"I don't think that's because of my offer," he said. "You need medical attention. The police can interview you later. The ambulance is here."

The paramedics cleaned Josie's wounds, removed six glass splinters with tweezers, and recommended stitches. Renzo said Josie needed to go to the hospital immediately.

Jane had quietly snagged Josie's purse out of the wrecked lobby. Josie marveled that her mother's age seemed to make her invisible to the police. Now Alyce and Jane paced the sidewalk away from the investigation. Josie's mom had her daughter's purse tucked under her arm.

When Josie was loaded into the ambulance, both women ran over to see her. "I'm going with you," Jane said, and Josie could tell by the set of her mother's jaw there was no point arguing with her. "I'll follow the ambulance in my car."

"But someone has to pick up Amelia at school," Josie said.

"I'll do that," Alyce said.

"Thanks," Josie said. "If you want, you can drop her off at the clinic. She likes helping there. And please ask Renzo what he wants to do about the leaves in my purse. I'm going to Summerdale General."

Josie was slightly disappointed she didn't get a siren with her ride. She expected—and had—a long wait in the ER. Jane wore herself out pacing and saying, "I shouldn't have asked you to do this, Josie. It's all my fault."

By two o'clock, Josie's arm was numb and painted with orange Betadine. The six stitches didn't hurt, but the pulling sensation was creepy. A newly hatched doctor had patiently extracted more shards of mirror and said he'd be right back to close the wound on her leg with butterfly bandages.

That's when Charlene, Renzo's motherly office assistant, found Josie in the ER cubicle. Charlene took the labeled bags of azalea leaves in Josie's purse. "These will go for plant DNA analysis this afternoon," she said with her sweet Texas twang. "The police will take your statement on Saturday, at ten a.m. at your home. Mr. Fischer said he will be present and you're too sick to be interviewed before then.

"Mr. Fischer said to tell you that your attacker, Sharon Pancera, has been arrested for first-degree assault—that's a felony in Missouri. He's working on getting her charged with the first-degree murder of Uncle Bob."

Jane burst into tears, and Charlene patted Jane's back and handed her a tissue. "Now, don't you worry, Mrs.

Marcus," she said. "That nice Mr. Hyzy is innocent. It's just gonna take a couple of days to free him. The sooner we get the DNA for these plants, the better."

"See, Mom?" Josie said. "It was worth it."

"Your friend Alyce was a big help, Josie," Charlene said. "She overheard the altercation with Sharon Pancera in the lobby on her cell phone. That was real smart of you to keep your phone on when that woman attacked you. She heard her confess to killing Uncle Bob."

"It wasn't smart of Josie to confront that woman alone," Jane said.

"Well, all's well that ends well," Charlene said. "And it will free Mr. Hyzy. I have to go now. You get well, Josie, you hear?"

At ten minutes after four, a worried, rumpled Ted ran into the emergency entrance of Summerdale General Hospital and found Josie in a wheelchair, being wheeled to the curb by a strong young woman. An exhausted Jane was at her side.

Josie wore scrubs. Her arm was bandaged and the Betadine dabs on the small cuts on her neck and face looked like orange measles. She greeted Ted with a happy smile.

"Ted! You shouldn't have come," she said. "Your work is important."

"Not as important as you," he said, kissing her gently on a spot with no cuts.

"Alyce said you had emergency surgery this morning. How's the patient?"

"I think the cat's going to make it," he said. "He was hit by a truck. Dr. Chris and Laura have everything under control at the clinic. I'm here to take you home."

"Ted, why don't you drive Josie," Jane said. "I'd like to go home and rest."

"Come with us for dinner," Ted said.

"Thank you, but I'm tired. Josie, you took a huge

risk," Jane said. "I'm glad it worked. If anything had happened to you, I would have never forgiven myself."

Jane's face was as gray as her hair, and she looked her age as she walked to her car.

"Poor Mom," Josie said. "I wish she wouldn't take this so hard."

"When your child hurts, you feel her pain," Ted said. "You also feel helpless. As a mother, you know that. How are you?"

"A little sore," she said. "The pain shot's wearing off. But the crisis is almost over, Ted. If Frank goes free, I'm glad I took the risk."

She yawned. "Where's Amelia?"

"Alyce left her at the clinic and she's helping Dr. Chris. I'm picking up her and the animals. How about pizza for dinner and then you go to bed?"

"Sounds like a plan," Josie said, and stifled another yawn.

Ted parked his orange Mustang in the clinic lot, and Amelia ran out with Festus and Marmalade. The three piled into the backseat. "Dr. Chris said you caught Uncle Bob's killer, Mom, and there was a big fight with blood and everything. That is so cool."

Josie didn't want to glamorize her role in Sharon's capture. "Sharon hasn't been charged with Uncle Bob's murder yet," she said. "And it was more a scuffle than a fight."

"But you got stitches," Amelia said. "I'm texting Palmer, Emma, and Bailey. Nobody else's mother catches killers. They shop and go to lunch."

Josie let her daughter celebrate her triumph. She drifted off to sleep for the rest of the short drive home, then ate a slice of pepperoni pizza. That's all she remembered until the alarm woke her Friday morning.

"Ouch!" Josie said when she sat up.

"Go back to sleep," Ted said. "I'll take Amelia to school." Josie heard Amelia say, "Today's the day!" and then she fell back to sleep. When the pain woke her up, she knew she'd been asleep for hours. From the slanting shadows, she guessed it was afternoon. Harry was sleeping at the foot of her bed. Josie sat up and took a pain pill.

Her mother arrived at her bedside with a folding tray. "It's two thirty," Jane said. "I've brought you lunch."

Josie tried not to wince, but the cuts hurt today. Jane plumped Josie's pillows, then set the tray on the bed.

Josie inhaled. "Delicious. Hot coffee, homemade chicken salad, and cinnamon coffeecake. Thanks, Mom."

She devoured her lunch while Jane smiled in approval.

"Any word on Frank?" Josie asked.

"Not yet, but Renzo says Frank looks so much better since he found out Sharon killed Bob. He has hope now, Josie, thanks to you. I'm glad you ate your lunch."

"I need to pick up Amelia," Josie said.

"I'm doing that," Jane said. "You're not driving on pain pills. You go back to sleep."

"I want to be awake for Amelia's big night," Josie said.

While Jane was gone, Josie gingerly got out of bed. As she walked, the stiffness left her. She found her turquoise bracelet and left it in Amelia's room and laid out the "absolutely, positively final" outfit. She felt better after she washed, dressed, and combed her hair.

She was sitting in the living room when Amelia dashed through. "Hi, Mom, gotta get ready," she said.

At 5:10, Amelia raced downstairs in a swirl of coral and turquoise, brown hair shining, eyes aglow. That dreadful party didn't hurt my girl, Josie thought. She's alive with hope and happiness.

The limo arrived at five fifteen, white, sleek, and shining, like the promise of a bright future. A uniformed chauffeur opened the door and black-haired Bailey waved to her friend.

Amelia was gone. Josie waited on the living room couch, cell phone at hand, praying that it wouldn't ring.

Ted and his menagerie came home at six. Jane had fixed a light supper and Josie ate in a trance, waiting, hoping that her phone wouldn't ring.

When Jane left at eight, Josie turned on the porch light and left it on for Amelia. She knew tonight was the start of a new era. Until Amelia left home for good, Josie would hold a vigil whenever her daughter went out at night, waiting for her to come home and turn off the porch light. As Josie's mother had done before her.

"You look sleepy," Ted said. "Why don't you go up to bed? I'll call you when the limo arrives."

"I have to know she's okay, Ted," she said. "She can't have another disappointment."

"She won't," he said. "Trust me."

Josie did, but she stayed on the couch, her cell phone beside her. She watched it like a ticking time bomb.

It didn't ring.

Then at midnight, her tween Cinderella returned. The white limo was nearly as long as their driveway. The chauffeur opened the door, and Amelia hopped out. Josie heard thank-yous, good-byes, and giggles, and knew everything was all right.

Amelia burst through the door like a whirlwind, juggling a T-shirt, a program, a small gold box, and a champagne bottle.

"Mom! Ted! It was awesome. It was so cool. It started at six thirty and finished around ten thirty. One D came on about eight. They played almost every song on their album and answered, like, three questions on Twitter. It was so much fun, and it didn't feel that long at all."

She paused to take a breath and held up her loot. "Emma bought us these cool One D T-shirts, and Palmer got us each our own program, and Bailey's dad gave us each a box of Godiva chocolates and a bottle of sparkling white grape juice, which looks like champagne."

"Yes, it does," Josie said, and now, at last, she relaxed. Her daughter was safe and there had been no drinking.

"But it gets cooler, Mom," Amelia said. "When we got out of our limo"—Josie smiled at that, "our limo"—"Honey Butcher, the Channel Seven anchor, was there. She interviewed us and asked where we went to school and we said Barrington.

"Now everyone at school will see us. We're rock stars!"

Chapter 34

Amelia knocked on Ted and Josie's bedroom door at seven thirty Saturday morning.

"Mom! Ted! You'll never guess what happened last night! Can I come in? Huh?"

"Give us a moment," Josie said. "We'll meet you in the kitchen."

A groggy Josie slipped into a soft cotton shirt and pants that hid her cuts. Her injuries didn't hurt so much today, and the bruise on her arm was healing. But her face was still dotted with orange measles.

"You look much better," Ted said, kissing her good morning.

"I feel better," she said, and smiled. "What do you think is going on?"

Ted shrugged into his T-shirt. "Let's go downstairs and find out."

Amelia was brewing coffee and beating eggs for an omelet. Ted poured himself and Josie a cup of life-giving caffeine and they sat at the dining room table. Amelia had set it for three.

"We're sort of awake now," Josie said, rubbing her eyes. "What's happening?"

"You won't believe this," Amelia said. "Do you want cheese in your omelet?" She turned up the gas under the omelet pan.

"Yes," Josie said. "What won't we believe?"

"Toast?"

"Yes. Both of us. What won't we believe?"

Amelia dropped four slices into the toaster, then poured the eggs into the omelet pan and turned down the heat.

"Emerson Middleton texted Palmer last night and Palmer just saw the message this morning."

"She gets up this early?" Josie said.

"Mom! She was on her way to the bathroom and checked her messages. The police raided Zoe's pimps-and-hos party!" Amelia sprinkled shredded cheese on the open omelet, then deftly flipped it closed.

"Why?"

"The cops caught a bunch of Barrington kids drinking. Zoe's mother and stepfather may be fined five hundred dollars. They could go to jail."

Amelia cut the omelet, oozing melted cheese, into two pieces. She nearly danced across the kitchen as she carried plates with toast and the warm omelets to Ted and Josie. Then she went back for her own breakfast of milk and toast with grape jelly.

"We need to watch the Channel Seven news at eight o'clock," Amelia said. "Honey Butcher said that's when our interview about One D would run—if we made it. They might have Zoe's raid on, too. We can't miss it, Mom.

"Will you set up the DVR, Ted? It's twenty till eight."

Amelia ate in such a rush she didn't bother painting all four toast corners with grape jelly. Ted and Josie quickly finished their breakfasts and poured themselves more coffee. Josie stacked the dishes in the sink, then headed downstairs, where Ted was setting the DVR.

The family room looked cozy in the fall sunlight filtered through the narrow basement windows. Festus was in the backyard, but Marmalade and Harry lounged on the couch.

By 7:50, the DVR was ready to record. Amelia hunkered down on the couch between the cats, texting her friends. Josie glanced at her daughter's texts and thought she could translate them: Amelia wondered what Honey would say about them and if the pimps-and-hos party would make the news.

Texts flew back and forth. The four girls were on high alert, waiting for their moment of fame, hoping the mean girls would get a well-deserved payback.

At last, the eight o'clock news came on with Channel Seven's usual gaudy fanfare and overwrought sound effects. Amelia sat through a report on a presidential trip, a farm bill in Congress, and a fatal accident on Highway 40.

She paced the room during the commercial break, then fidgeted through a story about a puppy rescued from a sewer and a security video of a daring daylight holdup at a jewelry store.

"Come on," she moaned.

By the time sports came on, Amelia was in despair. She complained so much that Josie wasn't sure what teams had played or their scores.

But after the sports news the announcer said, "Last night, St. Louis fangirls were headed for One Direction. Honey Butcher will tell you about a group that may be bigger than the Beatles—and an alarming trend among St. Louis teens. After this message."

As far as Amelia was concerned, the next two minutes lasted longer than the nearly four billion years of the Precambrian period. She texted, shifted, paced, and jiggled like someone possessed. She picked up Harry and hugged him, then abandoned him on the couch.

Josie said nothing, knowing those hundred and twenty seconds wouldn't last forever. But they sure seemed like it. Ted double-checked the DVR settings.

Then Honey Butcher was standing in front of a turreted castle in Venetia Heights, a rich enclave in West

County, not far from Barrington. Streetlights softly lit a white stone mansion, and police light bars danced on the lawn.

Honey, shapely and sophisticated in a red-and-black color-block dress, frowned at the white stone house. "More than thirty minors were caught drinking at this Venetia Heights home," she said.

The video panned over teens and tweens pouring out of the house. The girls teetered down the drive in barely there skirts, slipping tube tops, and impossible platform heels. Their bodies were ghost white but their faces were deliberately blurred.

"Hah!" Amelia said. "No point in blocking out their faces. The girl in the green is Zoe and that's Jace in that stupid yellow halter top."

The boys could hardly run in their long fur coats and hats in purple, lizard green, and orange. Their necks dripped bling and Josie caught glittery flashes on their wrists and fingers and wondered if the boys wore real diamonds.

"We are not showing the faces of the underage party-goers," Honey intoned, "but police sources say most are students at the exclusive Barrington School for Boys and Girls.

"The party took place at the residence of socialites Tracy Henderson Delgado and Beall Jackson Delgado, according to Venetia Heights police. The Delgados are facing possible arrest and jail time for serving alcohol to minors.

"Venetia Heights police went to the Delgado house last night because of complaints that there was, according to the report, quote 'a huge underage party' unquote. Mr. Delgado refused to let the police enter, so law enforcement got a search warrant.

"Police cited thirty-one people for underage drinking and seventeen for resisting officers. They also cited the thirty-seven-year-old homeowner for serving and providing a place for minors to consume alcohol.

"According to the police report, officers seized twenty-two twelve-ounce beers, two one-liter bottles of rum, and a beer-pong table layout."

Honey looked into the camera and said, "Many young people, particularly in overprivileged communities, are served alcohol at parties in their homes, by parents. This practice is so prevalent that Ping-Pong balls for the popular drinking game of beer pong are sold in local supermarkets next to the beer.

"Statistics show that alcohol use among teens is on the rise, after a decade-long decline. It's against the law in Missouri to allow anyone under twenty-one to drink or possess alcohol. Adults are required to stop underage persons from drinking or possessing alcohol.

"Local law enforcement often turns a blind eye to underage drinking parties, especially in wealthy West County."

Honey paused and put on a serious expression. "But we here at Channel Seven urge the police to make an example of this blatant infraction of the law and charge the Delgado adults to the fullest extent of the law.

"The Delgados and their attorney have not responded to repeated attempts by this station to contact them."

"I wonder why?" Josie said. She was shushed by Ted and Amelia.

Now Honey had shifted her tone from serious to smiling. "Fortunately, not all the Barrington students were at that drunken party. These four Barrington girls were at the One Direction concert in downtown St. Louis."

The camera panned over the gleaming block-long limo. The uniformed chauffeur gravely held open the door, and Amelia, Palmer, Emma, and Bailey piled out in a giggling group.

Honey held out her microphone to black-haired Bailey, a pretty, pillowy girl. "This is my first concert! And I'm a huge fan," Bailey said. "I'm so *superexcited*!"

"I'm here with my three BFFs," Amelia said. "Ted got me the tickets. Hi, Ted! Thank you!"

All four girls waved on camera and chorused, "We love you, Ted."

Josie smiled when she saw Ted's ears turn red.

"Which band member do you like best?" Honey asked, pointing the mic at Palmer.

"Harry," red-haired Palmer said. "He's the charming one."

"Niall is the cute one," Emma said.

"I like Harry, too," Amelia said.

"Zayn is quiet and mysterious," Bailey said.

"Don't fight, ladies," Honey said. "There's one for each of you." She smiled at the camera, and then the segment was over.

"OMG, I sounded so stupid," Amelia said, and threw herself dramatically on the couch. "My hair looked awful. And my scarf wasn't right."

"You were a star," Ted said. "And you remembered to thank me on camera."

"You rock!" Josie said.

Congratulatory texts flooded Amelia's phone. All the callers agreed with Josie. Others delighted in the embarrassment of the mean girls.

Either way, it was a night to remember.

Chapter 35

The One D hoopla was starting to level off by nine fifteen when Renzo Fischer called Josie.

"I need to talk to you before you give your statement to the police at ten this morning," the lawyer said. "We've got a pint-sized problem with Frank's case."

"What's wrong?" Josie asked. She felt like someone had punched her.

"Nothing serious," he said. "Doesn't amount to a hill of beans. I don't want you caught by surprise; that's all. I'll explain when I see you. I'm on my way."

Soon he was knocking on their door at Fresno Court. Amelia, fascinated by the lawyer's white cowboy hat and turquoise bolo tie, stared until Josie was embarrassed.

"Amelia," she said, "I believe you have a chore concerning Harry."

Amelia knew that meant clean the cat box. She quickly vanished. Josie wasn't sure if Amelia actually cleaned the litter box or simply made herself scarce. Either way, Josie was grateful.

Renzo's ostrich cowboy boots clomped across the hardwood floors, and they sat at the dining room table. He refused coffee and got down to business.

"Sharon Pancera says you attacked her and she never confessed to killing Uncle Bob," he said.

"What? But Alyce heard her," Josie began.

"I know, I know," Renzo said, and held up his hands. "Ms. Pancera says Alyce is your friend and you two conspired against her. But her neighbor, Mrs. Darla Combes, wants to testify that Sharon tried to pick her azalea leaves and Mrs. Combes chased her away. Darla Combes said she saw Sharon carry a big bag of leaves to her car shortly after that. And she remembers the day and time."

"Darla told me that," Josie said. "I'm glad she won at bingo that day."

"I do believe Mrs. Combes is looking forward to her time in court," Renzo said. "She says she doesn't want a killer living on her street."

"And it's her civic duty to put her in jail?" Josie asked, with a sly smile.

"Bless her public-spirited heart," Renzo said, and winked. "That's exactly what she said."

"What about Uncle Bob's landlady, Myrtle Billings?" Josie asked. "She saw Bob kick Sharon's dog and then Bob tried to pretend Angel wasn't hurt. Myrt called her niece at the day-care center to give her a heads-up, and Karen insisted Bob get that poor dog to a vet."

"Karen the dog groomer told the police all about her aunt Myrtle," Renzo said, "and Mrs. Billings is another highly observant woman who is willing to help the police."

"Any evidence placing Sharon at the crime scene?" Josie asked.

"Beverly—the day-care receptionist—says Sharon dropped by with more medicine for Angel the day Bob was murdered. Beverly didn't think anything of it because Sharon was there often checking on Angel. That's probably when Sharon wandered back and mixed the leaves into Bob's salad."

"But if Sharon popped in all the time," Josie said, "how can the police prove she was there the day Bob was killed?"

"They're looking into the security-camera tapes. They were confiscated the day of the murder."

"What if they don't show anything?" Josie said.

"We still have the plant DNA from Sharon's yard. Once those results are in, this will all go away, Josie. Don't you go worrying. I don't want that pretty brown hair turning gray. This will work out."

Josie's doorbell rang.

"I do believe it's time for the police," Renzo said.

Detective Dobbs and a Summerdale Crimes Against Persons detective named Ridgeway arrived precisely at ten o'clock. They joined Renzo at the dining room table.

Renzo permitted Josie to make a straightforward statement about Sharon Pancera's attack, but she was not allowed to say why she was at Sharon's apartment or answer any other questions.

"That's privileged information, Detectives," Renzo said. "As you can see, Ms. Marcus is looking a little peaked now. She needs her rest. She'll sign a statement for you and then we should let her recover."

Josie was relieved when the police and Renzo left. She collapsed on the couch, suddenly tired, when her mother called.

"I saw Amelia on TV," Jane said. "All four girls were cute, but she was the best looking and most articulate."

"You're not prejudiced, Grandma," Josie said, but Jane heard her smile. "She did sound good, didn't she? Ted and I are proud of her."

"How are you, Josie?" Jane asked.

"Much better, Mom," Josie said.

"I thought I'd stop by and see you after I visit Frank in jail tomorrow. We'd been planning to go to church Sunday, but now I'll have to see him behind bars."

"Plexiglas, actually," Josie said. "And he won't be there much longer." She didn't mention Renzo's "pint-sized problem." Jane was worried enough. More fretting wouldn't help her or Frank.

Josie spent the day relaxing in the warm sun and reading on the back deck, Marmalade on her lap, Festus at her feet. Ted barbecued their dinner.

By Sunday, Josie felt almost like her old self. Jane brought homemade chicken soup, a loaf of fresh-baked bread, and a German chocolate cake for the family lunch.

Josie had expected her mother to be upset after seeing Frank in jail, but Jane was chatty and cheerful.

"Frank is going to AA meetings in jail, Josie. He admits he has an alcohol problem. He's looking forward to his release, but he's worried he won't be able to get a job when he's out of jail."

"Any word on how close Frank is to freedom, Mom?"

"Not yet," Jane said. "But we have hope. Frank will be home soon and everything will be fine."

And he's just a renter, Josie thought.

Chapter 36

Monday morning, Amelia wore her "television outfit" — the clothes she'd worn to the One D concert — to recapture her moment of glory at Barrington. She seemed to run across the grass to school in her own personal spotlight. Josie was relieved to see her daughter so happy.

Back home, Josie had barely gotten through the door when Renzo called.

"Josie, I just talked to your mama and gave her the good news," he said. "Sharon Pancera has been charged with Uncle Bob's murder. The plant DNA evidence showed she used the azaleas in her own backyard. Her neighbor, Mrs. Combes, made a statement that Ms. Pancera had tried to steal her azalea leaves and then she saw her drive off with a bag of leaves less than half an hour later.

"And those security cameras you were so worried about? They showed her at Uncle Bob's at lunchtime and confirmed Beverly's statement: Ms. Pancera was at the day-care center the afternoon Bob was murdered. The cameras show her going into the kitchen with a suspiciously fat purse two hours before Bob was murdered. She was seen leaving home with the poison leaves; she was seen at the murder scene before Bob died. And the DNA proves those were leaves from the azaleas in her yard.

"Sharon was charged with first-degree murder," Renzo said. "That's LWOP, life without parole. Her public defender explained the facts of life to her and she pled guilty to second-degree murder. She should get life in prison with a chance of parole."

"That seems awfully chancy," Josie said.

"She'll probably serve twenty to twenty-five years if she behaves herself," Renzo said.

"Sharon killed Bob because he hurt her dog, didn't she?" Josie said.

"Sort of," he said. "But she wanted money. She used that poor dog. When she saw how badly injured Angel was, she thought she could sue Bob for major money. She spent all her savings—two hundred dollars—on a lawyer. The lawyer told Sharon she couldn't collect the big bucks because she'd given Angel to Bob at his apartment."

"A friend who knows the law mentioned that," Josie said. "Something about Bob not acting within the scope of his employment. If he'd kicked the dog at the day-care center, Sharon would have had a big lawsuit."

"But the injury happened where he, uh, had a rendez-vous with the lady," Renzo said.

"'Rendezvous' is grand word for that crummy dive where he lived," Josie said. "Bob's apartment was as romantic as a Dumpster. Myrtle, the apartment manager who heard Bob and Sharon arguing, said he laughed at her and said Sharon couldn't collect anything."

"That's technically right," Renzo said. "But if Ms. Pancera had gone to a good lawyer, like me"—Josie smiled at his Texas-sized ego—"I would have used the publicity for a potential lawsuit against Uncle Bob's. And I would have gotten her a big settlement. Once the media got ahold of how Bob hurt an innocent dog, he'd feel like he stepped in a nest of fire ants."

"You're about the only lawyer I know who could have

made it happen, Renzo," Josie said. "Back in 2000, Sharon was on TV for locking Angel in her car on a hot summer day. Bob knew that. He laughed at her when she threatened him and said he'd make sure everyone knew she'd nearly suffocated Angel. He told Sharon she should see her lawyer again."

"He was right," Renzo said. "Ms. Pancera should have seen that lawyer once more. Better yet, she should have seen me."

"Why?" Josie said.

"Because legally, it didn't make any difference that she'd locked her dog in the car all those years ago. It had no bearing on the current case. I think Bob would have settled out of court to avoid a major scandal."

"Except a smart defense attorney could have used the car incident to try to convince the jury that Sharon injured her own dog," Josie said.

"That's the key word," Renzo said. "Smart. Aren't as many of those around as you might think."

"At the very least, the jury wouldn't like Sharon very much, once they knew," Josie said. "And that would mean less money for her."

"It's a shame you can't spread me like lard," he said. "I could have handled that one easy."

By "handled" he means "manipulated," Josie thought, and was glad he couldn't see her grin.

"But Sharon didn't have enough money for a second visit to the lawyer," she said. "So she killed Bob. Serves him right. Sharon deserves jail, too, trying to get rich off that poor dog's suffering."

"I guess those two deserved each other," Renzo said. "But it sure wasn't a match made in heaven.

"Well, it's been a pleasure talking to you, Josie. I expect your mama will be calling you shortly with the good news."

Shortly didn't begin to describe the timing. Josie had

barely finished the call before her cell phone rang again. As Renzo had predicted, it was Jane.

"He's free!" Jane said. "Frank's free to go."

"I'm so glad, Mom. I was just talking to Renzo." She told Jane the details of the lawyer's call.

"Renzo is confident," Jane said, "but he's good, too. I don't think Sharon would have wanted to sue Bob, even if she had the money. When people knew how her dog was injured, Sharon's reputation would be damaged. Everyone would know she'd had an affair with a married man."

Mom is so last century, Josie thought.

"For Sharon, that would have been a small price to pay," she said. "Sharon already had a dinged rep, Mom.

"When is Frank free?"

"Tomorrow morning," Jane said. "Ten o'clock."

"I'll go with you," Josie said.

"Thank you, but no, Josie. I can get Franklin on my own. It's no big deal."

"Right, Mom. He's just a renter."

"Josie?" Jane said. "I—I wanted to say something. I had no right to criticize you for helping Frank. Thank you. I really appreciate all you've done."

Josie heard the tremor of gratitude in her mother's voice and it warmed her heart.

Five months later . . .

Josie could tell her mother had something special planned for dinner that Saturday night at her flat on Phelan Street. When Ted parked his Mustang in front of Jane's house, Josie saw candles glowing in her mother's living room.

Josie's heels clip-clopped on the sidewalk. She was glad she wore her chic little black dress and Ted had on his favorite navy blazer. Ted held a bottle of good burgundy. Red meat was on the menu. It was a chilly night in February, and Josie was in a hurry to get inside. The scars left in the lawn by Frank's drunken driving were long gone.

Upstairs, Jane's candlelit living room was fragrant with roses. Josie counted at least two dozen pink and red long-stemmed blooms in cut-glass vases.

Josie's mother glowed in the soft light. She wore a pink velvet pantsuit that seemed pettable, and her silver hair was softly curled.

Frank was at her side, handsome in a navy sport coat and tie, white hair thick and curly. Jane's home-cooked meals had put much-needed weight back on him. The fragile, breakable look he'd had in jail was gone. Frank seemed strong and happy. He held Jane's hand as if it were delicate china.

A bottle of champagne and a bottle of sparkling grape juice were chilling in a big silver ice bucket.

"I thought we'd have a cocktail before dinner," Jane said. She seemed nervous but happy, fluttering around the living room. Stuart Little pattered after her, wearing a red bow tie.

Ted and Josie sat side by side on Jane's green couch, holding hands. Josie watched Frank uncork the champagne. He filled three glasses, and Jane passed them around while Frank poured himself a champagne glass of sparkling grape juice.

Then he cleared his throat.

"I have an announcement to make before we toast," he said. "Then I hope we'll still be celebrating." He looked like he wanted to bolt out of the room.

Jane took Frank's free hand and patted it. Ted and Josie sat up, alert and expectant. Frank said, "Uh, where's Amelia, Josie?"

"She's at a sleepover at Palmer's house," Josie said. "Palmer is the red-haired girl in the One Direction interview. I'm sure you saw the interview."

"Many times," Frank said. "Nice girls, Amelia's friends.

Polite and very pretty. Of course, Amelia's the prettiest, but . . ."

"Frank," Jane said gently. "The crown roast is going to dry out. Just tell them."

"Yes, yes, of course," Frank said, and downed the whole glass of grape juice. Jane poured him another glass.

"Josie, Ted, Jane and I are getting married," Frank said.

Josie started to stand up, but he said, "Hear me out first. Last September, I had a drinking problem. I still have a drinking problem, but now I admit it. But back then I had too much to drink and drove up onto your mother's lawn and nearly ran over Mrs. Mueller's azaleas.

"I made excuses. I told myself and Jane that I was lonely and needed more work to do. That's when I got the job at Uncle Bob's. And you know how well that turned out.

"But I was still an alcoholic. When I was in jail, I went to AA meetings. That's when I had the courage to admit I am an alcoholic.

"I've been sober for five months now, and I will stay that way. I still want a drink and I still go to meetings. I have a job now, too. I work at the Book House on Manchester. That gives me something to do. I meet interesting people and talk about books. And bookstore work is hard. So I'm busy, too, and that's good.

"I need only one thing to make my life complete, and that's Jane. I love her. I've loved her since the day I met her. We want to get married this summer."

Jane clung to Frank, smiling at him. Josie had never seen her mother look so happy—or so young.

"Jane has agreed to take a chance on me as long as I honor my promise and keep going to the AA meetings.

"So that's what I wanted to say. Ted and Josie, can I marry Jane? Is it okay?"

"Okay?" Josie said. "It's wonderful. I'm thrilled for you and for Mom. I wish you every happiness."

"You don't mind?" Frank said. "I know you're grown up and everything, but I'll be your stepfather."

"I never had a real father," Josie said. "The man who married Mom left us long ago. I'd love to have a father. It's never too late."

She gave Frank a hug and a kiss and said, "Congratulations. Welcome to the family."

Ted shook hands with Frank and slapped him on the back. "The Marcus women are keepers," he said. "Congratulations. You make a terrific couple. I hope you'll be as happy as Josie and me."

He kissed Jane and said, "Congratulations, Mom."

They raised their champagne glasses and toasted, "To Jane and Frank!"

"Oh, Josie, let me show you my engagement ring," Jane said. She held out her pink-manicured hand.

"Two diamonds," Josie said. "In a rose gold setting. It's beautiful, Mom. A classic style."

Josie hugged her mother and kissed her.

"We got engaged last Saturday, on Valentine's Day," Jane said shyly.

"And you kept it quiet for a whole week?" Josie said, and hugged her again. "How could you?"

"It wasn't easy," Jane said. "But I wanted our announcement to be a special occasion. And, Josie, I'd like you to be my maid of honor."

Josie blinked back the tears and thought, Always my daughter, now too my friend.

"I'd be honored," she said gravely, and kissed her mother on her forehead.

"Well, come on, everyone," Jane said. "Don't just stand there. Sit down at the table before the roast dries out."

Epilogue

After Frank Hyzy's release from the St. Louis County Jail, Josie got a surprise in the mail—a fat four-figure check from Frank's lawyer, Renzo Fischer. He really did pay her for her investigation.

You did a better job than that so-called professional, Renzo wrote. *Think about becoming a private investigator, Josie. You're a natural. When you get your license, look me up. I could use a good in-house investigator.*

Me? A private eye? Josie thought. Go from high heels to gumshoes? No, I'm a mystery shopper. But it's something to think about if Suttin goes belly-up.

Josie put away enough money to cover Amelia's school expenses for the coming year, plus a mother-daughter shopping trip. There was still enough left for a weeklong vacation to the Caribbean with Ted during the long, cold St. Louis winter.

Candice Ellen Manning sold Uncle Bob's Doggy Day Camp after Frank's release from jail. She waited too long. Sharon Pancera's confession and her story of Uncle Bob's cruelty to her little Angel damaged the value of his dog day-care franchise. Bow-Wow Heaven bought it and the two dog day-care companies merged into one. Uncle Bob's Doggy Day Camp was now Bow-Wow

Heaven. All traces of Uncle Bob's empire were erased and the city soon forgot him.

"How do you think that dump could afford Uncle Bob's?" Josie asked her friend Alyce.

"Easy," Alyce said. "Bow-Wow charges dog owners a fortune, and they sure don't spend it on the animals or the facilities."

Angel, the taffy-colored Pomeranian who was so cruelly treated, was adopted by Mrs. Meyer, Sharon's next-door neighbor. The little dog recovered from her injury and enjoys being petted and spoiled by her new mistress.

Candice got a job walking and playing with the dogs at Westminster Dog Day Care. She rarely deals with the customers, and to date, no one has recognized her as the woman who killed Miss Patti Sue, darling of St. Louis's kindergarten set. Candice may have served five years in jail for the hit-and-run accident, but she paid for that crime for the rest of her life.

Karen is now a groomer at Westminster and enjoys her work. As expected, her faithful clientele followed her to the new day-care place.

Westminster Dog Day Care was awarded the Certified Pet Care Centers seal. Neither Bow-Wow Heaven nor Uncle Bob's Doggy Day Camp was given the coveted award.

After an exposé in the local free paper headlined BOW-WOW HEAVEN IS CANINE HELL, business dropped off sharply at the day-care center. Bow-Wow Heaven was overextended after it gobbled up Uncle Bob's. It folded six months after the story ran.

*   *   *

Heidi, the former Annabelle Lee Cody, met a nice retired man with a Boston terrier. They moved to Tampa, Florida, where they live in his trailer.

Jared, the Rove School student who passed out at the Rivingtons' wild party, recovered from his alcoholic coma, though he spent several months in therapy. He now goes to Alcoholics Anonymous and his mother goes to Al-Anon, to help support her son in his battle against addiction. She sued Simon and Eve Rivington for serving alcohol to her son and for his medical bills. The suit was settled out of court for an undisclosed amount.

Because of the scandal over the party, Simon Rivington resigned his position as CFO and the family left St. Louis. They now live in Detroit.

The Delgados were fined five hundred dollars for serving alcohol to minors and served six months' probation.

After a rocky start, Alyce settled into a comfortable pregnancy—as least as comfortable as that state can be. She did not want to know the baby's gender when she had an ultrasound. "It's a girl," she said. "I know it."

She and Josie enjoyed shopping for girls' baby clothes and a dream layette. "Alyce, what are you going to do if you have a boy?" Josie asked her.

"It's a girl," Alyce said. "And if I'm wrong, then some poor mom who needs baby clothes will have fabulous things for her baby and I'll have had all the fun of shopping for them."

Amelia and Ted spent weeks planning the menu for Alyce's shower. A month before the baby was born, Josie held Alyce's shower on the back deck at their Fresno Court home.

"Am I really going to be an honorary aunt?" Amelia asked.

"You're already Justin's aunt Amelia," Alyce said. "Now you'll be a double aunt."

Josie was happy for her mother when Jane and Frank announced their engagement. But as the weeks wore on, Josie began to worry. Frank was an alcoholic. He was going to meetings, but what if he fell off the wagon and had another car accident? Jane could lose her house and her savings.

Even Ted noticed Josie's sleepless nights. "What's wrong?" he asked her. "Why are you awake at three a.m.?"

"I'm worried about Mom," she said. "What if Frank starts drinking? What if he drives drunk again and hits someone? Mom could lose everything."

"Your mother is a smart woman, Josie," Ted said. "I'm sure she's considered that."

But Josie thought her mother was blinded by love. A dozen times, she tried to bring up the subject with Jane, then lost her nerve. One warm spring day, Josie gathered her courage and invited her mother to lunch at the Boathouse in Forest Park, one of her favorite places.

The St. Louis park, bigger than New York's Central Park, and more than a century old, was a tender spring green. The Boathouse Forest Park restaurant sat beside a lake near the St. Louis Zoo.

"It's a perfect day," Jane said. "We'll watch the paddleboaters and feed the ducks. You used to love to feed the ducks."

An hour later, Josie and Jane were sitting at a lakeside table watching the paddleboats and sipping white wine. Jane chattered about her wedding plans while Josie tried to figure out how she would bring up this difficult subject.

She didn't have to. Jane stopped talking and said, "Josie, what's going on? Why are we having this lunch?"

Josie was taken aback by her mother's bluntness.

"Uh," she said.

"Let me help you out," Jane said. "You have doubts about me marrying Frank."

Josie recovered enough to say, "Well, yes. He is—"

"An alcoholic," Jane finished. "And he is going to meetings. But one of your friends probably told you some horror story about what happens to women my age when we remarry. We fall for the wrong man and he cleans out our bank accounts and gets our house and leaves us penniless."

"Well," Josie began, but never got to finish.

"That isn't going to happen," Jane said. "Renzo gave me the name of a good lawyer and Frank and I signed prenups before we announced our engagement. I'm protected financially, and so is he."

"But—," Josie said.

"But what about me?" Jane said. "What if Frank starts drinking again and doesn't stop? Then I divorce him, Josie. I survived one divorce and I can survive another."

Josie studied her small, determined mother in the soft spring sunshine. Jane looked happy, and yes, she had the glow of a woman in love.

"It's hard for a young woman like you to understand," Jane said, "but now is the right time for me to remarry. Frank and I still have our health. That's important, Josie. I'm not going to be a nurse with a purse, just for the privilege of being married.

"We're both financially comfortable. We can travel. We enjoy each other's company and we love each other. I thought that kind of love only happened once, Josie, but now I have another chance and I'm taking it."

Josie took a long drink of her wine and helped herself to the last of the artichoke dip.

"I did the safe thing when I married your father," Jane said. "I loved him, but he was also a good catch, a lawyer with prospects. I ran our home, helped his career, and gave him a beautiful daughter. Then he dumped us and moved to Chicago, where he married that woman and started a new family.

"Your father didn't even give me the child support to which I was entitled," Jane said, "and I couldn't afford to take him back to court."

Your father, Josie thought. Him. Twenty-five years later, Mom still can't say my father's name. And I can't remember what he looks like anymore.

"I was still a young, attractive woman when your father left, not much older than you are now, Josie. I had to go back to work with outdated office skills, and life was a struggle. All I had was that flat. I could have married one of my colleagues at the bank, but I didn't love John."

Josie patted her mother's hand. "I know you worked hard for me, Mom, and I appreciate it."

"I'm old enough to know my own mind and the risks I'm taking, Josie. I'm going to enjoy life."

Josie kissed her mother's soft cheek. "Then I wish you a long and happy marriage. You're entitled."

On the first warm weekend in May, Ted, Josie, and Amelia held an engagement party for Jane and Frank. Frank's daughter, Laura, and the rest of the St. Louis Mobo-Pet clinic staff, plus the staff from the Book House bookstore, where Franklin worked, and scores of the bride's and groom's friends toasted them at the party.

Jane buried the hatchet and invited Mrs. Mueller to the engagement party, but her neighbor refused to attend.

"Really, Jane, I don't understand why you're getting married at your age," Mrs. M said.

"Because I'm pregnant!" Jane said. She enjoyed seeing Mrs. M scandalized.

*   *   *

After Jane and Frank's engagement party, Ted and Josie cleaned up the deck. Amelia and CJ were in the living room, eating leftovers and giggling over her iPad. Josie thought their brown-haired neighbor could have passed as the sixth member of One Direction.

When the deck was swept, the dishes carried in, and the trash bagged, Josie brought out a half-empty champagne bottle and poured herself and Ted a glass. They clinked glasses and sat together, sipping champagne and enjoying the warm spring sunshine.

Josie studied the details of their pretty Tudor Revival home—the white rusticated stone around the doors and chimneys, the mellow yellow-orange brick, and the art glass and the gabled windows.

"I'm so happy," Josie said, leaning her head on Ted's shoulder. "And so lucky. I have you. My mother, after years of struggling on her own, is engaged to a good man. My daughter is dating the cute boy next door. No wonder Amelia calls this a fairy-tale house."

"She's right," Ted said. "And you know what happens in fairy tales?"

"Tell me," Josie said.

"You live happily ever after," Ted said, and kissed her.

Shopping Tips

Your pound hound, Max, is terrific company. He's almost human. No, better than human—he's loyal and loving. Max goes everywhere with you, except to the office.

Then Betty, the company workhorse, retired. You got her workload and no extra money. Now you're working sixty-hour weeks, running hard to stay in place. And Max is home alone.

Your animal companion is starting to look like a four-legged beer keg. He chewed your Jimmy Choos and tore the stuffing out of a pillow. He's lonely and you're feeling guilty. You know this is no way to treat your best friend.

You start noticing all the dog day-care centers on your way to work. Are they the answer? At day care, Max could make new friends, swim, play Frisbee, frolic with other pooches, even get fitness training.

Before you pack Max off to day care, here are some questions you should answer.

How Can I Tell If the Day-Care Place Is Any Dog Gone Good?

Visit the facility—more than once.

My friend Jinny Gender knows dogs. We visited several

dog day-care places to research this book. Their picture-perfect Web sites showed dogs romping on emerald lawns and had slews of favorable customer reviews. Most lived up to those reviews.

But one dog day-care place was as appalling as Bow-Wow Heaven in Chapter 13. Jinny and I were disgusted by its indifferent staff, dirty "private suites," and dogs penned in a tiny corral for their so-called supervised playtime. The grim, smelly place looked nothing like its Web site.

Get recommendations from friends and neighbors.

But don't trust those recommendations until you see the day-care facility yourself. One friend raved about the place I call Bow-Wow Heaven. But she'd never been there. The facility picked up her dog and delivered it back to her home.

Does the day-care facility smell good?

Your dog should be in a clean, well-ventilated facility to prevent diseases. Accidents happen, but they should be cleaned up immediately. If the day-care facility is smelly, pick up your pet and run.

Is the equipment in the indoor and outdoor play areas well maintained?

Your dog can get hurt on broken equipment. Grassy play yards look inviting, but make sure there's plenty of room for pets to play. The ASPCA recommends that play areas have seventy-five to a hundred square feet per dog.

Are big dogs separated from small dogs by size?

Bigger dogs can bully small ones, especially rambunctious breeds like boxers and German shepherds. Some small dogs see themselves as ferocious and attack big dogs—at their peril. The bigger dogs regard the brave little yappers as lunch.

Are the dogs also separated by temperament?

This is especially important. Jack Russells and Yorkies are both small dogs, but a hyper Jack Russell can intimidate a shy Yorkie. An active border collie, with its instinctive urge to herd, can annoy a laid-back Lab. If the day-care center laughs at that question, look elsewhere.

Does the day-care facility have a screening process?

Some dogs do not belong in day care. They don't like other dogs. They're too scared or too aggressive. A day-care facility should ask how your dog behaves around other dogs. Does your dog growl or snap at strange dogs? Is it shy or frightened? Is it a bully?

Yes, your dog is a furry bundle of cuteness, but if you give the day-care screener an accurate picture of his personality, your dog will have the best day-care experience. And if your pet doesn't belong in day care, there are alternatives.

Does the day-care facility ban certain breeds?

Ideally, it should consider dogs on a case-by-case basis, experts say.

My day-care facility says I can't drop in and visit my dog on my lunch hour. Is that right?

Day-care centers are busy and may not be able to give you a private tour without advance notice. But if you can't stop by and see your pet play, think about another place for your dog.

Beware of any dog day care that doesn't allow you to visit your dog or watch the playgroups. Look for overcrowding. The ASPCA's Web site says, "a rule-of-thumb for adequate staffing is to have, at a minimum, one employee per ten to fifteen dogs."

I plan to breed my dog. What if she isn't spayed?

Many day-care centers will not take unaltered dogs. A female should not go to day care when she's in season.

Questions You Should Ask about Dog Day Care

Many of these are from the ASPCA (www.aspca.org):

What professional training do the employees have? Have they been to seminars or watched videos by experts with academic credentials in animal behavior?

Ask about the day care's relationships with local trainers tested by the international Certification Council for Professional Dog Trainers (www.ccpdt.org).

How many people on the staff are trained in emergency first aid and CPR for dogs? If it's only one person, what's the procedure when that person is off duty? What happens if your dog is injured? Will your pet be taken to a vet or an emergency clinic?

Were you greeted at the reception desk? If the staff ignores you, they'll also ignore your dog.

What shots does the facility require? Make sure the day care's required shots match the shots your vet recommends. If the day-care facility says a dog with no shots is no problem, go elsewhere. The facility should ask to see proof of those vaccinations.

Does the facility have a flea prevention plan? Fleas,

like head lice in schools, can happen in the nicest places.

Can you see into the grooming area? It should be visible to all visitors.

Is there lots of fresh, clean water in kennels and play areas?

More Questions to Consider
(Nobody said it was easy caring for your canine companion.)

How much downtime will my dog have?

Even active dogs need to rest. Some day-care facilities will let your dog rest in a crate. This isn't punishment. Dogs need their privacy and that crate is their cave. Other facilities give the dog a break in a quiet place.

No breaks? Not a good policy. All-day play can be stressful and exhausting.

The question dogs owners dread but have to ask: Have there been any deaths or serious injuries at this facility?

Sometimes day-care deaths or serious accidents are publicized and an Internet search answers that question. One pup in day care died of apparently natural causes, but an investigation showed that the dog had been left muzzled and unattended and the pup suffocated. If the day-care facility dodges this question, find another one.

How often should I take my dog to day care?

Most offer half days or full days, and many have pickup and delivery, as well as grooming services. After that, there are extras you can tack on—personal playtime, "yappy hour," and special treats, including organic cookies or ice cream. Many people start their dogs off with half a day, to see if the pets enjoy it. Watch your dog carefully when you bring her home. Does she seem stressed or worried? If your dog is tired after a full day-care day, it may mean she's exhausted because she was unable to relax.

How can I tell if my dog is right for day care?

Is dog day care the answer for your best friend? Depends on the dog, experts say.

How does your dog behave when you take her to the dog park? Is he well behaved when he's on a leash but turns into a canine fiend when he's off it? Does she enjoy playing with other dogs? Does he lack the canine social graces and refuse to politely sniff butts? Is she scared by energetic dogs? Does he snap and growl when he meets another dog?

Those dogs are probably not good day-care candidates.

My Dog Will Never Fit In at Day Care.

Glad you recognized that. You've saved yourself and your dog a lot of trouble. Here are some alternatives to day care:

Hire a dog walker. A half-hour walk runs $15 to $20 in most areas. An hour walk is $22 to $30. If you're a two-dog family, the second dog is usually half price. Many dog-walking services have discount passes if you buy several days' walks at once. In that case, five half-hour walks range from $60 to $85 a week.

Come home at lunch to walk and play with your dog. It's good exercise for you both.

Make play dates with a neighbor's dog. If your dog gets along with the Lab next door, and the neighbor has a fenced yard, your pet will enjoy the company.

Ask your nice neighbor, who loves dogs but doesn't want one full-time, if she'll visit your dog during the long afternoons. Pay her, please. If she won't take money, reward her with gift cards for her favorite bookstore, coffee shop, or restaurant every month.

Puttin' On the Dog

You can't make this stuff up. Well, I can't, anyway. Many day-care spas have full grooming services, facials, massages, nail clipping and nail polish, and skin and hair treatments, including emulsifying, exfoliating, moisturizing, and coat conditioning for posh pups. Acupuncturists, aromatherapists, and pet psychics are common. I could write another book about dog suites, canine weddings, organic treats, and more, but here are two favorites:

Blueberry facials are all the rage for pampered pets. South Bark in San Diego, California, says it's the home of the blueberry facial. That facility's wash packages ($16.50 to $22.50) come with a free blueberry facial. Or you can shop online for South Bark's Blueberry Facial and give your dog the spa treatment at home. A twelve-ounce bottle is $18.99 at www.shopsouthbark.com.

Doggy disco. Many day-care centers have doggy discos, but the Zoom Room, a franchise with indoor places for city dogs to socialize, has doggy disco parties for birthdays, adoption anniversaries, animal welfare charity fundraisers, bark mitzvahs, pet weddings and more. For information, go to www.zoomroomonline.com.

Sunscreen for dogs?

Many vets recommend it, especially for dogs who are shaved, hairless, light haired, or white, or if the breed is prone to skin tumors.

"Dogs that like to sunbathe on their backs can also get tumors in the space between the back legs," one expert said. "Any area where the skin is thin and there is no hair should be protected."

Human sunscreen, especially if it contains zinc oxide, can be toxic to pets. Use sunscreens designed for babies. Get a spray-on sunscreen for easy application, and you don't need to apply sunscreen where the hair is thick. One sunscreen is designed for dogs and horses—but not for cats. It's safe if your dog licks it off, and it's water-repellent. Epi-Pet Sun Protector Sunscreen Spray is $17.95 for four ounces (www.epi-pet .com/sunscreen.aspx).

DogTV?

Arf! DogTV is the first television network designed for dogs, available on DIRECTV. DogTV claims its programing is "scientifically developed to provide the right company for dogs when left alone."

The network supports the Humane Society of the United States. DogTV costs $4.99 to $9.99 a month.

And while you can watch it with your dog, the colors,

contrast, sound, and music may seem off to humans. DogTV says these are "adjusted to fit your dog's hearing and seeing abilities." Check it out at www.dogtv.com.

Favorite subjects? Supposedly, dogs like to watch other dogs playing in the snow, romping, and riding in cars. Oh, and they love watching letter carriers.

Read on for a sneak peek at the next
Dead-End Job Mystery
by Agatha and Anthony Award–winning author
Elaine Viets,

Checked Out

Coming in hardcover from Obsidian in May 2015

"I need your help," Elizabeth Cateman Kingsley said. "My late father misplaced a million dollars in a library book. I want it back."

Helen Hawthorne caught herself before she said, "You're joking." Private eyes were supposed to be cool. Helen and her husband, Phil Sagemont, were partners in Coronado Investigations, a Fort Lauderdale firm.

Elizabeth seemed unnaturally calm for someone with a misplaced million. Her sensational statement had grabbed the attention of Helen and Phil, but now Elizabeth sat quietly in the yellow client's chair, her narrow feet in sensible black heels crossed at the ankles, her slender, well-shaped hands folded in her lap.

Helen studied the woman from the comfort of her chrome-and-black partner's chair. Somewhere in her fifties, Elizabeth Kingsley kept her gunmetal hair defiantly undyed and pulled into a knot. A thin knife-blade nose gave her makeup-free face distinction. Helen thought she looked practical, confident and intelligent.

Elizabeth's well-cut gray suit was slightly worn. Her turquoise-and-pink silk scarf gave it a bold splash of color. Elizabeth had money once, Helen decided, but she's on hard times now. But how the heck did you leave a million bucks in a library book?

Phil asked the question Helen had been thinking a

little more tactfully: "How did you misplace a million dollars in a library book?"

"I didn't," Elizabeth said. "My father, Davis Kingsley, did."

"Was it a check? A bank book?"

"Oh, no," she said. "It's a watercolor."

Elizabeth sat with her hands folded demurely in her lap, a sly smile on her face. She seemed to enjoy setting off bombshells and watching their effect.

"Perhaps I should explain," she said. "My family, the Kingsleys, were Florida pioneers. My grandparents moved to Fort Lauderdale in the 1920s and built a home in Flora Park."

The Kingsleys might have been early local residents, Helen thought, but this pioneer family didn't rough it in a log cabin. The Kingsleys had built a mansion in a wealthy enclave on the edge of Fort Lauderdale during the Florida land boom.

"Grandpapa Woodrow Kingsley made his money in oil and railroads," Elizabeth said.

"The old-fashioned way," Phil said.

My silver-haired husband is so charming, only I know he's calling Woodrow a robber baron, Helen thought.

"For a financier, Grandpapa was a bit of a swashbuckler," Elizabeth said, and smiled.

Helen decided maybe Elizabeth wasn't as proper as she seemed.

"He enjoyed financing silent films. He often went to Hollywood. Grandmama was a lady and stayed home."

The old gal was dull and disapproving, Helen translated. Grandpapa had to travel three thousand miles to California to go on a toot.

"Grandmama would have nothing to do with movie people. She dedicated herself to helping the deserving poor."

Heaven help them, Helen thought. Their lives were miserable enough.

"Grandpapa put up the money for a number of classic films, including *Forbidden Paradise*—that starred Pola Negri—and Erich von Stroheim's *The Merry Widow*."

Films with scandalous women, Helen thought. Did Grandpapa unbuckle his swash for some smokin'-hot starlets?

"Impressive," Phil said. "Von Stroheim was famous for going overbudget. He ordered Paris gowns and monogrammed silk underwear for his actors in *Foolish Wives* so they could feel more like aristocrats."

A tiny frown creased Elizabeth's forehead. She did not like being one-upped.

"When he was in Hollywood, Grandpapa would drink scotch, smoke cigars and play poker," she said. "He played poker on the set with the cast and crew, including Clark Gable."

"Wow!" Helen said.

"Oh, Gable wasn't a star then," Elizabeth said. "Far from it. He was an extra and Grandpapa thought Gable wouldn't get anywhere because his ears were too big. Many men made that mistake. Until Gable became the biggest star in Hollywood."

There it was again, Helen thought, that glimpse of carefully suppressed glee.

"Gable was on a losing streak that night," Elizabeth said. "He was out of money. He'd lost his watch and his ring. He bet a watercolor called *Muddy Alligators*."

"A painting?" Helen said. "What was Gable doing with that?"

"I have no idea, but he was quite attached to it," Elizabeth said. "He thought gators sunning themselves on a mud bank were manly. Grandpapa won the painting with a royal flush, but he didn't trust Hollywood types. He

made Gable sign it over to him. Gable wrote on the back,
'I lost this fair and square to Woodrow Kingsley—W. C.
Gable, 1924.' Gable's first name was William. He changed
his name to Clark Gable in 1925.

"Grandpapa admired the watercolor, and was surprised that a roughneck like Gable owned a genuine
John Singer Sargent."

"Sargent painted muddy reptiles? I thought he did
portraits of royalty and beautiful society women," Phil
said.

"He did, until his mid-forties," Elizabeth said. "Then
he had some kind of midlife career crisis and painted
landscapes in Europe and America. Sargent painted at
least two alligator watercolors when he stayed at the
Florida home of John D. Rockefeller."

"Sargent switched from society dragons to alligators,"
Helen said, then wished she could recall her words. Elizabeth's grandmother was definitely a dragon.

"Dragons in training, usually," Elizabeth said, and
again Helen caught a flash of well-bred amusement.
"Most of his society belles were young women.

"Grandmama refused to display the painting in her
house. Grandpapa couldn't even hang it in his office. She
said it was ugly. I suspect it also may have been an ugly
reminder of his Hollywood high jinks. She banished the
alligator watercolor to a storage room.

"Sargent died the following year and Grandpapa had
a fatal heart attack seven years later, leaving Grandmama a widow with one son. The watercolor was forgotten for decades.

"Until about five years ago," Elizabeth said. "My father inherited the family home in the fifties. Papa was
eighty when he found the watercolor in the storage room.
Sargent's work was fashionable again. Papa had it au-
thenticated and appraised. The watercolor wasn't worth
all that much, maybe three hundred thousand."

Helen raised an eyebrow and Phil gave her a tiny nod. Three hundred K might not be much to Elizabeth, but the PI pair thought it was a substantial chunk of change.

"But it was worth much more, thanks to what the art world calls 'association.' A painting owned—and signed—by a film star brought the price up to more than a million dollars. The story behind it helped, too.

"Papa told everyone he'd discovered a lost family treasure. My brother, Cateman, and I begged him to have it properly stored and insured, but Papa said it wasn't necessary. 'It's in a safe place,' he'd say. 'Safer than any vault.' But we were concerned. Papa suffered from mild dementia by then.

"He died in his sleep six months ago, leaving his estate to Cateman and me. Papa gave me the Sargent watercolor and my brother inherited the family home. When the will was made five years ago, I was happy with that arrangement. I was a single woman with a comfortable income."

Comfortable. That's how rich people said they were rolling in dough, Helen thought.

"Since then, I've had some financial reversals. That watercolor has become important. I need that painting to save my home, and we can't find it."

"It was stolen?" Helen said.

"Worse," she said. "I believe it was accidentally given away. We've looked everywhere in the house, checked Papa's safe-deposit boxes and the safe, but we've found no sign of the missing watercolor. My brother even hired people to search the house. We can only conclude that my father hid it in one of his books that were donated to the Flora Park Library."

"Who gave it away?" Helen asked.

"Scarlett, my brother's new wife. Cateman recently married his third wife. It's a May-December marriage. He's sixty and she's twenty-three."

Did Elizabeth disapprove of her new sister-in-law? Helen thought Elizabeth had made a face, like she'd bitten into something sour, but it was hard to tell.

"Cateman and Scarlett moved into the family home immediately after Papa's funeral, and Scarlett began re-decorating.

"Papa had let things slide in recent years. Scarlett doesn't love books the way he did. I doubt she reads anything but the magazines one finds in supermarket check-out lines."

Yep, Helen thought. Elizabeth definitely doesn't like her brother's new wife.

"Her first act was to get rid of what she called the 'dusty old books' in my father's library, which dates back to Grandpapa's time. Scarlett donated more than a thousand books to the Flora Park Library. Most of the books were of little value. Papa was a great reader of hardcover popular fiction, and the Friends of the Library began selling those while they had the more valuable books appraised.

"The Friends put ten mysteries on sale for a dollar each, and the hardcovers were bought within a few days. But a patron found the birth certificate for Imogen Cateman, my grandmama, in her thriller. She returned it to the library. Then a man discovered the deed to property in Tallahassee in a spy novel."

"The Flora Park Library has honest patrons," Phil said.

"People of quality live there," Elizabeth said. "I would expect them to return family papers."

Elizabeth sat a little straighter. She considered herself one of the quality.

"We concluded that my late father hid valuables in his books, and the missing watercolor was in a donated volume. I'd like you to look for the painting."

"Why don't you look for it?" Phil asked. "Don't you know the people at the library?"

"Of course I do," Elizabeth said. "But my job as facilitator for my college alumni association takes up all my time."

Helen had no idea what a facilitator did, but Elizabeth said it so gravely, Helen felt she should have known.

"I could have taken the books back and searched them myself, but that would cause talk.

"I can only give you a small down payment," Elizabeth said. "But if you find the watercolor, I'll pay you ten thousand dollars when it's sold at auction. The library director is a family friend and she's agreed that you can work as a library volunteer, Helen, while you discreetly look for the watercolor."

"Me?" Helen said. A library, she thought. I'd like that. I'd get to read the new books when they came in, too.

"If Helen takes this job," Phil said, "how do you know Scarlett didn't keep the watercolor?"

Helen thought her husband would make a fine portrait—eighteenth-century British, she decided. He had a long, slightly crooked nose, a thin, pale face and thick silver hair. She dragged herself back to the conversation.

"I showed her a picture of one of the alligator watercolors," Elizabeth said, "and she said it was 'gross.' She prefers to collect what she calls 'pretty things,' such as Swarovski crystal."

"What about your brother?" Helen asked. "Does he have the watercolor?"

"Cateman is an honorable man," Elizabeth said. "Besides, he has more than enough money."

Rich people never have enough money, Helen thought.

"Why else would he hire people to search his house?" Elizabeth asked.

"The search was done after the books were donated to the library?" Phil said.

"Of course," Elizabeth said. The frown notched deeper into her forehead. She was annoyed. "My brother is most eager to help me find that artwork. He has sufficient means for himself and Scarlett, but he doesn't feel he can also support me. His two divorces have cost him dearly."

Now that's convincing, Helen thought.

Also available from
national bestselling author

ELAINE VIETS

The Josie Marcus,
Mystery Shopper Series

Dying in Style
High Heels Are Murder
Accessory to Murder
Murder with All the Trimmings
The Fashion Hound Murders
An Uplifting Murder
Death on a Platter
Murder Is a Piece of Cake
Fixing to Die

"Elaine Viets writes exciting amateur sleuth
mysteries filled with believable characters."
—*Midwest Book Review*

Available wherever books are sold or at
penguin.com

facebook.com/TheCrimeSceneBooks

OM0107

Also available from
national bestselling author

ELAINE VIETS

The Dead-End Job Series

Shop till You Drop
Murder Between the Covers
Dying to Call You
Just Murdered
Murder Unleashed
Murder with Reservations
Clubbed to Death
Killer Cuts
Half-Price Homicide
Pumped for Murder
Final Sail
Board Stiff
Catnapped!

"Clever."
—Marilyn Stasio,
The New York Times Book Review

Available wherever books are sold or at
penguin.com

facebook.com/TheCrimeSceneBooks